Praise for

A Place for Us

"A beautiful testament to true love and the right of every person to pursue a life with the ones they cherish."
—**BookLife Reviews**

"A fascinating journey into the LGBTQ world with an emphasis on lesbian relationships and marriage, especially as it applies across cultures and over time. . . . a beautifully crafted novel with emotional depth and memorable characters."
—*Readers' Favorite*, **5-star review**

"In this wise, intelligent, involving story, two women, confronted by the daunting cost of sharing their lives, search within themselves for their best selves. Their pathway illuminates the power and beauty of women drawn inexorably together, the complexity, breathtaking risk and authentic challenges specific to our lesbian lives."
—**Katherine Forrest**, author of *Curious Wine*

"A spectacular novel of love and resiliency. *A Place for Us* brilliantly exposes the real-world barriers the LGBTQ+ population face just to be in love. As a retired US Navy veteran and someone who had to hide my love for decades, I found the systems depicted in this book to be tragically relatable. I applaud Grayhall on writing this stunning masterpiece and reminding me that love always finds a way."
—**Karen Solt**, author of *Hiding for My Life: Being Gay in the Navy*

"Patricia Grayhall's *A Place for Us* is a poignant and immersive lesbian romance that celebrates resilience, love's triumph over barriers, and the enduring power of connection."

—Felice Cohen, author of *Half In:
A Coming-of-Age Memoir of Forbidden Love*

"*A Place for Us* is a fast-paced story that compels the reader to experience emotionally how far two lovers will go to overcome societal injustice to become family."

—Adele Holmes, MD, author of *Winter's Reckoning*

A Place for Us

A Place for Us

A Novel

Patricia Grayhall

SHE WRITES PRESS

Copyright © 2025 Patricia Grayhall

All rights reserved. No part of this publication may be reproduced, distributed, or transmitted in any form or by any means, including photocopying, recording, digital scanning, or other electronic or mechanical methods, without the prior written permission of the publisher, except in the case of brief quotations embodied in critical reviews and certain other noncommercial uses permitted by copyright law. For permission requests, please address She Writes Press.

Published 2025
Printed in the United States of America
Print ISBN: 978-1-64742-912-6
E-ISBN: 978-1-64742-913-3
Library of Congress Control Number: 2025900962

For information, address:
She Writes Press
1569 Solano Ave #546
Berkeley, CA 94707

Interior design by Stacey Aaronson

She Writes Press is a division of SparkPoint Studio, LLC. Company and/or product names that are trade names, logos, trademarks, and/or registered trademarks of third parties are the property of their respective owners and are used in this book for purposes of identification and information only under the Fair Use Doctrine.

This novel is inspired by true events. However, it is a work of fiction. The characters and narratives are created by the author's imagination, and any resemblance to actual events, businesses, governments, locales, or persons, living or dead, is entirely coincidental.

NO AI TRAINING: Without in any way limiting the author's [and publisher's] exclusive rights under copyright, any use of this publication to "train" generative artificial intelligence (AI) technologies to generate text is expressly prohibited. The author reserves all rights to license uses of this work for generative AI training and development of machine learning language models.

To my wife, Linda

PART I
October–November 1981

chapter one
London

AT TWENTY-NINE-YEARS-OLD, LAUREN HAD YET TO experience being held in a woman's arms and feeling time had stopped. Tonight, she found herself in a bustling pub in Central London on women's night, the air thick with anticipation. She'd shared a kiss with a woman the first night she came to this pub, but both she and the woman were novices, awkward and fumbling. That fleeting encounter left her wanting more: a taste of the electric connection she'd imagined could exist between women. New to lesbian life, she yearned to dive into the passion and fulfillment that dating men never offered.

Maybe this will be my lucky night. She leaned against the bar, watching the dancing. The night was warm for early October. So many women energetically strutting their stuff on the crowded dance floor generated a lot of heat, and the bass of the disco-inspired music pulsed through her body. Lauren sauntered to the end of the bar and opened the window, drawing a deep breath of the cooler night air.

A low, commanding woman's voice beside her said, "Can I order a dry white wine, please?"

The accent piqued Lauren's interest. She turned her head toward the voice. "Hi," she said. "Are you American?"

The woman appraised her before answering. Her warm brown eyes met Lauren's and pulled her in. "Yes. I guess I'll hear that question a lot while I'm here." Her full lips broke into a smile that made Lauren's body signal high alert.

"And how long are you here for?" Lauren asked while she racked her brain for something intelligent to say. A woman coming off the dance floor jostled her arm as she brushed past, her musky scent lingering.

The American woman pushed a strand of long, dark hair behind her ear, revealing a prominent cheekbone. "Just one more night before I leave for a conference in Paris. I'm Jo, by the way."

Lauren took the outstretched hand. Her palm was smooth, her grip firm.

"Lauren. How do you do?"

"That's a pretty name, and I'm doing well."

Lauren returned her smile. "For the British, 'How do you do?' isn't a question. It's a greeting." Jo's dark eyes sparked a buzz in Lauren's stomach, a new and surprising feeling for someone she'd only just met.

"Well, if you're going to educate me in British speak, I'd better buy you a drink."

The pulse of the base kept time with the pounding of Lauren's heart. She had to tear her gaze away from those dark eyes.

"Chris!" Lauren called to the bartender. "Do I have time for a G and T?"

"Okay, luv, but it's the last one."

Jo furrowed her brow. "Why is this the last drink? Is there somewhere you need to be?"

Lauren shook her head. "It's a pub. They close at eleven. In fifteen minutes."

"Oh." Jo's face fell.

Jo's apparent disappointment matched her own. Then Sheena Easton's "Morning Train" came on. "Forget the G and T," Lauren called to the bartender. She reached for Jo's hand. "Shall we dance?"

A coy smile played at the corners of her mouth. "Sure."

As they gyrated to the beat, Lauren checked out her new acquaintance. Tall and stylishly dressed in a high-collar white shirt and tight black jeans, she turned heads. She had to keep her engaged.

The last song was "Lady" by Kenny Rogers. Lauren raised her eyebrows in question and held out her hand. To her delight, Jo took it and pulled Lauren to her, slipping her hand around her waist. Lauren placed her left hand on Jo's shoulder, their bodies only an inch or two apart. Close enough for the orange, spice, and wood notes of the perfume Opium to make her lightheaded. Or was it the nearness of this alluring woman? As they swayed to the music, Jo pulled her closer and her silky, dark hair brushed against Lauren's cheek. Her pulse raced. She had little time.

"Where are you staying?" Lauren asked.

"Nearby, in Bloomsbury. I've read all of Virginia Woolf's novels and wanted to visit some of her haunts." Jo's low voice and breath, warm against Lauren's ear, sent a shiver through her.

She pulled away to smile at Jo, captivated again by her dark eyes. "What's your favorite?"

"*To the Lighthouse.*"

"Mine too!" A literate woman, even better. Lauren let Jo pull her back into an embrace, making her hyperaware of the firm pressure of Jo's hand on her back. She let herself mold into Jo's lithe, lean frame. They fit nicely. *Oh my god. Is she interested?* Lauren had only moments now to keep the conversation going before closing time.

"I'm leaving for New York tomorrow with a friend and colleague from work. We'll spend a couple of days in the city, then travel to New England for leaf peeping. But tonight . . ."

The song ended, the bartender flicked the lights, and women drifted away from the dance floor. The bartender began collecting glasses. Lauren's heart hammered as she and Jo stood looking at each other. *I can't just let her walk away.* "Would you like to join me at my flat for a drink?" she blurted.

Jo hesitated for several beats before she replied, "No, I don't think so."

Lauren's face grew hot with embarrassment, and she bit her lip. She must have misread the signals. This wasn't to be her lucky night after all. Together, they walked back to the bar and collected their jackets from the stools. Lauren averted her face to hide her disappointment.

Outside, they both hesitated in the cool night air as women streamed out around them, chatting and calling out to each other. Lauren couldn't bring herself to look into those dark eyes that had so captivated her she'd made a fool of herself.

Jo turned and briefly touched Lauren's arm. She cleared her throat. "I have a . . . sort-of girlfriend back home. So going to your flat is probably not a good idea. It would be nice to continue our conversation, though."

Lauren's pulse quickened. An opening! She screwed up her courage again. "Are you hungry? There is a great Indian restaurant close by that stays open late. Shall we grab a late dinner and talk?"

"Sounds good. It's dinnertime for me in DC."

Lauren grinned and finally met those dark eyes. And, oh, there was that buzz again. Maybe, just maybe, this *would* be her lucky night.

chapter two

THE STOP IN LONDON WAS PART OF JO'S QUEST FOR distraction on her first trip abroad. When her boss in Washington, DC, offered to send her to Paris, she'd accepted. Immersion in her first international conference on environmental law would keep her from ruminating about the imminent flameout of her affair with Sharon. Lauren's perfume, with hints of jasmine and sandalwood, and the sensual pleasure of her body pressed against her on the dance floor, provided an intoxicating distraction as well.

At the Indian restaurant, Jo encountered another first: vindaloo. She'd ordered spicy Indian dishes before in the States, but this was something else. Her eyes watered, she broke into a sweat, and her hair was on fire. She coughed and reached for her water.

"Not water. It makes it worse," Lauren told her. "Try yogurt." She pushed the side dish toward her.

Jo downed several spoonfuls, then coughed. She fumbled for her napkin, her eyes and nose streaming.

Lauren eyed her with concern. "Sorry about that. I told you it was spicy. We can switch dishes." She reached for Jo's vindaloo and pushed her own barely touched chicken tikka masala to Jo. She asked the hovering server for more napkins.

"That's more than a bit of spice," Jo croaked. Her throat no longer felt as if the top layer had incinerated, but her eyes and nose still streamed. *Not an impressive look.* Surprisingly, she cared what Lauren thought of her.

Lauren offered her another napkin. "Spicy in London is true Indian spice. Not the watered-down version they served in the US when I was there last."

Normally, Jo liked a bit of spice. Was that on offer tonight? When Jo's eyes and nose stopped streaming and her composure returned, they chatted about books, travel, and Lauren's upcoming trip to the States. She did not have it all planned out, as Jo would have.

When there was a comfortable lull in the conversation, she sensed Lauren regarding her.

"At the pub, you said you had a sort-of girlfriend. What did you mean?" Lauren asked.

Jo stopped eating and focused on her plate while she considered how to respond. Her stomach churned, and she rubbed her hands up and down her thighs before she looked up at Lauren. "I'd hoped we might live together, but she's ambivalent about loving a woman," she admitted.

"Is that why you call her your 'sort-of girlfriend'?"

Again, Jo took her time answering, flashing back to the early days. When Sharon walked into a restaurant in her form-fitting business suit and high heels with her blond curls falling over her shoulders, she took her breath away. Sharon's blue eyes used to light up at the sight of Jo, her smile dazzling. *For me?* Jo had thought, unable to believe her good fortune. But not anymore.

"She's attractive. Very femme. But paranoid about being outed. Her high-powered job as a lobbyist for the pharmaceutical industry brings her into contact with the industry's movers and shakers. Lately, she's become more and more unavailable." Jo paused, fingering her napkin. Lauren held her gaze, concern showing in her eyes.

Should I tell her more? But why shouldn't she? She would not likely see Lauren again. It might do her good to talk about it.

"I suspect she's seeing someone else. And it's probably not a woman."

"Oh." Lauren reached for her hand. "I'm sorry."

Lauren's kindness made Jo's eyes prick with tears. She might as well get it all out. "After the conference in Paris, I'd planned to travel to Greece for a week. I asked Sharon to join me, thinking it might spark a return of romance. I bought my plane ticket. But when I boarded the plane for London, she hadn't yet bought hers, so I may cancel the trip."

Lauren kept her hand on hers. She noticed Lauren's long, tapered fingers, cool to the touch, and her smooth, unblemished skin. *Beautiful hands.*

"It's just as well, really. I need time on my own to sort things out." Jo straightened her shoulders and withdrew her hand. "But let's talk about happier subjects. Have you been to Greece?"

"As a teenager, I traveled to Lesbos with my parents," Lauren told her. "The history and mythology fascinated me. I imagined I'd lived a former life in the sixth century on Lesbos as a member of Sappho's inner circle. I'd comb her long, dark hair as she composed her lyrics. That should have been my first clue I loved women, but it's taken me years to accept it."

Jo held Lauren's gaze as she spoke, enjoying her British

accent. Her hooded eyes when she smiled were captivating and mysterious and the dimple at the side of her mouth beguiling. Her honey blond hair kept falling over one eye until she flicked it back. Jo recalled the softness of Lauren's breasts and the curvy fit of her body that invited further intimacy during their slow dance. But she was getting ahead of herself.

"My clues began earlier," Jo shared. "At eight, I begged my parents for a Davy Crockett outfit for Christmas, complete with a coonskin cap. I imagined myself rescuing Elizabeth Taylor from a bear and carrying her off to my cabin in the woods. At that age, I didn't understand what to do with her after that."

Just as I don't quite know what to do with you right now. She took a sip of her lukewarm tea and regarded Lauren over the rim. *Should I invite her to my hotel room?* Jo had been faithful to Sharon throughout their tumultuous relationship. But did monogamy matter to either of them at this point? Sharon couldn't even commit to a trip to Greece. And a night with this cute Englishwoman would be a welcome distraction from thoughts of her.

They continued their conversation through several more cups of tea until almost one in the morning. The server came and went, bringing more tea and more water. Jo glanced around at the empty restaurant, then smiled into Lauren's eyes. "Would you like to see my hotel?" she asked. "My room is not very plush. This afternoon, I wanted a shower but there was only an old-fashioned claw-foot bathtub. I had to become a contortionist to wash my hair." *Why was she being so indirect? This was not like her.*

"I'd love to," Lauren said.

Jo smiled, then bit her lip. *Holy shit. Am I really doing this?*

But then again, why shouldn't she? Who knew what Sharon was doing in her absence?

The night air had turned chillier, and Jo pulled up the collar of her jacket on the short walk to the hotel. Lauren shivered and wrapped her arms around herself. *Is she nervous? Or just cold?*

Once upstairs in her hotel room, Jo turned on a small table lamp to create a soft glow. Lauren removed her jacket and threw it over a chair, and Jo did the same. The bedside alarm clock ticked loudly, and a door slammed in the hallway. Lauren stepped toward her, Giorgio perfume intoxicating, but not as much as the want in her eyes. Lauren took another step, closing the distance between them, then pressed her body against Jo's. She brushed her lips softly against Jo's, causing her to forget all about her sort-of girlfriend in DC. She kissed Lauren, who moaned and responded hungrily as she deepened the kiss and slipped her hand under Lauren's shirt.

She drew back when she found Lauren trembling. "Are you okay?" Jo asked. "We don't have to continue if you're uncomfortable."

"No, I want to," Lauren said, her voice barely above a whisper. "I've never made love with a woman before."

Lauren's admission startled Jo. *A lesbian virgin? Did Lauren really want her first time to be with someone just passing through? Shouldn't it be more . . . special?* "Are you sure you want this?" she asked.

Lauren responded by pulling Jo backward, tumbling with her onto the bed.

Okay then. She was game. She lay on top of Lauren, kissing and fondling, turned on by her responsiveness. Craving more skin, Jo reached under her shirt and unhooked her bra. Lauren shuddered when Jo cupped her full breast, smooth and warm, and ran her thumb over her nipple. "I'll move as slowly as you wish. Just tell me if you feel scared or uncomfortable and we'll stop."

Lauren sought Jo's mouth for a deep, lingering kiss. Not once that night did she tell her to stop.

It was five in the morning before they slept.

Jo awakened from a deep slumber with Lauren nudging her shoulder. "It's nearly ten o'clock and I need to go home and pack," she said. "My flight leaves for New York this afternoon."

Jo groaned and rubbed her eyes. "You don't leave yourself much room for error, do you?"

Lauren was already up and slipping into her jeans. Jo admired her tight, shapely bum and wished for another go. But when Lauren buttoned her blouse and stumbled into her shoes, Jo sprang out of bed.

"Wait, I don't even have your number and address. We can write or call each other sometime," she said. She produced a business card from her briefcase, wrote her home phone number on the back, and handed it to Lauren.

Lauren jotted her own number and address on the bedside pad. Then she kissed Jo long and hard, picked up her jacket, and headed for the door. She paused and turned, smiling. "This was lovely. Just how I'd hoped it would be. But I wish . . ." Her smile faded as she looked wistfully into Jo's eyes for a long moment, then seemed to brush a thought away with a slight shake of her head. With a sad smile, she said, "I wish this wasn't goodbye."

Then she was gone.

Jo lay back on the bed, staring at the ceiling. She wasn't likely to see Lauren again. But it was an exciting start to her trip—so many new experiences in just thirty-six hours.

chapter three

AS SHE RODE THE CROWDED TUBE TO HER HOME IN North London, Lauren took the card out of her pocket, running her finger over Jo's name. Would she ever see her again? The train rocked gently, and she pictured Jo's face and recalled her touch as she had so competently pleasured her body. She shuddered and hugged herself.

The woman in the opposite seat stared at her. A glance at her watch revealed she had less than an hour to pack if she was to meet Nina at Heathrow Airport on time. *Pull yourself together.*

Lauren caught only two hours of sleep on the plane. As they waited in the line for customs at JFK, Nina said, "Where are we going to stay?" As usual, they made few plans, leaving room for spontaneity.

A bearded young man behind them cleared his throat, and they turned. "I can recommend a hotel. It's in midtown Manhattan, but it's not too expensive. Do you want to go there together? Share a cab?" he said.

Nina looked him up and down and turned to Lauren. "What do you think?"

Uh-oh. She hoped this wasn't the start of Nina's adventures with men. They'd have to get separate rooms. Despite her reservations, she conceded. "I'm knackered after that flight and the gin and tonics. Let's go."

As they crept along the streets of New York in the cab with the window open, Lauren inhaled the aromas of caramelized, sugar-coated nuts and fresh pizza. Wailing sirens and honking horns accosted her ears, and the flashing neon lights they passed gave her a slight headache.

The young man's leg pressed against hers in the back seat. She relaxed when he mentioned meeting his girlfriend, who was driving up from Connecticut the following morning. Lauren fantasized she was meeting Jo, driving up from DC, then shook her head. *I'll probably never see her again.*

When they spilled out of the cab, Lauren dismissed the young man with, "Thanks, Jack. This was very sweet of you. Enjoy New York."

The two women took a tired-sounding elevator up to their room on the eighth floor. Lauren dropped her bag on the dingy carpet, visited the cramped bathroom, and flopped onto the twin bed, falling asleep with her clothes on.

Lauren awoke early after a sound sleep. Memories of the night with Jo drifted into her mind and made her stomach drop. She cherished her long-awaited experience of passion, even if she would never see Jo again.

Nina appeared dead to the world, her long sandy hair splayed across the pillow. Lauren got up, splashed water on her face, searched for her wallet in her handbag, and quietly let herself out.

She returned with two cups of black coffee and fresh donuts. She'd never eaten donuts for breakfast, but she enjoyed trying new things while traveling. Nina emerged from the bathroom and said, "What'd you bring us?"

"Donuts." Lauren took a bite of the sweet treat. "Yum. Let me finish this. Then I'll take a quick shower. You can start thinking of a plan while I'm in the bathroom."

Their plans took them to Windows on the World at the World Trade Center, the Empire State Building, and Times Square. After three days, Lauren yearned to leave the crowds, the sirens, and the never-ceasing honking. The huge cockroach that scurried over her sandaled foot while she was standing in line at the theater clinched her desire to move on.

But Boston enchanted her with its youthful college culture and hangouts. In Harvard Yard, they picnicked on the cool grass under maples, the leaves already turning color and drifting upon them while they ate. Watching the students laughing and talking as they hurried by between classes, Lauren regretted not going to college. She went straight to work at eighteen, though her bosses recognized her competence and intelligence and promoted her through the ranks. *Would a highly educated professional like Jo even consider partnering with me?* Jo appeared to be the woman of her dreams, even if a relationship with her loomed tantalizingly out of reach.

On Martha's Vineyard, they rented a motorbike and tootled around the island, stopping to admire the gingerbread houses painted in playful, bright colors and adorned with elaborate wood carvings. As it was the offseason, the restaurant owners were glad to see them and offered extra-large portions. Lauren enjoyed her first taste of fresh lobster dripping in warm butter. Satiated, she removed her lobster bib and took a sip of a crisp, light chardonnay. Day after tomorrow, they planned to return to London via New York.

"Nina, I know this sounds last minute, but I'd like to stay in the States for a few more days. I have a cousin living on Long Island I haven't seen yet. She might let me crash with her."

Nina licked her fingers and shot her a knowing look. "You just want to hook up with that American woman."

Lauren laughed. "You know me so well."

"What should I tell the office? That you met this hot American woman and you're staying in the States to shag her?"

"Don't be crude." Lauren couldn't suppress a smile as she pondered it. "I'm not due back at the office until next week."

"Right. Well, be careful. Even if you hook up, it's not likely to lead anywhere, given the distance. Just have a good time."

Lauren didn't reply, but she resolved to call her cousin when they returned to the hotel, hoping Jo had canceled her trip to Greece and returned to DC.

Lauren said goodbye to Nina at JFK Airport and continued riding the train to Long Island. Before calling her cousin from the station to pick her up, she found a phone box, dropped in some coins, and dialed Jo's home number. No answer. Her shoulders sagged as she hung up, and the coins jingled into the slot below. Chewing on her lip, she turned the card over and called Jo's office.

"Carter and Hobbs, attorney's office. Can I help you?"

"May I speak with Jo Turner, please?"

"Are you a client?"

The receptionist's voice was frosty, and Lauren almost hung up. She gulped and cleared her throat. "Ah . . . no, a personal friend."

"I see."

Lauren rubbed the back of her neck. *What does she see? This was not a good idea.*

The receptionist put her hand over the receiver to speak to someone. "I'm afraid she's not available."

Was she asking Jo if she wanted to take the call? Well out of her comfort zone now, Lauren said, "Do you know when she might become available?"

"She's out of the office, but I can take your number and have her call you when she returns."

"No, that's okay. I'll call back, thank you." Lauren hung up the receiver and sagged against the side of the phone booth. *Damn.*

Lauren's cousin and her husband welcomed Lauren and pampered her with home-cooked meals and stimulating conversation. But they must've wondered why she excused herself to walk to the phone booth on the corner several times a day and always returned to the house looking dejected.

Was it futile to stay in New York? Even if Jo returned, would she want to see her? Maybe it *was* just a one-night stand.

After three days, she surrendered to the obvious and flew home to London.

chapter four

Paris

AS SHE RECLINED IN HER SEAT ON THE FLIGHT TO PARIS the evening after meeting Lauren, Jo relived her night with her. She marveled that she experienced so little guilt about it. True, she had detected no love in Sharon's distracted farewell and tepid kiss when they said goodbye at the airport in Washington, DC. Would Sharon still meet her in Greece after the Paris conference? And if so, should she tell her about spending the night with Lauren?

In Paris, Jo sat with other international conference participants in a semicircle in the large meeting hall, each with a microphone connected to a translator in a glassed-in booth above. She gradually developed a scratchy throat and hoarse voice. *Damn.* She did not want to lose her voice at her first international conference. Her mind wandered to Lauren, her soft, lovely curves and passionate responsiveness, until she realized she'd completely lost track of what the Swiss presenter was saying.

Jo refocused on the conference, tuning in to the discussion

of laws surrounding the safe use of asbestos. By late afternoon, however, she pined for a respite, her throat burning.

A young Jewish attorney from Sweden named Micael took Jo under his wing. "What you need is some hot matzo ball soup. I know just the place."

Jo followed him down several winding streets, the sidewalk cafés bustling with patrons, the smell of roasting meats, fresh bread, and cigarette smoke assailing her one unblocked nostril. The French spoke so fast, gesturing with their hands. It was a wonder they didn't knock their wineglasses and espressos from their tables.

Jo's head throbbed. She was about to renege on their plans when Micael ushered her into a cheerful kosher restaurant. Micael ordered for them, and soon a steaming bowl of matzo balls swimming in a savory chicken soup sat before her. Another new experience. She inhaled the steam, and her blocked nostril opened. She looked up to find Micael gazing at her with a quizzical look.

"Do you have a boyfriend?" he asked in his accented English, his bushy eyebrows raised in question as he stroked his trim beard.

Uh-oh. "No, I have a girlfriend. At least, I think I do. If she's still my girlfriend."

Micael's face brightened. "Ah, good, that's what I thought. Would you be up for checking out the gay bars with me? Some mixed, both men and women."

Micael apparently saw no problem with cruising when one had a girlfriend. Or with spreading germs around when one is sick. Well, perhaps she didn't either, given her behavior in London. Despite her preference for monogamy, what did that say about her commitment to Sharon?

Jo swallowed a steaming spoonful of soup. "No, I had a wonderful experience in London. I think I'll find my way back to the hotel and crash. Thank you for this fabulous soup, though."

True to her word, as soon as she arrived at the hotel, she showered and crawled into bed, falling into a deep sleep.

The jangling of the telephone woke her. She glanced at the clock: 3:00 a.m. *Who would call at this hour?* She groaned and groped for the receiver. "Hello," she croaked.

"Hi, Jo." Sharon's voice sounded flat, lacking the warmth and seductive tenor of her greetings early in their courtship.

Irritation propelled Jo upright, causing her to knock her elbow against the hard headboard, eliciting a stab of pain. "Are you aware it's the middle of the night here?" She blew her nose, her throat still on fire.

"Yes, sorry. You don't sound well. But I wanted to tell you I'm not meeting you in Greece. When I put you on the plane in Washington, I felt nothing but relief. I just can't be . . . gay." Sharon paused while Jo coughed. "I'm dating men again. I'm telling you now so you can make other plans."

Jo let this news sink into her foggy brain. *Not a surprise.* Still, her chest tightened and her breathing grew shallow. While anger kept her tears at bay, she said, "So kind of you to tell me now in the middle of the night when I'm sick and alone in a foreign country." A coughing fit interrupted her. "I'm going back to sleep." She didn't wait for a response and hung up.

But sleep eluded her. Though Jo knew this breakup was coming and she'd had months to process, it still hurt her pride and self-esteem as much as her heart. It had always galled her that Sharon forbade even the most innocent sign of affection in public. Jo had thought their trip to Greece, including a stop on the island of Lesbos, might loosen Sharon's inhibitions and rekindle their flagging romance. A Hail Mary too late.

With her thoughts jabbing her, Jo got up to go to the bathroom and drink water. On the toilet with her head in her hands, she allowed herself a good cry.

When her tears ran out and numbness replaced the pain, an idea occurred to her. *What if I cancel my trip to Greece and return to London?* She raised her head and considered it. How long did Lauren say she'd stay in the States? Seven days? She could spend an extra day or two in Paris after the conference finished and then go to London. Lauren should be back by then. Her tear-streaked cheeks stretched into a broad smile. *I'll see Lauren again!*

Calmer now, she staggered back to bed and fell asleep.

Over the next week, her cold gave way to a nagging wet cough. The bouillabaisse offered at one of the arranged dinners tasted bland. The conference occupied her thoughts during the day. But most evenings, as she wandered the busy streets of Paris alone, Sharon's words rankled her.

How could Sharon return to men after the pleasures of lesbian love? Had Jo misinterpreted her enthusiasm in bed, or was Sharon faking it like she had with men? Ruled by ambition in her career, was her paranoia about being outed her main motivation to return to men? How had Jo let herself get involved with a woman ambivalent about her sexuality?

After the conference finished, Jo revisited the kosher restaurant for more chicken soup with Micael. Her cold was nearly gone. As she cut into the grainy matzo ball with the edge of her spoon, he regaled her with stories of his adventures cruising.

"You want to join me now that you have no girlfriend?" he said with a wicked smile, fingering his mustache.

"No, thank you. I've met someone in London. Someone I hope to see again."

"Ah, I see. You have a backup girlfriend," he teased with a wink.

Jo flinched at his suggestion. *I'm not like Micael.* She swallowed a spoonful of soup. "She's not my girlfriend," she said. "We've only met once."

Bidding farewell to Paris, Jo boarded the plane to London and imagined how surprised Lauren would be. Happily surprised, she hoped.

chapter five
London

JO CHECKED INTO THE SAME BLOOMSBURY HOTEL IN London in the early afternoon, bursting with excitement to see Lauren. As soon as she dropped her bags in her room, she hurried to the pay phone in the lobby and called her number. It rang and rang. No answer. Jo slumped back to her room, deflated, and flopped on the bed. *Have I gotten the dates wrong?* She stared at the ceiling, immobilized with disappointment. A half hour later, she rose and put on her coat. *I might as well explore London.*

Jo contacted her office before leaving the hotel. She answered questions about her pending cases and gave her secretary her contact information.

Drawn to the Greek Revival architecture of the British Museum, she entered the imposing structure to find herself overwhelmed with the prospect of exploring two million years of human history, art, and culture. She chose the exhibit of the Parthenon dedicated to the goddess Athena, then moved on to the Egyptian sculpture exhibit. Standing before the colossal granite image of King Ramesses II, she sighed. *I wish I had a romantic partner to travel with.*

As she emerged from the museum into the fading light, Jo pulled up her coat collar in the evening chill. On Sicilian Avenue, she found a red phone box and again tried Lauren. No answer.

The avenue bustled with people, trendy shops, and restaurants. At first, the human buzz lifted her spirits, but the couples sipping wine and laughing together in cozy restaurants reminded her of her lack. After another try of Lauren's number, the smell of garlic and basil drew her into a small Italian restaurant. The server seated her in a corner near the kitchen. The pans and plates clacking together and the whoosh of the kitchen door opening and closing reinforced her status: a single woman dining alone. As she sipped her chianti, she reflected on her situation: jilted by her girlfriend, and with little prospect of connecting with Lauren. Traveling solo was not as enjoyable as she'd hoped. She might change her ticket and return to the States early.

The following morning, Jo ordered a full English breakfast complete with baked beans and a fried tomato, but she only picked at it. No answer again when she tried Lauren's number. She flicked through the phone book for local bookstores and found Gay's the Word nearby. Strolling out of the hotel into the watery sunlight, she reminded herself to first look to the right when crossing the street.

Pausing on a bench in Russel Square in the cool crisp morning, she people watched. Women pushed baby prams, dogs walked their owners, and an old man read *The Times*. Two women joggers brushed by, talking and laughing. *No one sees me.* Sharon didn't see her either. Not her feelings. Not her vulnerability.

Why did she let their affair go on so long? She vowed to never again get involved with a woman who was bisexual, ambivalent, and unavailable. She shook off her painful musings, stood, and set off at a brisk pace for Gay's the Word.

Hardly anyone was browsing in the bookstore when she entered. The woman at the counter smiled. "Can I help you find something?"

"I'm a tourist and looking for something to do today."

The woman directed her to a bulletin board. Jo found a discussion group on feminist theory taking place that afternoon. She also noted a women's restaurant nearby that would do for lunch, as she'd eaten little of her breakfast. While she jotted the address down, a husky woman's voice behind her made her jump.

"I go there often. The food's pretty good."

Jo turned. A lanky woman in torn jeans and a plaid shirt smiled at her.

"Is it open for lunch?" Jo said.

"Yes, it is." The woman looked her over and apparently liked what she saw. "I'm headed there as soon as I buy these books if you'd like to join me?"

Lunch with a companion for a change was appealing. "Yes, I would."

They found a booth and slid into it, a scarred oak table between them. A long-haired young woman in a granny dress brought their soups and salads. They chatted amiably through mouthfuls of food. Judith hailed from the north of England and punctuated her questions with "luv" and "pet." During Judith's discourse on how she ended up in London, Jo appraised her new acquaintance. Though not pretty, she exuded health and fitness in a handsome, soft-butch sort of way.

Judith caught her looking. "Are you keen on seeing some London sights this afternoon? I have the whole day off."

"Maybe, but I need to check something first." Jo excused herself to find a pay phone. No answer again. *I should give up.*

After they paid, Jo accompanied Judith on foot to Hyde Park. As they walked along the lazy Serpentine, two scruffy puppies scampered by them in a game of chase, their leashes flying behind, delighting her. The cool, crisp fall air; the trees sporting hues of saffron, rust, and crimson; and the rhythm of walking allowed Jo to release some of her disappointment at not connecting with Lauren. As they swished through the fallen leaves on the footpath, Judith walked very close, bumping into Jo's side.

Is she coming on to me? Jo was a single woman now, and Judith was not unattractive. If she was still in her twenties, enthusiastically sampling women like a kid in a candy shop, she might consider a romp. But she viewed attraction differently now; she was no longer satisfied with short-term conquest. Despite only knowing Lauren for less than twenty-four hours, she'd returned to London hoping for a repeat of their promising first encounter. Who knows where it might lead?

As they left Hyde Park, Jo said, "Thank you, Judith, for a lovely afternoon. I must get back to my hotel. My girlfriend is flying in from New York this evening." *If only that were true on both counts.*

They exchanged their farewells and a quick hug, but no contact information. Jo watched Judith disappear around a corner, and a dull ache filled her chest. *Will I ever have a stable love?*

chapter six

THE FOLLOWING EVENING, AS LAUREN FUMBLED WITH keys to her London flat, the phone rang inside. She dropped her bag and searched for the right key. She unlocked the door and raced to answer it.

"Hello?"

"Lauren?"

Lauren's breath caught. She knew that low, sexy voice. "Jo?" *This is too good to be true.*

"I'm here in London. I was worried I'd missed you."

Lauren touched the bounding pulse in her neck. "Fantastic! I've just arrived from New York. Where are you staying?"

"Bloomsbury. Same hotel."

The fatigue of Lauren's long trip vanished, replaced by anticipation. "Come to my flat. Do you have a pen? I'll give you directions."

Lauren had enough time to shower, wash her hair, and change. Her chest buzzed with excitement. She tidied her flat and searched the refrigerator. Mostly empty. A rotten smell accosted her when she opened the produce drawer, and she quickly disposed of the soggy greens in the bin outside.

A quick glance at the wine rack revealed an expensive bottle of burgundy. She was just popping the cork when the doorbell rang. As she passed the hall mirror, she ran her fingers through her still-damp hair.

Lauren opened the door to find Jo dressed in jeans, hiking boots, and a leather jacket. A pair of gold loop earrings partially emerged from under her long, dark hair. She wore makeup and lip gloss. The butch-femme combination took Lauren's breath away. Jo's dark eyes searched Lauren's as her lips stretched into a tentative smile. She held out a grease-spotted bag of what smelled like fish and chips.

"Are you going to invite me in?"

Lauren could find no words to express her joy. She pulled Jo in, closed the door, and pinned her against it with a passionate kiss.

Jo's low moan of pleasure spurred Lauren on until Jo pulled away, gasping. "I guess I needn't have worried about whether you'd be glad to see me."

"Come and sit down. I'm so surprised you're here." Lauren led Jo to the soft cushions of her couch, and they sat side by side, legs and arms touching. Before Jo could begin speaking, Lauren threw her arms around her and kissed her again. "Just so there's no doubt I'm happy to see you. Now tell me what happened."

Jo sighed and pulled back slightly from Lauren's embrace. "While I was in Paris, I got a call from Sharon. She dumped me. Not a surprise, but I lost my enthusiasm for going to Greece. I changed my ticket to London because I wanted to see you again. I've been here two days already, calling you every few hours."

Warmth spread through Lauren's chest. *She came to London to see me.* "This is so incredible! Here I was extending my stay in New York, hoping you'd come back, calling your home number every few hours. I even called your office."

Jo's eyes widened. "We wasted precious time!"

Lauren stroked Jo's hair and looked into those dark eyes that melted her soul down. *Sharon's loss, my gain. Maybe.*

"Did it hurt when Sharon dumped you?"

"My pride, mostly. But the thought of seeing you kept my spirits up during the conference."

Though Jo smiled when she spoke, Lauren detected sadness in her eyes. *Am I Jo's consolation prize?* She'd never expected to see her again, yet here she was. Her body's reaction to Jo in the flesh, the lightheaded giddiness and warmth in her belly, told her to stuff the analysis. For now. "I'm so happy you're here! How long can you stay? What do you want to do?"

"Besides the obvious, we should eat dinner while it's still warm. I can stay at least three more days. We have time to enjoy each other and maybe explore a little of London. If you want to, and don't have to work."

"You must know the answer to that. And I don't return to the office until next week."

The mouthwatering aroma of crispy batter, tender fish, and golden fries coming from the paper bag reminded Lauren she hadn't eaten for hours. How thoughtful of Jo to think she might be hungry. "Let's eat. I can hardly wait for dessert."

Lauren awoke and reached for Jo. She wasn't there! She bolted upright but relaxed when she inhaled the rich scent of coffee brewing. The sound of cupboards opening and closing reassured her further. *Last night wasn't a dream.*

Jo walked in wearing Lauren's bathrobe with two steaming mugs of black coffee. "Good morning, sleepyhead. I had no luck finding any creamer. It's nine thirty already. I must return to the hotel and check out. I didn't do it last night, as I wasn't sure I'd be staying."

"Silly girl." Lauren took a sip, then put her mug aside, reached up, and kissed Jo, her lips soft and warm and tasting of coffee. "Come back to bed."

"With pleasure."

They sat together in the bed and finished their coffees before Jo dressed quickly and left for the hotel. Lauren settled back onto the pillow, languidly stretching, and remembering their night of lovemaking before falling asleep again.

Lauren woke again to the sound of Jo entering her flat and setting her bag down. Moments later, Jo perched on the edge of the bed, looking dejected.

Lauren's body tensed and she sat up. Had she talked with Sharon? She laid her hand on Jo's arm, searching her face for clues. "What's wrong?"

"There was an urgent message for me from my office to call right away. A situation has developed in California and our law firm is getting involved. A pesticide called ethylene dibromide apparently causes reproductive problems in men. It damages sperm with long-term exposure."

Lauren's body relaxed. Not Sharon. "Sounds like good stuff."

Jo flashed her a brief smile. "This has gone beyond worker's compensation, and a class action lawsuit is being filed. The senior partners want me out there ASAP to interview farm workers and take depositions. I need to leave for DC tonight or tomorrow, then fly to San Francisco the next day."

Lauren sighed and flopped backward on the pillow. *Damn.*

"I'm sorry." Disappointment clouded Jo's face. "I have to make my plane reservations and call the office as soon as possible."

"I'm sorry too." Lauren sat up again and rubbed Jo's back. "I'll go out and get us something to eat."

Once on the pavement, tears filled Lauren's eyes. *We could have more than a fling if we just had time.* She saw the potential for what she'd yearned for since she'd admitted to herself she was a lesbian: a long-term relationship.

After drying her eyes and blowing her nose, she popped into her favorite Chinese restaurant for takeout, then to the off-license liquor store for beer. As she trudged back to her flat, she reminded herself that Jo lived thousands of miles away, across an ocean. *How likely is it we can develop a lasting relationship, anyway?* Jo's job involved frequent travel to interesting cities. *Does she have a woman in every port?*

Jo was still on the phone when Lauren arrived at her flat. Lauren placed a plate of ginger chicken and vegetable spring rolls before her and sat next to her on the couch, their plates balanced on their knees. They ate in silence, punctuated only by Jo's one-sided conversation with her office.

Jo hung up. "Well, it's done. I fly out tomorrow, late morning. Then to San Francisco the next day. Thank you for the food. This ginger chicken is delicious." Jo licked her fingers and regarded Lauren. "I understand this change of plan is disappointing. For both of us."

"Yes." Lauren held Jo's gaze, then kissed her lips, tasting sweet ginger. She took Jo's hand and led her to the bedroom. *Who knows what the future holds?* But Jo had come to London to see her and had called her every day. So now, perhaps for the last time, Lauren intended to ravish her.

chapter seven
Washington DC

ON THE FLIGHT HOME TO DC, JO SLEPT MUCH OF THE way. Disparate fragments of events of the last couple of weeks filled her dreams. She was startled awake when her head drifted onto the shoulder of the woman in the next seat. Jerking upright, she pulled out her Rita Mae Brown novel, *Six of One*, and tried to read, but her mind wandered.

She didn't look forward to returning to her townhouse. Though they never lived together, traces of Sharon would still haunt the place, including her nightgown, toothbrush, and the tent they'd bought together for their trip to the Outer Banks. How would they split that? Sharon could have it. Along with the memories of their lovemaking in it on that rainy night in June.

Then more pleasant thoughts of Lauren brought a smile. *What an honor to be her first.*

That evening, as Jo unpacked from her trip to Europe and packed for her trip to California, she put Don McLean's "Castles in the Air" on the record player. She paused her packing and listened. Tired of urban life, he sought the peace of country living with a like-minded woman. The words resonated with her. Jo also yearned for the same with a woman. And a job that didn't require as much travel. And a dog. *Definitely a dog.*

Fourteen hours later, Jo boarded the flight to San Francisco. She scanned her briefing papers. Late that afternoon, she would meet with Cal/OSHA in San Francisco. They were about to issue an Emergency Temporary Standard for ethylene dibromide. The next day she would interview several members of the United Farm Workers union in Salinas.

Interviews and depositions occupied ten hours a day for most of the week. Hurried meals, meetings, and sleep filled the rest. When she had a moment, images of Lauren's hooded eyes, her smile, her lovely hands inevitably intruded. Sure, they might write letters and have an occasional expensive phone call. But maintaining an ongoing romantic relationship would be difficult. She knew she should file the experience away as a pleasant interlude, dulling the pain of her breakup with Sharon.

On Friday, after an exhausting week, an attorney, Jim, from one of the local law firms representing the farmworkers, stopped Jo in the hallway.

"Hey, my wife and I have a house in Marin County. Totally different vibe than San Francisco. We'd love to have you join us for dinner if you're not going back to DC right away."

He has a wife. Should be safe. "Sure, I'd like to. I'm not leaving until Sunday."

They served her a Mexican dinner on their deck: enchiladas with serrano chili sauce and Oaxaca black bean soup. And plenty of California wine, which was coming into its own to compete with the French wines. Jo floated through the evening on a pleasant high. Sitting next to her, Jim's wife smiled at her often and touched her hand when talking.

After dessert, Jim said, "Are you up for a dip in our hot tub?"

Jo squirmed in her chair. Was this normal California hospitality? "Ah, no, I don't think so. Plus, I don't have a bathing suit."

"No suit is required," Jim said and smiled.

Jo's brow furrowed, and she looked over Jim's shoulder at his wife beaming at her. *What the hell?* California hospitality includes a soak in the hot tub and a threesome? She'd definitely gotten a seductive vibe from Jim's wife, but the whole idea made her stomach wrench.

"No, I should get back. I need to review the depositions and contact my senior partner in the morning. Thank you for dinner."

"Are you sure you have to go so soon?" Jim said, laying a hand on her arm.

Jo jerked her arm away. "Yes, definitely." She grabbed her bag and hurried out the door, waving a hand without looking back. Fortunately, she'd driven her rental car. She hoped she was not over the limit for alcohol as she groped for the California map in her glove compartment.

The next morning, after she hung up the phone with the senior partner, Jo needed to be around other lesbians. She perused *The Bay Area Reporter*, a gay newspaper. Rita Mae Brown was reading and signing books at a San Francisco hotel. She could get her copy of *Six of One* signed, a prospect that lifted her mood.

Since parking was challenging in the city, she walked and

took an open-air cable car, holding on to a metal pole on the side as it clacked up and down the hills of the city, its bell dinging loudly next to her ear. At the hotel, women, many in jeans, plaid shirts, and sweater vests, filled the ballroom with their anticipation and energy. Already, Jo felt at home, although she stood out as East Coast formal in her gabardine slacks, white silk blouse, and scarf. She hadn't thought to bring her lesbian attire on this trip.

Rita Mae told stories for almost an hour. "If I were a straight man, I'd be considered the Mark Twain of our time." *What an ego.* Still, after Rita Mae published *Rubyfruit Jungle* in 1973, lesbians did consider her a literary icon.

As Jo stood near the back of a long line of fans waiting to get books signed, she chatted with the person behind her, an attractive woman in her fifties. "She's hot," the woman said, nodding toward Rita Mae. "I'd love to ask her out."

"Go ahead," Jo said.

"She wouldn't go out with a woman my age. Plus, she probably has a partner."

"If she does, she'll tell you. Nothing to lose by trying." That had been Jo's philosophy in her twenties, and it had worked for her then.

"Except my pride." The woman silently regarded Jo. "Why don't *you* ask her out? She'd probably go for you. Do you have a girlfriend?"

"I doubt it. And no, I don't."

"Go ahead, then. Ask her out. I'll enjoy it vicariously."

Jo smiled. Inviting Rita Mae out to dinner was something she might have dared to do in her twenties, but now? Still, it had been a long, taxing week in the straight world and conversation with the author would be a welcome cap to it. She pulled a pen and a small notepad from her shoulder bag and wrote, "Would you like to have dinner with me this evening?" She gave the name of her hotel and the phone number and signed her name.

Her coconspirator gave Jo a thumbs-up.

The absurdity of her audacity caused Jo to change her mind. She stuffed the note in her pocket. But as the line inched closer, Rita Mae's animated conversation, brown eyes, and toothy smile that deepened the creases at the side of her mouth enticed her. She took the note out and placed it inside the cover of her book.

When she arrived at the front, Jo handed Rita Mae her copy of *Six of One* with the note. Rita Mae pulled it out, read it, then placed it back inside. Without looking up, she signed Jo's book. Then, glancing up, she said, "Thanks, but no," and handed Jo her book. Disappointed, and a little embarrassed, Jo shrugged it off and left the hotel alone.

That evening, as she crunched her taco salad in the hotel restaurant, Jo ruminated on the last few weeks. Her girlfriend had dumped her and was dating men. She had a brief tryst with a woman who lived thousands of miles away. And she'd just asked a famous author to dinner on a dare who turned her down. None was likely to bring her any closer to a peaceful domestic life with a long-term relationship. She should stop looking for milk in a hardware store.

chapter eght
London

WHEN JO LEFT FOR THE STATES, LAUREN MOPED ABOUT with little energy for unpacking, grocery shopping, and the mundane tasks of living. In the lunchroom at work, Nina quizzed her about her extended time in the States, and Lauren updated her.

"Remember, she lives in DC. It will go nowhere, so don't get your hopes up," Nina warned.

Lauren shrugged. "Right." She trudged back to her desk and limply sorted through her backlog of work. She willed herself to stop thinking about Jo. But then she thought about her all the time.

On the weekend, Lauren returned to the pub where she'd met Jo.

Chris, the bartender, greeted her. "Hiya, Lauren, where've you been? We missed you the last couple of weeks."

"New York, Boston, Martha's Vineyard."

"World traveler, you. How was it?" Chris finished wiping down the counter and leaned forward on her elbows.

"I had the best time with a woman I met here. An American."

"Yeah, I remember her. Tall, slender, nice-looking. How could I forget? Lucky you." She winked.

Lauren smiled. "Indeed." She swirled the wine in her glass. She had to speak up over the Rolling Stones' "Miss You" thrumming in the background. "We didn't have enough time together, though. She's gone back to the States."

Chris threw her towel over her shoulder. "So, you going to stay in touch?"

"Yes, I hope so. We said we'd write and call. I'd really like to see her again. Soon."

"I can understand that, luv. But does she have a gal at home?"

"Not anymore. They broke up a couple of weeks ago."

"Ah." Chris signaled to a woman waiting at the far end of the bar. "Be right there, luv," she mouthed before turning back to Lauren. "It's not a good idea to catch someone on the rebound. Be careful." She sauntered off to tend to her customer.

Lauren had also heard that love affairs forged on the rebound rarely lasted. She should forget Jo and try to meet someone new. Someone local and available. She scanned the women in the pub but saw no one who interested her. Not even for a dance.

Two hours later, still on her own, Lauren headed back to her flat. She didn't want to meet anyone new. She wanted Jo.

When she arrived home, Lauren flopped on the couch and calculated the time difference before calling Jo. No answer. Perhaps she was still in California. Did she have to work on the weekend too? Did she have a date? Lauren hung up and told herself to chill.

She tried calling Jo again on Sunday evening. This time, Jo picked up. She sounded delighted to hear from Lauren, and Jo's low, sultry voice made her stomach quiver. After the initial conversation, Jo recounted how she had asked Rita Mae Brown out to dinner.

"I'm relieved she turned you down." No way would Lauren want to compete with Rita Mae.

"I expected she would, but she didn't even look at me." Jo laughed.

"Of course, that would have made all the difference," Lauren teased. "You're so vain."

"I am not."

No, she really isn't, although she has every right to be. The banter continued, until Lauren said, "I have something to ask you. You can say no and I will accept it, but I have to ask."

"Ask away."

"Can I come visit you in Washington?" Lauren sucked in her breath. Jo's silence unnerved her, and her heart pounded. Static on the line interrupted the silence. Lauren still held her breath, dreading Jo's refusal.

Finally, Jo said, "I think we can arrange that. When are you thinking?"

Lauren let out a long breath. "Soon? If my boss okays it. I've just taken leave, so it may be tricky."

"I'll return to California in a few weeks, so the sooner the better." After a pause, she added, "It would be wonderful to see you again."

A rush of warmth filled Lauren's chest. "I'll talk to my boss tomorrow."

The following morning, Lauren approached her sour-faced superior in her office at the North London Council. In response to her knock, Lauren received a brusque, "Come in."

Her boss did not look up from her paperwork.

Lauren cleared her throat. "Um, I know I just took some leave, but I would like another ten days off. Starting on Monday."

The older woman looked up and gave her a withering look, making Lauren flush. Then, waving her hand dismissively, she said, "That's ridiculous; you were just on holiday. You have several grant applications you've yet to deal with besides the backlog from your previous absence. So, no leave." With the matter settled, her boss returned to her paperwork.

Lauren's shoulders slumped as she slunk back to her desk. She sat drumming her fingers and swiveled from side to side in her office chair. For years, she had taken on extra work, completing her projects competently and on time. She'd worked through last summer instead of traveling and used no sick days. She deserved a little slack.

What if she called in sick? Would her boss fire her when she did not receive the required medical certification in three days? It wasn't like her to be so irresponsible. Her boss considered her a reliable and valuable employee. But despite warnings from her friends, she was eager to discover what could emerge from this affair with Jo. If she waited too long, Jo might find someone else.

That evening, after confirming with Jo, she called British Airways and booked a flight to Dulles Airport for the following Sunday. She'd be in DC when she'd call in sick to work on Monday. Her job might be gone when she got back. *I hope the risk is worth it.*

chapter nine
Washington DC

WHEN JO GOT THE CALL FROM LAUREN TO SAY SHE WAS arriving in DC on Sunday, she agreed without thinking it through. Several depositions and background research on the health effects of ethylene dibromide awaited her attention. Discovery boxes were still arriving with medical records, and she had yet to line up her medical experts. And she'd just resolved not to date women who held little prospect of a long-term relationship. Yet she'd agreed to a visit from just such a woman.

Am I an incurable hedonist? Probably. Perhaps she should relax and enjoy the time they had, with no expectations. She'd better hunker down even harder at work for the next two days. The late nights she'd been putting in at the office to avoid thinking about Sharon would not be possible, or desirable, while Lauren was visiting.

When Lauren strode through Passport Control and Arrivals at Dulles Airport on Sunday evening, Jo rushed forward to embrace her. She did not give the straight-woman, quick squeeze and pat on the back but held on tight, forgetting she was not out to clients who might see her.

Lauren bubbled over with chatter as they waited for her bags. When they got to the car, Jo pulled her in for a proper snog, as Lauren called it, until the windows fogged.

As they drove through Jo's Logan Circle neighborhood, Lauren eyed the run-down Victorian homes, the graffiti on the equestrian statue, and the groups of young men on the street corners. Once they got to her gated community, Jo reached for the remote control to open the tall iron-barred gate.

Lauren's eyes widened with astonishment. "Wow, this is bizarre."

"The neighborhood is not that safe. Sadly, there is still much poverty and drug dealing, though it's getting better. While I'm at work, you shouldn't go out on foot. Take a taxi."

Lauren shook her head. "I walk around London all the time and feel perfectly safe."

"It's different here. You'll see." The gates opened slowly, and they drove in.

Knowing Lauren would be tired from her trip and in need of a quick bite before bed, Jo had picked up a vegetarian pizza on her way to the airport. As they sat at the dining table munching their warmed pizza and sipping beers, Jo outlined possibilities for what Lauren might enjoy doing.

"Are you interested in the play, *Evita*? It's at the National Theatre, and I can try to get tickets. While I'm at the office, you should definitely visit the Smithsonian museums."

"I don't care what we do, as long as I'm with you."

Lauren's smile made Jo shiver. She rose to clear their plates, biting her lip. *For Lauren, I'm the primary attraction.* She'd have to be careful not to raise their expectations—just enjoy a good time like she'd planned.

That night, they started with gentle kisses that soon caught fire. Despite Lauren's long journey, she enthusiastically pursued making love, and Jo needed no persuasion.

The following morning, Jo stumbled out of bed but let Lauren sleep. As she drove to the office, she made plans. Tickets for *Evita*. Some dinners out. A party of lesbian professionals. The Smithsonian, the Mall, and the monuments.

Late morning, Jo called home. Lauren had already rummaged in her kitchen, taking inventory of the food. "You must not eat at home. Your refrigerator is mostly empty."

That's the problem. I need a home life with a partner to want to come home to eat. "Yeah, mostly I eat out," she admitted.

"How about I make you dinner tonight?"

Was Lauren reading her mind? "That would be lovely. I should be home by six thirty. Don't forget to take a taxi to the grocery store." The anticipation of a home-cooked meal with an erotic dessert put a spring in Jo's step as she sailed down the hall to her next meeting.

Jo arrived home on time. The aroma of onions, mushrooms, and herbs greeted her at the door. She found Lauren in the kitchen wearing her apron, a gift Jo had never worn. She encircled her arms around Lauren from the back and nuzzled her neck, planting kisses up to her ear.

Lauren shivered. "Keep that up, and there'll be no dinner."

"Okay, I'll do a quick change and be right back to be your sous chef."

In the bedroom, Jo donned soft, worn blue jeans, a flannel

shirt, and fuzzy socks. She kept on her earrings and light makeup. She smiled at her reflection in the mirror. Lauren in her kitchen cooking dinner for her was better than any outing. *I could get used to this.*

Jo returned to find Lauren had everything under control. "The beef bourguignon has been cooking for four hours. Only one more hour to go. I just finished the panna cotta and put it in the freezer so it'll set up more quickly. Let's enjoy a glass of wine and I'll tell you about my shopping trip."

They sat together on the couch. Jo slung an arm around Lauren and turned her body toward her to listen, the pot simmering softly in the background.

"I left the compound on foot, not in a taxi, as you suggested," Lauren began.

Jo's eyes widened. "Not a good idea."

"Yes, I know. So, I picked up the beef, vegetables, and herbs, but the liquor store was weird." Lauren took a sip of her wine.

"How so?"

"Everything was locked up behind plastic. I pointed to the burgundy wine I needed, and the proprietor whispered to me to wait until everyone else had left the store. Then he hurriedly took it down and wrapped it for me, saying that if his customers knew I was buying an expensive wine, somebody might mug me."

Jo tensed. "Sounds about right." She regretted not emphasizing enough her warning to Lauren not to go out on foot.

"When I left the store, three guys started following me, but it didn't worry me. Not until I sped up, and they sped up. And when I crossed the street, they crossed the street. They were talking and laughing all the while."

"Oh, no." Jo tightened her arm around her.

"Mind you, I was carrying grocery bags in both arms, a purse over my shoulder, and an umbrella."

Lauren's vulnerability alarmed Jo. "Holy shit! What did you do?"

"I came to a bus stop. Then I laid my bags on the bench, held out my umbrella, and said, 'The first one of you who touches me gets this in the balls.'"

Jo's breath caught. "Oh. My. God. They could've overpowered you."

"I know. My heart was in my throat. But then one guy said, 'Hey sister, you're British! That's cool,' and they kept on walking."

Jo let out her breath, set aside their wineglasses, and took Lauren in her arms. "I'm so glad you're okay." *Lauren has guts. She didn't take shit from anyone and stood up for herself.* Jo admired her chutzpa. She kissed Lauren, and a surge of desire sent blood rushing to her sensitive parts. But first, there was the hard-won dinner whose tantalizing, oniony aroma wafted from the kitchen.

"I'm fine. Let's eat," Lauren said, pulling Jo up from the couch.

When they sat down to dinner, Jo took her first bite of tender, savory beef bourguignon. *This is the life.*

chapter ten

JO'S SHOULDER PRESSED AGAINST LAUREN'S IN THE National Theatre. During the emotional singing of "Don't Cry for Me Argentina," Jo took her hand and held it under her coat. Warmth spread through Lauren's chest with a light giddiness, a sensation she'd had often during the past week. *Is this what it's like to fall in love?* A new experience for her. While Jo was at work, she daydreamed about waking up with her every morning. Could they ever live together? Would the passion continue? The improbability of ever living together threatened to spoil her mood, and she pushed it from her mind.

When the play finished and they were filing out of the theater, Jo said, "It's a beautiful evening, not too cold. Let's walk to the Mall and check out the monuments. They're all lit up at night."

"Sure, I'd love to. Is it safe?"

"Perfectly safe. The Mall is crawling with Capitol Police and National Park rangers, as well as quite a few tourists."

Lauren put her arm through Jo's and leaned against her as they walked. A gentle breeze rustled the fallen leaves and the soft hum of the city accompanied them, with an occasional plane rumbling overhead. The Capitol Building mirrored in the reflective pool was impressive, but the Washington Monument was too phallic for her taste. The warm, floaty feeling enveloped her as Lauren took in the sights.

"My favorite historical figure is Abraham Lincoln," Jo said as she urged Lauren toward the memorial along the elm-lined promenade. Its lighted Doric columns and the white marble of the imposing structure contrasted with the inky sky. They climbed the stairs holding hands and stood before the massive nineteen-foot statue of Lincoln. He grasped the sides of his chair with one hand clenched and the other relaxed, staring ahead with a pensive expression.

"As a child, Lincoln seemed a larger-than-life hero to me. As I learned about his life, I realized he was just a flawed man of his times who suffered from melancholia. That made his vision and determination even more impressive." Jo turned and ran her fingers over the *Gettysburg Address* etched into the wall. "Once I could recite this by heart."

Lauren smiled. "Try it, now."

Jo stood with her back against the wall and delivered it flawlessly, without pause.

Lauren had a sudden urge to touch her. She drew Jo close and kissed her, her hands wandering until she found bare skin. Just as she was about to reach her breasts, footsteps and a woman's voice startled her.

"Excuse me, what are you doing?"

Lauren jerked back to see a woman in a park ranger uniform staring at them with her eyes wide.

"Um . . . kissing?" Lauren's neck flushed with embarrassment, as if she'd been caught with her hand in the cookie jar. *Well, almost.* She hoped her British accent would alert the ranger they were tourists. She so didn't want Jo to get in trouble.

The ranger frowned. "This is not the place for it. Go somewhere private."

They hurried down the steps, giggling like teenagers.

Once they reached the car, Jo pulled Lauren into the back seat and locked the doors. Her body yielded to Jo's insistent kisses as the windows fogged. Jo reached around and undid her bra while sliding her leg between Lauren's thighs. She felt herself falling, unaware of her surroundings, only Jo's hands, her mouth, and the weight of her body as she surrendered to desire.

Monday, after Jo went to work, Lauren took out the teapot covered in painted roses Jo had bought her because she said all Englishwomen must drink tea. She set the pot of tea to steep and flopped on the couch with a guidebook to plan her day. She would start with the Museum of Natural History, then find lunch nearby. Then, if she had time, she'd pop over to the Air and Space Museum.

She wondered if Jo preferred a stay-at-home partner. Or did she want a professional woman with a career of her own? She knew little about Jo's previous girlfriends, other than Sharon. Only that Jo had had quite a few.

She stood, then sat, then stood again and paced. She'd put a lot on the line to come here. Her job for one. Her heart for another. Did Jo also want more than a fling and great sex? She rubbed her arms and reached for the teapot. She hoped so.

As Lauren approached the swinging door of the Museum of Natural History, she stumbled into a man exiting. "Oh, excuse me," she said quickly as he pivoted aside with acrobatic grace.

"It was my fault, really. I was daydreaming and not looking," he said in a posh British accent.

Lauren looked at his handsome features more closely. She lifted an eyebrow and cocked her head. "You're Cary Grant!"

"That I am," he said, smiling. "Enjoy your visit." He turned and strode away, leaving Lauren open-mouthed.

Wow. What were the chances of literally running into Cary Grant? Perhaps as good as her chances of remaining in the US with Jo. Maybe it was a good omen.

Lauren was just finishing chopping vegetables and cutting up pork loin for a stir-fry when the front door opened, heralding Jo's arrival. She put her briefcase down with a thud and hung up her coat, then she strode into the kitchen and wrapped her arms around Lauren. "I've been looking forward to this all day." Her mouth sought Lauren's for a lingering kiss. "Wow, you taste like wine. Is there a bottle open?"

"Yes, let me pour." Lauren turned the heat down on the stir-fry. "Come, let's sit for a few minutes."

When they settled on the couch, Jo said, "I've had a frustrating day. My prime expert witness reviewed the medical records and concluded there were no illnesses related to chemical exposure. My claimant's sexual dysfunction had other causes, like depression, alcoholism, and a cheating wife."

"Isn't that a good thing? To have treatable causes?" Lauren took a sip of her wine and regarded Jo in her dark-blue business suit, white silk blouse, and scarf, the light catching one of her gold earrings. Jo crossed her long, shapely legs at the knee, one high heel dangling. She looked so feminine, yet she came on so butch in bed. The memory set butterflies loose in Lauren's stomach.

"They won't see it that way," Jo said, "but enough about my work. How about your day?"

Lauren blew out a breath and set her glass on the side table. "My day was interesting. I'll finish up cooking while you change, and I'll share with you over dinner my story of running into Cary Grant."

When Jo disappeared into the bedroom, Lauren returned to the kitchen with that warm, floaty sensation in her chest again. While she watched the water come to a boil for noodles, Lauren considered bringing up the possibility of their having a future. It was unlikely Jo would abandon her law practice to relocate to the UK. Logic would demand that Lauren give up her government job —if she still had one. Then what employment opportunities would she have in the US? Could Jo sponsor her somehow, even though they couldn't legally marry?

Her brow furrowed as she rubbed the back of her neck. *Now isn't the time.* It was too early to bring up a subject of such magnitude. Lauren knew not to pressure Jo, who'd just gotten out of a relationship with Sharon.

Jo appeared from the bedroom in her signature jeans and plaid shirt. Lauren enveloped her in a tight embrace, breathing in the fresh smell of shampoo clinging to her hair. *If only I could hold on to her forever.*

chapter eleven

DESPITE HER INTENT TO JUST HAVE A GOOD TIME, Lauren was growing on her. Jo's mind skipped ahead to the possibility of something more long-term. The following day, she flipped through her Rolodex and jotted down the number of a friend from law school, an immigration attorney.

This is premature, Jo admonished herself. She put the number aside.

Later that day, though, she retrieved the number and dialed. Her friend was in the office.

After the preliminaries, Jo got to the point. "Let's say a British citizen wants to come to the US to work for six months or a year. What do they need?"

"They can get a visitor's visa as a tourist, but they can't work. To get a job, they need an employer who sponsors them and proves they couldn't find a qualified US citizen for the position. Then they might be eligible for a nonimmigrant work visa."

Jo's shoulders slumped, and she let out a long breath. "So, a British citizen without a college degree working in a London government office would not likely qualify for a job that a US citizen can't fill."

"Probably not."

Jo thanked her friend and hung up. Swiveling back and forth in her office chair, she chewed her pen. She'd told herself to hang loose with Lauren, with no expectations. Despite this, she'd caught herself placing Lauren into her fantasy of a stable home life. But this was unrealistic. And Lauren was leaving the next day.

Their last evening should be memorable. She could take Lauren out for a dinner at the 1789 Restaurant. Or they could eat in the adjacent F. Scott's since Lauren was a fan of F. Scott Fitzgerald. Or maybe she could cook for her at home. Her repertoire included buttermilk pancakes and tacos, but she'd already made both during Lauren's stay. Or she could pick up some Indian takeout reminiscent of their first night together.

Whatever they did, she must avoid any suggestion that their affair could continue. This might be their last night together. She dialed F. Scott's for reservations.

Jo left work early, announcing to her paralegal she'd be in late the next morning. She gave him a stack of medical records to organize and rushed to catch the elevator before the door closed.

At the restaurant, the host seated them among travel posters from the twenties and thirties. They admired an original cartoon by Hirschfeld from *The New York Times*, cut glass blocks from the Chrysler Building in New York, and an art deco stained-glass window.

"Did you know F. Scott failed the entrance exams to Princeton several times but talked his way into being admitted? He neglected his studies, though, and never graduated. He was too busy writing," Lauren said. They discussed writers of the Jazz

Age in America until the conversation drifted to British politics and the Falklands War.

It surprised Jo to learn that Lauren had voted for Margaret Thatcher. "Why did you vote for her?" she asked.

"Because the Labor Party had no economic policy. The country was going to rack and ruin, and she offered concrete solutions."

As Lauren talked, Jo studied her in the candlelight. She couldn't describe the color of Lauren's eyes; they seemed to change with the light, sometimes hazel, sometimes dark blue. Her slightly crooked front tooth did not detract from her alluring smile. That Lauren was also intelligent and literate added to her appeal, despite her lack of a college education. *Why does she have to live so far away?*

Throughout dinner, Jo steered the conversation away from Lauren's imminent departure. But the knowledge that their affair had an uncertain future cast a pall over an otherwise lovely evening.

On the way home, Lauren brought up the inevitable. "When will we see each other again?"

"I'm not sure," Jo said. "I have to go to California again for several weeks. You have a lot of catch-up to do, having been away so much."

Lauren remained silent on the journey home. Once they arrived and parked, she reached for Lauren's hand. "We'll keep in touch—write and call." Jo wouldn't lose contact with this woman who had so many qualities she admired.

That night in bed, despite Jo's despondency, she savored Lauren with an urgency and passion borne of the knowledge it might never happen again.

With Lauren safely back in London, Jo investigated the requirements of becoming a solicitor in the UK, but the obstacles gave her a headache. She leaned her elbows on her desk and covered her face with her hands.

When she and Lauren said their goodbyes at the airport, Jo despaired. How could they get in deeper, falling in love, when there was no hope of even living in the same country? It made little sense to carry on. The impossibility of their situation would only make parting worse. She must protect Lauren and herself.

The following evening, she stopped off for some Chinese takeout and ate alone at home, the silence like a heavy cape around her. After dinner, she sat at her desk and wrote to Lauren.

> *Lauren, because we live in different countries and moving is not an option for either of us, continuing to see each other as lovers will only become more painful. Though it hurts me to write this, we have to stop.*
>
> *I will always care for you. You are an amazing woman. If you will accept my long-distance friendship, we can still write and call one another. I am truly sorry we can't experience what could have grown even stronger between us.*

When she undressed and opened the shower door, her eyes landed on Lauren's shampoo on the ledge. Her absence punched her in the gut. Here she was, traveling down a dead-end road again, letting her feelings get out of control, her dream of a stable, loving relationship as distant as ever. She turned on the shower and let the water mix with her tears.

On the other side of the Atlantic, Lauren was dealing with the fallout of her unauthorized absence from work. "It's only because of your past record of reliability that you even have a job," her boss said, frowning at her over her glasses. "You're on probation for the next six months."

What a relief. Lauren returned to her desk, determined to put in extra hours to catch up. By midafternoon her mind wandered to the last day with Jo. Lauren hadn't pushed her for any commitment, and Jo had offered none. Still, Lauren couldn't help planning what they would do together on Jo's next visit to London. They could go see *Wild Wild Women* in the West End if it was still showing. Or *Annie*. Jo might even enjoy a football game featuring her home team, Millwall. After work, she wandered through a Christmas market amid busy chatter, the clink of glasses, and the calls of the vendors. She fingered brightly colored wool scarves as she considered what to get Jo for Christmas.

Lauren wrote to Jo to let her know she still had a job. She shared her ideas for what they might do together in London and enclosed two novels by the French author, Colette.

Several days later, Lauren received Jo's letter. She tore it open. Standing just inside her front door, she read and reread it, her hands shaking. The letter dropped to the floor as she swayed, letting out a grief-choked sob before collapsing on the couch.

PART II
May–June 2003

chapter twelve
Paris

LAUREN TURNED THE KEY IN THE APARTMENT DOOR. *What mood will Delphine be in this evening?* she wondered.

"You're late, and I wanted to speak to you." Though this sounded like an accusation, Delphine didn't say it in the harsh tone she used when she was angry, which was often.

"Sorry. The Périph was all snarled up," Lauren replied as she toed off her shoes. The Parisian ring road was unavoidable in her commute. "So, what did you want to talk about?"

Delphine had been lying on the couch watching television. She'd become quite sedentary over the twenty-one years they'd been together. She flicked it off, pulled herself up, and shuffled to the bookshelf for the atlas.

"I'd like to revisit the US this summer. It's been ten years since our last trip, and I haven't been to as many places in the US as you have."

They usually spoke in English, which Lauren also spoke at

work, translating French film scripts into English for subtitles and dubbing.

The residual odor of cooked cabbage and sausage wafted from the kitchen. "Can I have some dinner before we talk?"

Delphine bristled. "I've eaten. If you didn't spend so much time at the studio..."

Here we go again. Lauren worked long hours to afford their Parisian lifestyle. Delphine worked part time, studying who knows what. They now owned the apartment, but Paris was an expensive city. "Did you leave some dinner for me?"

"No."

Lauren sighed. In the kitchen, she began chopping vegetables for a stir-fry. She was careful about her diet. Late-onset type 1 diabetes had been a shock in her late thirties.

Delphine hovered as she chopped. "I'd like to visit California. You have a friend in San Francisco, don't you? We could stay with her and save money."

Lauren didn't look up. "I've not seen her in years. I wouldn't be comfortable just calling her up out of the blue and asking to stay with her." Tears ran down her cheeks from the onions. She scraped them into a frying pan.

As usual, Delphine persisted. "I have no desire to tent camp the whole time. Email her."

Lauren scooped the remaining vegetables into the pan. They sizzled along with her resentment. *You've been home most of the day. Why couldn't you make dinner for both of us? And then you insist I contact a woman who you know once broke my heart?*

"I'm not asking her. We'll have to come up with other options for accommodation or not go at all," Lauren said. *Go away and leave me alone.*

"Oh, what do you care if it's an imposition if she allows us to stay? It's not like you have an ongoing friendship with her."

Lauren didn't answer. She turned down the heat on the stir-fry, strode into their bedroom, and shut the door. Her resentment continued to smolder as she changed out of her work clothes. Delphine would not let up once she got something into her head. She would badger, cajole, and manipulate until she wore Lauren down and got her way.

Even after twenty-two years, it would be difficult to see Jo again. Especially staying in her house. Over the years, they'd written, sometimes very long letters, sharing their thoughts and feelings about significant events in their lives, along with birthday and Christmas cards. Lauren once carried a letter from Jo in her purse for a year. There had also been the occasional expensive long-distance phone call. Lauren knew Jo had lived with a partner for the past four years. *It would be so embarrassing for Jo to witness the state of my relationship with Delphine.*

Delphine pounced on Lauren as soon as she emerged from the bedroom. "You've talked and talked about wanting to visit Yosemite National Park. We can stay with your friend in San Francisco and use it as our home base. We can also go tent camping in Yosemite and see the famous waterfall you've always wanted to visit. Email her. It won't hurt to ask."

Lauren shot her an exasperated look. "I just don't think it's a good idea to stay with her. She has a partner, and I don't know how much room they have."

"Just ask her. Do it tonight. I've heard it's hard to get campsite reservations at Yosemite, so we need to do it soon."

Lauren sighed. There would be no peace until she agreed to ask. She did want to see the giant waterfall at Yosemite. And

Delphine was right. They could only go to San Francisco if they saved on accommodation. She ate dinner alone at the dining table and wrestled with the options. Delphine plonked into a chair in the living room, perusing the atlas and calling out places to visit near San Francisco. When Lauren finished her meal, she rose. "Okay, I'll email her," she threw over her shoulder at Delphine as she headed for the computer in the spare room.

That evening, after deleting several drafts, Lauren wrote:

> *Hi Jo, I hope you are doing well. Delphine and I are thinking of coming to California in late June. Would it be possible for us to stay with you in San Francisco for a week or less? Only if it isn't inconvenient and you have room for us, of course.*

She paused, then added: *It would be lovely to see you.*
How should she sign it? *Love? Warmly? Sincerely?* She settled on: *Best, Lauren.*

That night, she was more restless than usual. Delphine poked her in the ribs. "Stop thrashing! You've ripped off the duvet and I'm cold." Lauren had trouble getting back to sleep, worrying about the possibility Jo would say yes to their visit.

The next day Lauren stayed at the film studio late, checking her email every hour. If Jo responded, she wanted time to process it before Delphine hounded her. At seven that evening, with no response from Jo, she gave up and left. *It's just as well if she* doesn't respond. It would be awkward seeing each other again. Exchanging letters was one thing, but seeing Jo in the flesh could tear the scab off an old wound. And Delphine might well have one of her hissy fits in front of Jo and her partner. She couldn't bear that. They should stay in Europe this summer and go to Corsica or Italy.

Lauren arrived home after 7:30 p.m., and before she'd even hung up her bag, Delphine demanded, "Well? Did you hear from her?"

"No. Don't ask me again. We should make other plans. It was a bad idea to ask."

"It's only midday in California. She probably hasn't read her email yet."

Lauren ignored her and went into their bedroom and closed the door. She sagged against the door, fatigue overtaking any desire for dinner. But she had to eat. Her diabetic regimen demanded it.

After a hurried meal, Lauren retired to the spare room. She paid bills and perused the internet for sites to visit in southern Italy. As she was viewing pictures of the Amalfi Coast, her email dinged, startling her.

Dear Lauren,
How nice to hear from you! Of course, we would love to have you visit and stay with us. We have a guest room and, fortunately, I will probably have a week of vacation at the end of June. Please send me your dates and flight information. One of us will pick you and Delphine up at the airport if the timing works.
Warmly, Jo

Lauren paced the room, breathing hard until lightheadedness forced her to sit. She'd thought of Jo so often over the years, now a senior partner in a prestigious law firm in San Francisco. *What will Jo think of me?* She'd changed, no longer the amorous young woman game for adventure. The joy had mostly vanished from her life; she experienced a sticky heaviness at home and work was the only bright spot. Would Jo find her boring? And then there was Delphine, whose behavior she could neither predict nor control.

Lauren rubbed the back of her neck. After Jo's warm response, part of her longed to see her again. *I've set this ball in motion, so I'll see it through.* She wrote back to Jo, thanking her. Then she checked the Air France site for flights.

chapter thirteen
San Francisco

JO GAZED OUT THE WINDOW AT THE MONTEREY PINE tree, partially obstructing her view of the Golden Gate Bridge. *I must cut it back.* She refocused her attention on the questions for tomorrow's cross-examination. When her back reminded her to get up and stretch, she walked around the top floor of her house, then checked her email.

She startled to see one from Lauren. Wanting to visit and stay a few days with her partner, Delphine. Jo leaned back in her chair and smiled. They had exchanged heartfelt letters over the years. She'd sometimes called up memories of their time together when feeling down, unloved, or misunderstood. They reminded her of what could've been. But for the ocean, immigration barriers, and her ambition.

Jo wrote back immediately and told Lauren to come. She and her partner Brenda didn't have firm plans for the last week in June. By then, she expected her most recent trial to be over and she'd have time to spend with her guests. Jo needed to do this for herself. If it was a problem for Brenda, she could stay in her part of the house or make plans with her friends.

How would it feel to see Lauren in the flesh after twenty-two years? Would she feel a familiar rush of excitement? Probably not. It had been far too long. Jo returned to her cross-examination questions.

That evening, just after seven, the door slammed downstairs. Brenda was home. Jo closed the lid on her laptop and descended the stairs to the first floor. "Hi, Bren. How was your day?" She pulled a beer from the refrigerator and sat on a bar stool at the kitchen island.

"I got stuck with reviewing piles of documents for a case of patent violation. Sometimes, I wonder why I ever went to work for an intellectual property rights law firm. It's so boring."

Jo smiled. "I can imagine." Brenda was an adrenaline junkie. The climbing gym and careening at top speed down a ski slope were more her style. Thirteen years older than Brenda, Jo often found herself stretched to the limit of her capabilities on a mountain scramble or snowshoe hike. It had sometimes been a source of conflict when Brenda plowed ahead, not moderating her pace or making sure Jo was doing okay. Brenda's philosophy was that every woman should take care of herself. Often, Jo felt she was on her own. Perhaps then she shouldn't feel guilty about agreeing to a visit from an old lover without consulting Brenda.

Brenda plopped onto the couch with a packet of potato chips. "When is our appointment with the couple's counselor next week?"

"Five thirty on Tuesday," Jo said. "Try to get there on time."

"I can't go. Anne invited me to go kayaking after work that day." Silence except for the crunching of potato chips.

Jo took a deep breath through her nose and let it out through her mouth, repeating it three times. She counted to ten while visualizing her old dog, as their counselor had suggested. It didn't work. A tight, angry knot clenched her chest.

"What the hell? Kayaking with someone you hardly know is more important than working on our relationship?"

"Go see her by yourself. She likes you better anyway. She's always taking your side." *Crunch, crunch, crunch.*

Jo clenched and unclenched her jaw. "There are no sides, Bren. She's trying to help us both to communicate without exploding."

Brenda finished her potato chips and crumpled the bag. "Besides, it's normal for couples to fight. It's only you who thinks we need therapy."

Jo's eyes grew wide. "You think it's normal to kick a hole in my office door? To throw my attorney notes out the window? To nearly get us killed driving crazy because you're so angry? That's *not* normal."

Brenda got up and paced the floor. "You make me feel trapped. You push and push with your words and your logical arguments and you won't stop. I need you to back off."

Jo sighed and pursed her lips. This was their dance. She didn't know how to stop it. "That's why we're seeing the counselor. To learn how to avoid triggering each other." *Or, more accurately, for me to learn how not to trigger you.*

In moments like this, she wished she had another dog. But she didn't because she couldn't trust Brenda not to take out her anger on an innocent animal.

"I'm getting dinner," Brenda said as she headed for the refrigerator. She pulled out one of the prepared dinners Jo arranged for a chef to make once a week. "You eating?"

Jo's body still buzzed with adrenaline from their recent exchange. It amazed her that Brenda could flip from anger to casual so easily.

"I'll eat later." Perhaps now wasn't the best time to bring up Lauren's visit. *But then, when is?* "An old friend from London who now lives in Paris emailed me. She and her partner are coming to San Francisco in late June, and I offered to host them here for a few days."

"I thought we might go somewhere at the end of your trial."

Jo ran her hand through her short, dark hair. "We've made no plans. Maybe we can all do something together?"

"We'll see." Brenda put the frozen dinner in the oven and poured herself a glass of wine.

Noncommittal as usual. "I'm going to finish up in my office," Jo said, skipping dinner. She retreated to what was usually her safe place. The hunter green walls of her office soothed her. Bookcases groaned with law books and classic literature, and file cabinets lined the opposite wall. Jo ignored her computer and sat staring out the window.

When did I lose control of my life? In the early days, it had been fun to flirt with the younger woman on group hikes. Brenda had the most amazing sapphire-blue eyes and long lashes. Her short, spiky auburn hair gave her an edgy look, not unlike her personality. Plus, she worked as a paralegal.

Then, Jo was recovering from a brief but disastrous affair with a married woman. At breakfast with her walking group, she announced, "I'm swearing off women for six months. If I even so much as give a woman a peck on the cheek, I will pay you a hundred dollars each. That's a promise."

A month before the six months were up, Brenda kissed Jo on

the summit of aptly named Mount Diablo, and she was out $1,200.

Those early days were fun, though. Brenda left quirky notes in her briefcase after a night of sex: *You're a beast and certifiable. We have no choice but to call the MHPs to haul you away.* Or when Diana Krall sang "I've Got You Under My Skin" at an outdoor concert, Brenda passed Jo a note saying: *I'm suffering from the same skin condition. Touch me now.*

Jo did not allow Brenda to move in right away. She'd lived alone for a decade and was content with her solitary life. She even rescued dogs she'd cherished until they died. But she should have heeded the warning signs: Brenda's rage when she could not reattach the chain on her bicycle. Her "Fuck you!" when Jo pushed the wrong emotional button.

However, after two years of dating, Brenda did move in. Now they stepped in tandem to a toxic approach-avoidance intimacy dance. Sometimes Jo questioned her own sanity. She'd sought individual therapy with Ellen, then couples counseling with Dianne. But for the latter, she needed a willing partner.

I hope Brenda will stay calm while Lauren and Delphine are visiting.

Jo finished her trial questions and glanced around her office. Hidden somewhere in the back of a drawer was a folder containing all the letters Lauren had written her over the years. She rummaged until she found them. A smile formed as she took the folder to her desk and began to read.

chapter fourteen

JO RESCHEDULED THEIR VISIT TO THEIR COUPLES counselor, Dianne. This time, Brenda did not renege, and Dianne let Brenda do much of the talking. At the conclusion of the session, Dianne said, "I'd like you both to come up with a contract stating what you will do, and not do, when either of you is triggered."

On the way home in the car, Brenda said, "In your contract, I'd like you to respect my request for a time-out and not approach or talk to me until I tell you I'm ready."

Jo completed a left turn before she answered. "I can do that. If your time-out doesn't last for days. At some point, we'll need to talk."

"Right, but I'll decide when I'm ready."

Already Brenda is digging in, pushing me away. "I'd like you to agree there will be no yelling, damage to property, or dangerous behavior. Call a time-out before you get to that point," Jo said.

Brenda gave no reply. She crossed her arms and turned away to stare out the side window.

Jo let the matter drop. They were nearing their favorite Thai restaurant.

"Do you want to stop for Thai food?" Jo asked. She didn't fancy another chef-prepared frozen dinner. It was unfortunate that neither of them had the time or inclination to cook at home.

"Sure, but no more therapy talk," Brenda said.

They were seated in a booth next to a family of four. A toddler with curly blond hair and a runny nose stood up behind Brenda and peeked at Jo over the back of the booth. Jo smiled at her, and she ducked, then raised her curly head again. Jo smiled and winked at her. The child giggled and ducked. This game of peekaboo went on for several minutes.

"Tell me about your recent case," Brenda asked, ignoring the child.

"Residents of a town are suing companies for contaminating their water supply with perchloroethylene," Jo said. "The defense is putting forth their arguments with expert after expert striving to mislead the jury about the safety of this toxin." The food arrived, and she inhaled the aroma of peanut sauce before digging into her noodles.

"It looks like the trial will finish before the end of June." Jo couldn't elaborate on an ongoing case, so she changed the subject. "If our visitors are up for it, do you want to go somewhere with them? Or shall we tackle cleaning out the storage shed and have a yard sale?"

"I can't decide now. Tell me about your friends." Brenda popped a cube of tofu into her mouth.

"I've never met Delphine. And I haven't seen Lauren for over two decades. Delphine is French but speaks English well, because she used to live in London. Which is where she met Lauren. In a pub."

"What's your connection to Lauren?" Brenda stopped eating and directed her gaze at Jo.

"I met her in London on my way to a conference in Paris

years ago. We had a brief affair but decided we couldn't sustain it over such a long distance." Jo waited a beat to gauge Brenda's reaction. She believed in full disclosure and hoped Brenda wouldn't now object to the visit.

"Well, I hope she doesn't still lust after you."

Jo laughed. "Oh, I'm sure she doesn't. She's been with her French partner for over twenty years."

The following week passed without friction. They each made up their contracts, as their couple's counselor suggested. It took some cajoling, but Brenda agreed to early and limited time-outs and to avoid scary behavior.

On Saturday, they went for a brief hike up Mount Tamalpais. Despite the urban encroachment, there were still towering old-growth redwood trees, madrone, and live oaks. As they strode along the leaf-carpeted path by the creek, Jo's body relaxed, and she emptied her mind of thoughts of the trial. Brenda's renewed commitment to therapy helped restore the easy camaraderie between them.

"Hey, I'll race you to the top of that ridge," Brenda said.

Jo looked up at the steep ridge. "Are you trying to kill me, Bren?"

Brenda gave her a quick kiss. "Come on. You're a beast. You can do it."

Jo took off at a lope, which soon became a scramble. Brenda was hot on her heels, both of them panting their way up the steep slope. Jo's competitive nature kept her pounding upward, grabbing branches along the way. But Brenda's youthful advantage prevailed near the top.

They both collapsed onto a fallen log. "This is no way for a fifty-three-year-old woman to behave," said Jo, panting.

Brenda dropped a kiss on Jo's head. "But you're no ordinary woman. That's why I love you."

The following week, Jo and Brenda sat side-by-side in Dianne's small office. "How did you do with your contracts?" Dianne asked. "Brenda, why don't you start?" She flashed her an encouraging smile.

Brenda put her takeout coffee aside and leaned forward. "Okay. One night this week we were cuddling on the couch watching TV. I wanted to go to sleep, as I had an early meeting the next morning. Jo wanted to finish watching *The West Wing*. I felt angry that she didn't respect my work or need for sleep."

"How did you deal with your angry feelings?" Dianne asked. She appeared to listen intently with a solemn expression.

"I took a deep breath and let it out slowly. I told myself I didn't know for sure what Jo was thinking. She probably just wanted to watch the show."

Dianne smiled. "That's excellent, Brenda. Then what did you do?"

"I went upstairs and got ready for bed. Jo soon followed. I pretended to be asleep, and she prepared for bed without bothering me."

Dianne turned in her chair. "And how was that for you, Jo?"

"When Bren left without saying good night, I knew she was pissed. I watched the show for another fifteen minutes. There was no banging around upstairs, so I turned it off and joined

Bren in bed. I got the cold shoulder, but there was no fight. For that, I was grateful."

Dianne smiled again. "The two of you are making progress."

A week before Lauren and Delphine were due to arrive, Jo returned home at 6:45 p.m. from a grueling day in court for a prearranged date with Brenda. She called out to her: "Hello, I'm home. Sorry I'm late. The judge held us over. The traffic and the rain were terrible."

An empty house greeted her. Rain pounded on the skylights. She and Brenda were supposed to have dinner together and discuss plans for a trip in early fall.

Jo checked the refrigerator. They were out of frozen dinners. *Why is it always up to me to make sure there is food in the house?* She poured a glass of wine. *Where's Bren?* She checked her phone messages but there were none from Brenda.

Half an hour later, the rain continued to pound on the skylights. With no sign of Brenda, Jo ordered a pizza. If Brenda was held up at work, why wouldn't she call? The roads were slick. Had she had an accident?

Time ticked by as Jo paced the living room with a slice of pizza in one hand, wineglass in the other. She stopped pacing to call Brenda's cell phone multiple times, but it just went to voicemail. She poured another glass of wine and sat on the couch, jiggling her knee up and down. *Where could she be? Is she okay?*

At 9:15, the sound of the garage door opening alerted Jo. *Brenda's home.* Her shoulders relaxed.

Brenda walked through the front door, turning to shake water off her umbrella. No apologies, just a "Hi."

Jo stiffened. "Where have you been?" she demanded. "We agreed to have dinner and plan our trip."

"Out for drinks with a couple of women from the firm. I've eaten so many appetizers, I'm not hungry for dinner."

"So you just blew off our date?" Jo forgot to take a deep breath. Forgot to name her feelings. Forgot to take a time-out.

"I guess. Sorry." Brenda turned her back and walked to the fridge, taking out a beer.

She doesn't sound sorry. Irritation rose in Jo's throat like bile. "Our time together is such a low priority, you just blew it off?"

"These two women hardly ever ask me to join them for drinks. I thought it was important to be collegial."

"More important than your commitment to our date?" Jo couldn't help herself, despite an inner voice telling her to take a time-out.

"Look, I said I'm sorry. What do you want me to do, grovel at your feet?"

Jo knew she should take the hint that Brenda's flash point was imminent and back off, but she couldn't. Rare thunder rumbled, and Jo glanced up at the water streaming down the window.

"You could have at least called." She was on the verge of tears. Brenda did not respond well to tears. Usually, she ran for the hills. But Jo couldn't help it. She wanted more caring, more consideration, more commitment.

"You just don't care," Jo choked, heading for disaster. *Stop it. Time-out. Now.*

But it was too late. Jo ducked just as a beer bottle whizzed by her left ear, hitting the wall behind her and crashing to the tile floor. Beer foamed around the broken glass.

Jo raised her head and locked eyes with the defiant woman across the kitchen island, her heart pounding. Without a word, she turned and climbed the stairs to her office, leaving Brenda to clean up the mess.

chapter fifteen

JO CLOSED THE DOOR TO HER OFFICE AND SAT IN THE dark, staring out at the Monterey pine and the city lights below. *Brenda has really crossed the line this time.* She could hardly remember what had drawn her to this woman whose hair-trigger temper erupted whenever Jo had need of consideration and care. Ellen, Jo's personal therapist, said her ability to tolerate such behavior arose from her dysfunctional family of origin. Regardless, Jo's tolerance had limits, and she had reached hers.

Her hands shook from residual adrenaline when she opened her laptop and stared at the screen. Lauren and Delphine were arriving in a week. She couldn't imagine entertaining them now. They would have to find somewhere else to stay. She composed an email.

> *Lauren, I'm embarrassed to write you that my relationship with my partner is on the rocks and there will be much tension in the household. You may want to find alternative accommodation. I'm sorry for this late notice, but things have deteriorated since my last correspondence with you.*
>
> *Of course, should you stay in the San Francisco area, I would love to meet you for a drink or dinner.*

She hit send and slumped against the back of her chair. *My life is shit.* Once again, she'd been looking for milk in a hardware store with a woman who was incapable of giving her the love and care she needed. She couldn't even accommodate an old friend in her own home. Let alone get another dog. But she'd decided. *I'll tell Brenda tomorrow it's over.*

Jo rose from her chair and opened the office door, relieved that the door to their bedroom was closed. She took off her shoes and padded to the guest room, where she eventually fell into a fitful, dreamless sleep with her clothes on.

Brenda was up and gathering her things to head out the door when Jo shuffled downstairs for coffee, her head throbbing. Brenda didn't speak before leaving, and no note of apology waited for Jo on the kitchen island.

Jo made coffee and spooned yogurt and blueberries into a bowl. She took both upstairs and opened her laptop to check her email. Five were from the office. The trial was to resume at noon that day. Would she take over the cross-examination of the defendant's final expert witness? Did she notice the inconsistencies in his deposition?

The email from Lauren popped out at her.

> *I'm so sorry, Jo, that things are rocky and tense in your relationship.*
>
> *We have already paid for our plane reservations and cannot afford the high price of accommodation in San Francisco. May we still stay with you as planned? We will respect your need for privacy and understand it isn't the*

best time for you to entertain guests. If you prefer, we will stay out of your way and give you and your partner the space you need.

It rankled Jo to have to urge Lauren at the last moment to find other accommodation. *No, I won't do it.* She'd let them have the guest room, and she'd sleep on the couch or set up her air mattress and sleeping bag in her office. She wrote back to Lauren that they should stay in her home as planned.

After a long day of cross-examination, the defendants rested their case. Another attorney in her firm would present the plaintiff's closing arguments. Jo grabbed a quick burger at a restaurant near the courthouse and drove home with a sense of foreboding. She could not stomach another blowup.

The chef apparently had been there that afternoon, as Brenda was eating a prepared dinner of grilled chicken and broccoli on the kitchen island. Jo pulled out a ginger ale from the fridge and sat across from her. She rolled her shoulders to relax them, took a deep breath, and began, "How was your day?"

"It was okay. The old goat wasn't in the office today, and I mostly did research on one of his copyright-infringement cases."

It amazed Jo that Brenda had held down this job for almost five years. How did she control her temper at work? And why couldn't she do the same at home?

"When you're finished eating, let's go into the living room and talk."

Brenda frowned. "Look, I'm sorry I threw a beer bottle at

you last night. It's just that you're so needy and smothering. I feel I can't have a life of my own."

As Brenda crunched her broccoli, Jo regarded her in silence. Who was Brenda talking about? Was it needy and smothering to expect her partner to keep a date? Or to call if she couldn't make it? Or did Brenda put the face of someone else from her past on Jo? *It doesn't matter. I'm finished trying to understand.*

"Let's have this discussion in the living room," Jo said, turning away.

Brenda joined her on the couch ten minutes later. Jo looked into her big blue eyes with the long lashes, and a dull heaviness settled on her chest. She swallowed and said, "Bren, I realized last night that I just can't do this anymore. I know we've been going to couples therapy, and it seemed we were making progress. But last night was the final straw. I'm not happy, and apparently neither are you."

Jo braced for Brenda's anger. Instead, she burst into tears, startling her. Brenda never cried. But here she was sobbing, great racking sobs, like her heart would break. "You said . . . we were making . . . progress," Brenda said between shuddering breaths.

"Yes, some. But I feel like I'm walking on eggshells all the time. I also don't like the person I've become around you. Our relationship is toxic."

Brenda still sobbed. "But . . . you said . . . you loved me."

The hard knot in Jo's chest softened. "I did love you. We had fun together. In the beginning." Her heart bled for this woman, whose central nervous system was so primed to respond with anger when she felt threatened, powerless, and out of control. Feelings Jo had experienced herself way too often lately. *But do I still love her?* Yes, some, if she dug deep enough through the hurt. "I still care, but..."

"I'll... try... harder. Go...back on medication."

Jo rubbed Brenda's back. Early on in their relationship, Jo thought she could help her. Provide her with a stable home, take care of her financially, make her feel safe. But Brenda could not tolerate intimacy and was not capable of filling Jo's need for a stable, loving partner. Still, Jo dreaded the whole breakup scene, admitting to her friends and herself she'd failed again. She sighed.

"Go back on your medication. We'll talk to Dianne one more time."

chapter sixteen

Paris

LAUREN'S MIND WANDERED, MAKING IT DIFFICULT to focus on her work. Since Jo agreed to their stay, Lauren dreaded visiting her with Delphine in tow. She'd have to convince her to be on her best behavior. Fortunately, they got along best when on vacation having adventures together.

She looked up from her dubbing and addressed her colleague, Jane. "One of my French actors attempted his own English translation. He said, 'In the morning, I make my toilet.'"

Jane said, "Really? He makes toilets?"

Lauren imitated the French actor. She had a talent for mime, often rendering her colleagues helpless with laughter.

Her interactions at work lightened her spirit, fed her intellect, and contrasted with the heaviness and lack of control at home. There she never knew what awaited her when she walked in the door: amiable companion or raging bitch.

That evening, she encountered the former. She grabbed the opportunity to lay out their strategy for their upcoming trip to San Francisco. "I got an email from Jo. She and her partner, Brenda, are having difficulties, and the atmosphere will be tense. We should keep to ourselves. Go out in the evenings."

"I don't care, as long as we have a place to sleep. But we should also make meals there to save on expenses."

"Only if it is comfortable for them. We can't be part of the problem."

In a rare moment of concern for Lauren's feelings, Delphine said, "Will it be strange for you to see your old lover?"

Of course, it will be strange. When Jo quashed any possibility of a future together, Lauren despaired of finding someone to truly love her. To come face-to-face with Jo again might well resurrect the pain she'd buried in a corner of her heart years ago. But she was curious. *What will I feel?* Feeling something would be a welcome contrast to the gray numbness of her existence with Delphine. But Lauren hesitated to disclose any personal vulnerability Delphine might exploit in a future argument. "Oh, that was so many years ago. I've forgotten all about it, and I'm sure she has too."

Delphine looked skeptical but said nothing.

"Let's plan what we want to do in California," Lauren suggested, to change the subject. She pulled out the atlas.

Delphine settled into a chair next to her and poked a forefinger at Yosemite. "I got reservations for a campground. It's near Yosemite Falls—we were lucky to find one in the park." They passed two pleasant hours making lists of places to explore and charting their course.

After a late dinner, Lauren lounged on the couch with a glass of port. The friction-free evening prompted her to recall glimmers of what had attracted her to Delphine so long ago.

Before she met Jo, and later Delphine, she and a friend took two marvelous trips to Paris, which enchanted her with its sophistication and culture. They usually stayed in the Latin quarter, reveling in lively cafés in the evening, imbibing carafes of wine and savoring delicious food. By day, they meandered among the gravestones in the Cimetière du Père-Lachaise, where Oscar Wilde and Sidonie-Gabrielle Colette were buried, or they stole a quiet moment in Le Sacré-Coeur at the top of Montmartre. When not hanging out on the terraces of cafés, drinking strong coffee, eating buttery croissants, and people watching, they prospected the boutiques for the latest fashions. Lauren always came home lugging bags of dresses, scarves, and shoes. *I was quite a clothes horse then*, she recalled with a smile.

Lauren refilled her glass and continued her muse.

She met Delphine in a pub in London two months after she received Jo's letter of rejection. Only nineteen, Delphine worked as an au pair to learn English. Fresh-faced and lively, her French accent charmed Lauren, who thought of her as little more than a child. But Delphine seduced her with her intelligence and wicked sense of humor, and they became lovers.

When Delphine finished her job in London and her family recalled her to France, she convinced Lauren to follow her. Lauren, still rebounding from Jo, wanted a change and another adventure to pull her out of her funk. She loved French wine, French food, and French fashion. Why not also learn to love this French woman who seemed so smitten with her?

Lauren gave up her government job, her flat, her friends, and moved to Reims in the Champagne region of France. Having to function in French beyond her high school knowledge of the language challenged her. She picked grapes in the late summer and worked in the shipping department of a winery. This provided the novelty she needed to keep her from thinking about Jo. But soon, she discovered Delphine's sexual energy extended beyond their relationship.

When her thoughts strayed into painful history, Lauren finished her port and wandered into the spare bedroom, where Delphine was tapping on the computer keyboard.

"Look, we can camp at Glen Campground at Point Reyes National Seashore," she said. "Does your old girlfriend have an extra car she'll let us borrow?"

Lauren stiffened. "That's totally over-the-top. You will *not* ask her that." Delphine controlled their finances, and her penchant for penny-pinching irritated Lauren. She didn't want Jo to think they were just looking for a free ride. Though clearly Delphine was.

"Look, Delphine, Jo's agreed to have us as guests, despite her current relationship problems. That's enough. You will *not* ask to use her kitchen or her car or impose on her any further. If you do, we're leaving. We'll have to pay for hotels if you don't want to camp. Got it?"

Delphine looked up, her eyes widening in surprise. She was usually the one laying down the law, not Lauren. "Okay," she said, apparently at a loss for a comeback.

"Promise?"

"Yeah, sure," Delphine said, rolling her eyes.

Lauren still harbored doubts.

chapter seventeen
San Francisco

ON TUESDAY EVENING OF THE FOLLOWING WEEK, JO waited in baggage claim at San Francisco International Airport, scanning the board for arrivals from Paris. She'd left Brenda with the car. A buzz of excitement coursed through her, and she paced. *Will I recognize Lauren?* In the last picture Lauren sent, she looked so very thin.

When Lauren arrived in the baggage claim area, Jo immediately recognized her. Her hair was now short and stylishly cut, with blond highlights. Glasses perched on top of her head. That was new. Her broad smile when she spied Jo revealed the same crooked tooth and dimple in her right cheek, but crow's-feet now appeared around her eyes with her smile. Jo's pulse raced at the sight of her and she suppressed a desire to grab hold of Lauren and hug her tight. Instead, she gave her a straight-woman hug, patting her back and pulling away quickly.

Delphine straggled behind. She was a head shorter than Lauren, with a dimpled, pretty face. Her thin blond hair clung to her damp forehead, and she appeared out of breath.

Jo slung her arms around both women. "Welcome to San Francisco. How was your trip?"

At first, Lauren stiffened slightly under Jo's arm, but then she seemed to relax. "It was long, but I slept a little until Delphine spilled her drink in my lap," she said.

Delphine huffed. "You elbowed me in your sleep."

Lauren said, "It's good to see you, Jo," with a warmth that made Jo's heart leap.

"It's good to see you too, Lauren. And to meet you, Delphine."

Jo let go and struggled to calm her racing heart as they walked to the luggage carousel.

Lauren pushed through the crowd to pick up their bags, and Jo waited with Delphine, who spoke English fluently as they exchanged pleasantries. Jo's mind was elsewhere, though. To see Lauren again in the flesh roused her, flooding her with feelings she did not expect.

When Lauren staggered toward them with the bags, Jo reached for the heaviest-looking one, while Delphine managed her carry-on.

Luggage stowed, and the visitors settled in her Mercedes SUV, Jo clutched the wheel to steady herself. *What will this visit be like if the mere sight of Lauren makes my pulse race?* During the journey home, she discreetly glanced at Lauren in her rearview mirror. She spoke to Delphine in French, and both women looked tired. Brenda kept up a steady chatter in the passenger seat, but only Delphine replied.

Despite the tension in her household, Jo intended to make her guests feel welcome. As they passed through the living room, Lauren halted, apparently looking at the sleeping bag and pillow on the couch.

"You needn't put yourself out," she said. "We can sleep out here. We'll buy an inflatable mattress."

"I'm fine," Jo said. "I'm perfectly comfortable on the couch. You two are in the guest room."

After they were settled, Jo put out the sushi she'd bought earlier, and the four of them ate around the kitchen island, Delphine chatting about their plans in her charming French accent. Lauren was noticeably quiet during the meal. Jo attributed this to their long flight from Paris.

As they were clearing up, Jo said, "Tomorrow you can sleep in and just relax. I work at home on Wednesday, so I'll be upstairs in my office most of the day. I'll have coffee made, and breakfast stuff is available. Just help yourselves when you feel like getting up." Then she added, "Oh, and just in case you still drink tea, Lauren, I put a teapot and bags of English breakfast tea on the counter." She wondered if Lauren would notice that she'd kept the flowered teapot she bought for her in DC all those years ago.

"I drink coffee now," Lauren said. She didn't mention the teapot, and Jo looked away to hide her disappointment.

Delphine turned to Jo, blocking her way to the sink. "Lauren tells me you're a lawyer. What kind of lawyer?" She tilted her head to the side, gazing into Jo's eyes.

"I'm an environmental attorney. The work usually isn't that exciting—not like in the movie *Erin Brockovich*. It's long hours slogging through boxes of medical records and contamination measurements."

"Do you work for companies?" Delphine moved a little closer. Too close.

"No, I represent individuals or groups who believe companies have polluted their air, soil, or drinking water with toxins," Jo said, shifting the dishes to her other arm and wishing Delphine would move out of her way.

"That sounds like very important work." Delphine gave Jo a seductive smile and held eye contact with her in a way that made her uncomfortable. Jo glanced at Lauren, whose face remained impassive.

"And Brenda is a paralegal for a firm that deals with intellectual property law," said Jo, to deflect Delphine's attention from herself. She dodged Delphine and brushed past her with the dishes.

The only time Lauren engaged was when they discussed their plans to visit Yosemite. *Curious*, Jo thought. *Does she feel shy? Or is she just tired?* This reticence contrasted with the woman she remembered.

That night, Jo lay awake. Heat rose to her neck and face, and she tossed the top of the sleeping bag aside and stuck her leg out to cool off. After several minutes, she covered her leg again and turned on her side. *What has Lauren's life been like with Delphine? What does she think of me now? Does she still think of our time together?* Jo rolled over to look at the clock. Then she sat up and turned on the light, reaching for her book to distract her mind from such thoughts.

The visitors were up early, so Jo joined them for coffee and croissants. Lauren still said nothing about the teapot, so Jo put it back in the cupboard. They took their food and drink out to the deck with a view of San Francisco and the Golden Gate Bridge. Hoping to engage Lauren in conversation, Jo turned in her chair to address her. "Tell me more about your work in France."

Lauren swallowed her bite of croissant. "I translate French films into English. You probably remember from my letters that when I first moved to France, I picked grapes and did other odd jobs. I went back to college—night school—and got a degree in applied languages, while I worked during the day."

"Yes, I remember. That must've been hard."

"It was, especially since we were caring for Delphine's three-year-old niece while her brother, a single parent, got his act together."

Of course, whip-smart Lauren would ace college. All while working and caring for a three-year-old. "How did you end up doing translations for films?" Jo noticed Delphine, looking bored, had finished her croissant and was staring straight ahead.

"I've always loved film and took courses in England. After I got my degree, a film company hired me to do English translations for subtitles and dubbing. After a few years, they promoted me to project manager. I work with the translators to ensure deadlines are met, budgets are balanced, and quality standards are maintained."

Jo detected pride in Lauren's voice. She opened her mouth to ask more, but Delphine interrupted, speaking to Lauren in French. Lauren shot Jo an apologetic look, excused them both, and followed Delphine into the house.

Jo finished her breakfast alone, wondering what dynamic motivated those two. In the brief time they'd been together, it seemed Delphine ordered Lauren around quite a lot. *What happened to the woman who didn't take shit from anyone?*

Deep into a pile of discovery depositions, Jo was concentrating hard when Delphine wandered into her office. She perused the framed photo of Jo and Brenda at Berry Creek Falls in hiking gear, their arms around each other. "Nice photo of you two," she said. "You look hot in outdoor wear."

Oh, fuck.

Uninvited, Delphine flumped into the chair by Jo's desk.

"Are you getting on okay with your trip plans?" Jo asked Delphine. She had no time for this. She had to get through these depositions.

"We are." Delphine glanced around the office. "You have a lot of books. When do you have time to read?"

"Rarely." *Please leave.*

"I like lesbian romance novels. I enjoyed *Tipping the Velvet* by Sarah Waters. The sex is hot. Have you read it?"

"Um, no. I don't read romance." Jo turned a page of her deposition and read, or pretended to read, hoping Delphine would take the hint. But no, she continued to ask questions. Jo answered with as much gentility as she could muster. They were her guests, and she didn't want to appear rude. Eventually, though, she reached her limit of tolerance.

"I should finish this up around noon or so if I knuckle down. How about you leave me to it and then I'll join you and Lauren for lunch downstairs?"

"Can we borrow your car to go grocery shopping?"

"Sure." Jo said. "But we also have prepared meals in the freezer."

"Okay." Delphine rose from the chair. At the door, she turned and smiled. "You have nice energy."

"What?" Jo muttered before she resumed reading her deposition. *What is this woman playing at?*

At twelve thirty Jo descended the stairs, inhaling the sweet pungency of onions sautéing, and discovered Lauren preparing lunch. She'd also shopped; zucchini and strips of pork loin lay next to the chopping board. Lauren looked up and smiled when Jo stood next to her.

"You don't have to cook," Jo said. "You're on vacation. There are prepared meals in the freezer."

Though she protested, Lauren's cooking for them filled Jo with warm contentment. *Delphine is so lucky.* "It's the least I can do as we're crashing at your house."

They locked eyes, and Jo's pulse quickened, remembering kitchen scenes in DC. Then Lauren turned back to the stove.

As Jo set the dining room table, her hands shook slightly. *What's happening to me?* She took several deep breaths to calm herself.

At lunch with her guests, Jo asked Lauren, "You wrote to me years ago you were in an accident. It sounded serious."

"It was. I was off work for six months. Navigating our second-story apartment in a wheelchair was a challenge."

Jo was about to ask more when Delphine interjected, "What really helped her heal was a *magnétiseur*."

"Really? What's that?" Jo asked, annoyed that Delphine had again interrupted when she was just getting Lauren to talk.

"It's a healer who recharges a person with fresh energy so that she can heal herself," Delphine explained.

Jo quirked an eyebrow. "Did you try it?"

Lauren shot Delphine a reproachful look. "I did."

"And did you stick to the refrigerator afterward?" Jo asked with a grin.

Lauren smiled—it was the first time Jo had seen her do so all day.

Lauren and Delphine disappeared for the rest of the afternoon to explore Fisherman's Wharf and Ghirardelli Square. They returned with takeout fish and chips and chocolate brownies for Brenda and Jo. Conversation around the dining table flowed, and Jo relaxed. *Perhaps the visit will go smoothly with no drama.*

After dinner, as Jo and Lauren were clearing the table, Delphine put her hand on Jo's arm when she reached for her dish. "You have strong warrior energy. That's why you defend and protect people."

What the hell? Jo looked up at Lauren, but she ignored them, continuing to stack plates and clear empty boxes.

"Will you put your hands on my shoulders? I want to feel your warrior energy flowing through me."

Brenda raised an eyebrow.

This woman is totally bonkers. But Delphine was their guest, and Jo didn't want conflict. She put the plate down and tentatively placed both hands on Delphine's shoulders. Delphine moaned softly and closed her eyes. Jo jerked her hands away.

She glanced at Lauren to gauge her reaction, but she'd retreated to the kitchen.

Brenda stared at them across the table, frowning.

So much for no drama.

chapter eighteen

LAUREN GLARED AT DELPHINE IN THE GUEST BEDROOM that night. In an icy voice, she said, "What are you trying to pull with Jo? Your seduction routine? You're making a fool of yourself and me. Leave her alone." She clenched and unclenched her jaw.

"Are you jealous? Still have the hots for her?" Delphine knew how to dig at Lauren's tender spots.

"Don't be ridiculous. I warned you. One more scene like tonight and we're leaving." But Lauren didn't want to leave. Jo reminded her of how it felt to be around someone respectful and caring.

The following morning, Lauren was up before Delphine and was pouring the coffee Brenda made before she left for work.

Jo came downstairs dressed smartly in a dark-blue pants suit and high-collar white blouse, earrings, and makeup. Lauren couldn't help the flutter in her stomach at the sight of her. Delphine was right. She still had the hots for her. She'd have to do a better job of snuffing it.

"Good morning," Jo said. "Do you have plans for the day?" She poured herself a mug of coffee.

"I thought we'd explore Chinatown and North Beach and maybe do the Hop-On Hop-Off Bus Tour." She avoided looking directly into those dark eyes that still could hold her captive.

"Sounds good." Jo regarded her over the rim of her mug. "I was wondering . . ." She took another sip.

Lauren tensed. *Is she going to comment on Delphine's provocative behavior?*

"If you wanted to hike with me this Saturday? Bren's going kayaking with a friend, and I don't suppose Delphine is much of a hiker. I thought we could catch up a bit. Just you and me."

Lauren's breath caught. *Will she probe my relationship with Delphine? Mock me?* But the lure of time alone with Jo prevailed. "Sure, that would be great."

"Good. Will we see you this evening?"

"Probably, if that's okay."

Lauren watched Jo grab her briefcase and hurry to the door, smiling over her shoulder. "Of course."

There was that flutter again. *Stop it, Lauren.*

Tired of exploring, Lauren and Delphine popped into a crowded Chinese restaurant for dim sum. They sipped tea and waited for their next serving of steamed dumplings.

"Jo invited me to take a hike with her tomorrow. Brenda is kayaking. It's an excellent opportunity for you to visit the Museum of Modern Art, since I don't care about that."

"That's fine," Delphine said. "I'm not worried about you being alone with her. After all, she dumped you years ago."

Leave it to Delphine to twist the knife. The dumplings arrived, and Lauren ate hers in silence while Delphine rattled on.

Despite Delphine's comment, Lauren found her mood becoming lighter as the day grew close to evening. She planned to make an Icelandic lamb stew for dinner. They stopped by the grocers, and she collected the ingredients. Cooking at home in France felt like drudgery, but cooking for Jo made her heart happy. *Just for Jo?*

After Lauren placed lamb and vegetables into the Dutch oven, she recalled the teapot Jo had set out when they first arrived. She'd noticed immediately it was the one with painted roses that Jo had bought for her in DC, a bittersweet memory. *Jo kept it all these years. Why? Does she remember our time together with fondness?*

Lauren put the stew on simmer as Jo walked in.

"It smells divine in here," Jo said. She stood next to Lauren, their elbows touching, and lifted the pot lid. "Lamb stew, yum!"

The smile she gave Lauren made the effort worthwhile.

After a convivial dinner with everyone behaving themselves, Delphine said, "Let's play a game of Pigs." She pulled a compact case from her bag, and two half-inch plastic pigs rolled out onto the table. "You just shake them in your hand and toss them in the air. Then, whether they land on their snouts, their back, or their feet, you get points. I'll be the swineherd and keep score."

Jo raised her eyebrows at Lauren, who smiled and said, "It's mindless, but fun. You make a hog call and predict which way the pigs will land." Lauren explained the rules and scoring. Brenda looked skeptical at first but agreed to play.

Soon they were shouting, "Snouts! Razorbacks! Double Snouts! Oinker!" As the throws continued, Lauren laughed often, catching Jo's eye.

Jo tossed, and both pigs landed on opposite sides. Lauren elbowed her. "Pass the bacon."

Lauren tossed. One pig landed on the back of the other. "Piggyback!" Delphine and Brenda shouted. She was out of the game.

As she watched the others carry on, Lauren mused, *It's been forever since I've laughed so hard.* Being with Jo loosened something in her. She liked it.

chapter nineteen

AT NOON THE FOLLOWING DAY, JO FIDGETED IN THE waiting room of her therapist, Ellen. She'd read the same paragraph in the magazine several times. When Ellen called her in, she sat fiddling with her sand dollar necklace and didn't meet her eyes.

"It looks like you're uncomfortable about something," Ellen said, settling into her chair and adjusting her sweater around her shoulders.

Jo looked up to meet her gaze. "I have guests from France," she said. "Lauren and her partner, Delphine. They've been together for over twenty years."

"What is it that's got you thinking or feeling?"

"Lauren and I were lovers in 1981 before they got together."

"I see," Ellen said and waited.

Jo cleared her throat. "I'm the one who broke it off. Not because we didn't get along. We did. She cared for me in so many wonderful ways. But she lived in London, and I lived in Washington, DC, and it seemed impossible to continue." She looked down again and stared at her hands.

"Do you have regrets?" Ellen probed.

"I do."

"What are you feeling now?"

Tears pricked Jo's eyes. "She's just so solid, so steady. So *normal*. And she cared for me. I wish I'd chosen to fight harder for us to be together, despite the barriers. We could've had a wonderful life caring for each other. Instead, I've bashed my head against the wall with one unavailable woman after another."

Ellen leaned forward. "With twenty-twenty hindsight, what do you think was going on for you that you didn't fight harder for that relationship?"

Jo wiped her eyes on her sleeve and fingered her necklace. She looked up and met Ellen's eyes. "I don't know. Probably I believed I didn't deserve love. That it was unattainable. Or that love had to involve strife and drama."

The kindness in Ellen's voice enfolded her. "Of course you deserve love. Where did you get the idea that love must come with strings? Strife and drama, as you say?"

"My mother, I guess."

"So that's a powerful voice in your head. Is there another voice telling you to create a different life for yourself? That you *can* attain love without the strife and drama?"

"Maybe. Not with Lauren, though." Tears threatened to come again. Jo swallowed her pain.

"No, not with her. You said she has a partner of twenty years? She's clearly off-limits."

"I know," Jo said with a deep sigh.

The next morning, Jo rose early and rummaged in the garage for her hiking boots, poles, and backpack. As Lauren didn't have a pack, she pulled out an extra one for her, along with trekking poles. She chose the Mount Sutro Loop Trail for their hike because it would take at least two hours and had splendid views of the city. She hoped getting Lauren alone would allow her to talk.

Brenda wandered in. "You're up early."

"Yeah, it's best to get going before it's too crowded." Jo threw both packs over her shoulders and awkwardly held four hiking poles to throw in the back of the SUV.

Brenda stepped forward to take the poles. "How much longer do you plan on sleeping on the couch? I miss you."

"As long as the guests are here. Then I'll move back into the guest room." Jo turned away and threw the packs in the SUV.

"You still mad at me?"

Jo turned and took the poles from Brenda and tossed them in. "I'm not mad, Bren. I'm disappointed and discouraged that nothing changes." She closed the hatch on the SUV and turned to leave.

Brenda blocked Jo's exit. "I've gone back on medication. We've not had any more fights."

"We've not had much contact either. Have a good time today with your friend." Jo brushed by her.

"You too," Brenda called after her.

On the trail, Jo reminded herself not to ask Lauren questions resembling an interrogation or cross-examination as they walked through an ethereal fog under towering eucalyptus trees. "You must get to watch a lot of good French films," she said.

"Yes, but the French are into slow plot lines, less action, and more character development, with lots of dialogue and meaningful looks. Sometimes, it's hard to capture all that with English subtitles."

"I can imagine. Do you enjoy living in France?"

"I love France, but I can't say I love the French."

Jo also wanted to ask if she loved Delphine, but she refrained. "Really? So why did you decide to move there?"

"Because I so enjoyed France as a tourist. I thought moving there would be an adventure. I'd grown tired of going out to pubs in London to meet women and wanted a change. Delphine was different then, livelier and more fun."

Lauren's face clouded, and Jo decided not to press her for more. They were silent, except for their breathing as they climbed a set of steep stairs. With a break in the fog, they stopped on a bench to drink water and admire the view of the city spread before them.

Lauren said, "My turn. Why did you move to San Francisco? Was it a woman?"

Jo laughed. "No, I'm married to my work. A prestigious and dynamic law firm offered me a fast track to partnership. Plus, California is a great place to litigate environmental injustice."

A loud gaggle of young people appeared, stopping briefly to admire the view. Jo waited until they'd passed. "It's impressive you went to night school in your late thirties and got a college degree. Why did you decide to go back?"

"I considered going back to England. But I'd been in France for eight years. There was no way I could return to government work. By then, there were more stringent educational requirements. I wouldn't even qualify for my previous jobs. Getting a degree would give me more options."

"And did it?" Jo took another swig of water.

"Well, yes, I got my current job doing English translations for a French film company."

"So you stayed in France."

Lauren waited several beats. "There was nothing for me in London anymore. Most of my old friends had married or moved away. I couldn't afford the lifestyle I'd once had. My brother had his own family with kids. I missed my parents, though."

She's not saying she stayed in France because she loved Delphine. She stood, put her water bottle in a side pocket, and hoisted her day pack onto her shoulder. "Shall we carry on?"

Ten minutes later, Lauren wobbled and stumbled while going up a steep section. Jo grabbed her arm before she fell. "Are you okay?"

"I'm not sure," Lauren slurred.

Jo remembered Lauren had type 1 diabetes, and a jolt of alarm shot through her. "Do you have sugar with you?"

"I think so." Lauren held on to Jo's shoulder while she grabbed Lauren's pack and tossed things on the ground, looking for sugar.

"Where?"

"Pocket maybe?" Lauren wobbled again as if to fall, and Jo caught her in her arms. She held on while jamming her hand into the back pocket of Lauren's jeans. *Success!* She pulled out a packet of jellybeans. Still holding Lauren upright, she opened the bag with one hand and pushed four brightly colored beans into Lauren's mouth.

Lauren chewed the beans, then slurred, "I'll be okay. Takes time."

Jo guided her to a log. They sat side by side, and Jo slung an arm around her. Lauren's hands shook as she lifted her water bottle to drink. The gravity of Lauren's illness hit Jo. What if she didn't have sugar? She could die. Would she have been willing to take this on if they'd lived together? She would. Definitely. Jo shook her head. *Why am I even thinking this?* She dropped her arm from around Lauren.

Twenty minutes later, Lauren became more herself, the shaking gone. "Sorry about that. Usually, I get more warning. This one snuck up on me."

"I'm just glad you had sugar with you." Jo stood up. "Okay to continue?"

Lauren looked up and held her gaze. "Thank you for looking after me."

Jo hoisted her pack onto her shoulder and helped Lauren with hers. "Of course." *I would look after you always.*

chapter twenty

IN THE EARLY AFTERNOON, THEY RETURNED FROM THE hike to find Delphine in a pissy mood. She hadn't gone to the museum. She couldn't get her new e-reader to work, and Lauren wasn't there to figure it out. Lunch was late, and she'd misplaced her credit card.

Lauren fiddled with Delphine's e-reader but had to abandon it to fix lunch. Already she missed Jo, who had gone upstairs to work. Being around her was bittersweet, sometimes painfully reminding her of what they might have had. She worried her longing might be obvious. It was probably fortunate she and Delphine were leaving for Yosemite soon.

Once the three of them sat down to lunch and the spaghetti bolognese was served, Delphine said, "We have reservations at a campsite in Yosemite, large enough for two tents. We've also rented a car for that week. Do you want to join us?"

Just when I need to distance myself from Jo. She shot Delphine a reproachful look.

Jo finished her mouthful and drank a sip of water before answering. "It's an attractive possibility. I'll discuss it with Bren when she gets home this evening. We'll take our own car."

When Jo was out of earshot upstairs and they were clearing up, Lauren confronted Delphine. "We didn't discuss this."

"I thought you'd be fine with it, since you've gotten so chummy with Jo. Before you say anything, I'm not jealous. I know she wouldn't be interested in you."

"Most people respect other people's relationships and their own. Speaking of which, how can I be sure you won't try your seduction routine again?"

Delphine sniffed. "I'd hoped you'd be jealous and that it would enliven our sex life."

Lauren glared at her. "Quite the opposite." Their sex life had been dead for ages, and there was no hope of revival on this trip. "If they agree to go, promise me you'll behave."

"You're so British proper. Your rigidity gets worse as you age," Delphine said.

"Promise me." Lauren's eyes bored into her.

Delphine's mouth drew into a pout. "Okay."

That afternoon, Jo lent them a tent. Delphine and Lauren picked up their rental car and shopped for a cheap blow-up mattress and sleeping bags. Back at Jo's, the Subaru parked in the driveway with the kayak on top alerted them to Brenda's presence. As they organized their purchases in the garage, Jo appeared.

She leaned against the doorframe. "Looks like the answer is yes. We'll join you. Bren would rather camp in Yosemite than clear out our storage shed and host a yard sale."

This news pleased the part of Lauren that craved Jo's company, despite how it inflamed her longing. She looked up from rolling her sleeping bag. "That's great. I meant to ask you this morning, how did your trial turn out?"

Jo looked pleased she'd asked. "The jury decided in favor of the plaintiffs. They awarded them millions in damages and lifetime medical surveillance."

"Congratulations!" Lauren said, and Delphine echoed it.

"They'll reduce the award upon appeal, but the decision is cause for celebration."

Lauren raised her hand to meet Jo's for a high five.

Jo moved to a cabinet and opened the door to reveal shelves of neatly organized hiking and camping gear. "You're welcome to borrow our stoves, pans, and whatever other camping gear you need. Bren and I each had stuff before we got together, so we have many duplicates."

Apparently fed up with organizing, Delphine said, "Why don't you two continue to sort it out and I'll go make dinner? Would you like savory crêpes this evening?"

When Jo gave her an enthusiastic thumbs-up, she clambered up the stairs to the kitchen.

Jo pulled a camping stove, a plastic tablecloth, and two folding camp chairs from the cabinet. "Let me know if you need anything else." She hesitated, rubbing her hands up and down her thighs, then cleared her throat. "There's something important I need to talk to you about before we go."

Lauren tensed. Was her irrepressible attraction to Jo obvious? *Is she going to tell me off? Set boundaries?*

A flush colored Jo's cheeks. "Brenda gets angry easily. It doesn't take much to set her off. We've been working on it together and separately. If a blowup happens on the trip, we'll leave. That's why I wanted to drive our own car."

Lauren exhaled. *What a relief.* "Delphine has a short fuse too. You haven't seen it yet, and I hope you never do." She chuckled. "Let's pray they don't light each other's fuse on this trip and set the camp on fire."

Jo let out a quick huff. "Why do you think we both ended up partnered with volatile, angry women?"

"Why indeed, since we're both so reasonable and perfect?" Lauren winked.

"My thought exactly," Jo said, smiling.

When Jo left to go upstairs, Lauren loaded their gear into their rental sedan. "Jo *is* reasonable and perfect," she muttered to herself. She was kind, caring, and responsible—all the things Delphine was not.

chapter twenty-one
Sierra Nevada Mountains

AS THEY WAITED IN SEPARATE CARS IN THE LONG LINE to get into Yosemite National Park, Delphine jumped out of the sedan and hurried to the driver's side window of Jo's SUV. She banged on the window and motioned to Jo to roll it down.

When she complied, Delphine inquired urgently, "*Allo. Vous êtes lesbienne?*" (Hello, are you a lesbian?)

Jo had to laugh. "Yes, I am, but do I know you?" she asked, playing along.

Delphine feigned delight, put her hand on her cocked hip, and batted her eyelashes. "*Très bien! Voulez-vous coucher avec moi?*" (Great! Do you want to sleep with me?)

"*Non, madame,*" Jo replied, shaking her head.

Delphine feigned wounded surprise. She threw up her hands and shrugged. "*Pourquoi pas?*" (Why not?) she asked, before turning on her heel and flouncing back to the sedan.

Jo laughed and rolled the window up. "She really is bizarre, but funny sometimes."

"Hmm," Brenda said, not smiling.

The four of them surveyed their site at the Lower Pines Campground with a view of El Capitan and Half Dome and a short walk from Curry Village. Practiced campers, Jo and Brenda made quick work of setting up their tent. When they finished, Brenda plopped into her camp chair to read a book. Jo meandered over to help Lauren, who struggled to do it all while Delphine shouted instructions.

The setup complete, Jo said, "Why don't I make dinner for us tonight? Hamburgers with all the trimmings, if you can stomach such plebeian offerings."

Brenda glanced up from her book. "Sounds good to me."

Delphine pulled her camp chair out of the trunk of the sedan and collapsed into it. "Hamburgers are fine."

Lauren piped up, "I'm happy to help."

"Why don't you just relax, and I'll run to the village for a few extras."

On the way to the store, Jo thought of Lauren, so competent, so solid. What drew her to a woman like Delphine? What made her stay?

Upon returning to the campsite, she found Brenda still reading. The sound of arguing issued from Lauren and Delphine's tent. Jo tried to ignore it by focusing on the dinner prep—something she had to concentrate hard on since she did it so rarely. But tonight, she wanted to spare Lauren from having to cook.

Jo grabbed tongs and piled the patties on a plate. She laid out the buns, relish, ketchup, mayonnaise, lettuce, and tomato and called everyone to dinner.

Delphine and Lauren emerged from their tent, looking somber. Brenda laid her book aside, rose, and gave Jo a peck on the cheek. "Thank you, sweetie, it looks great."

Jo caught Lauren staring at her with a look that suggested longing. *It's just my imagination*, she told herself.

The next morning, Jo awoke to find Brenda pressed against her back. She crept away and rose so as not to wake her. She fired up the camp stove and put on water for coffee. A rustling behind her alerted her to someone coming. She turned to see Lauren, and the sudden urge to take her into her arms startled her. She hoped it didn't show on her face.

Lauren said, "Good morning. I woke early and took a walk."

"Hi. Coffee water's almost ready. How was it?"

"Lovely. I wish I were still young and could hike up to the top of El Capitan." She gazed up at the rock.

Jo followed her gaze. "You can still do it. If you take plenty of jellybeans, food, and water. And take your time. We could do it together." Jo bit her lip and resumed tending to the coffee. *What am I saying?* If she hiked it again, it should be with Brenda. "It's quite a challenge, though. It takes all day and is almost twenty miles. I haven't done it in years."

"I wish I'd been around then to hike it with you. Now I don't think I can."

Jo didn't look at her as she poured their coffee, but the regret in Lauren's voice didn't go unnoticed.

A half hour later, when Brenda emerged from the tent, she demanded coffee. After a few sips, she wrapped her arms around Jo from behind. "Let's hike the Mist Trail, just you and me. I have a surprise for you."

Jo turned around and guided Brenda's arms back to her sides. "What sort of surprise?"

"You'll see," Brenda said. "What's for breakfast?"

"Oatmeal," Jo replied. "I got out the dried fruit and nuts for you."

Nearby at the table, Lauren and Delphine were tucking into the eggs and bacon that Lauren had cooked. She'd offered the same to Jo, but she'd reluctantly declined. She didn't want Lauren to think she had to cook for her all the time.

Lauren had apparently overheard Brenda's invitation. "We can entertain ourselves for the day. You two go off and hike."

Jo wanted to stay with Lauren, but that did not bode well for the repair of her relationship with Brenda. She was still her partner, though barely. *Lauren is not and never will be.*

At the trailhead, Brenda set off at her usual breakneck speed, dodging other hikers, Jo panting to keep up. Forty-five minutes in, Jo begged for mercy and a rest stop and chugged her water. When her heart rate returned to baseline, she said, "So when is the surprise?"

"We have to make it to that flat rock near Nevada Falls."

Jo groaned. "Can we slow down just a little? Or I'll be dead when we get there."

Brenda slackened the pace ever so slightly. They climbed stone steps through the cool mist of Vernal Falls, then stopped on a footbridge to admire them before pressing on. Upon reaching the flat rock, Brenda said, "Turn around."

Jo dropped her pack, turned her back to Brenda, and chugged more water. Rustling suggested Brenda was searching through her pack.

"Okay, you can look."

Jo turned to find a two-foot-square cloth checkerboard spread out on the flat rock. Red and black pieces were in place for a game of checkers.

"You force-marched me up here to play checkers?" Though she sounded indignant, Jo shook her head in pleased disbelief. She and Brenda played this game early in their courtship. And laughed their asses off for no reason. Just as she had with Lauren when they played Pigs.

Jo reached out and took Brenda's hand. "You remembered."

Brenda beamed. "I did."

They played and Jo won, as she always did. Passing hikers gave them curious looks.

Trekking the rest of the way to Nevada Falls, they paused, cooled again by the mist. Brenda wrapped her arm around Jo from behind and nestled her head on her shoulder. Jo sighed, wrestling with her mixed feelings. Brenda had much sweetness under the anger. Jo had tried to give her a stable base from which to recover from childhood sexual abuse and her dysfunctional family. But how long could she sacrifice her own domestic peace and happiness to nurture Brenda's recovery? *If she can ever recover.*

chapter twenty-two

WHEN JO AND BRENDA SAUNTERED INTO CAMP, appearing relaxed and tired, Lauren offered them chilled wine from the cooler. She'd been to the store for ice and groceries and already had a chicken stew simmering on the camp stove. Delphine was lying down in the tent after complaining of a backache. Brenda left for the village to buy more film for her camera.

Jo sat down across the picnic table from Lauren. "How was your day?"

My day has just gotten better since you arrived. "Pleasant enough. We drove to the parking lot at Yosemite Falls, then did the short hike up to it. I've always wanted to see them, and they didn't disappoint." But seeing the falls with Jo would be even better. Perhaps they could go, just the two of them.

"How about you? What was your surprise? If you want to tell me."

Jo chuckled. "Checkers."

"What?" Lauren's eyes widened.

"Brenda pulled a cloth checkerboard from her pack, and we played a game just off the trail." Still smiling, Jo shook her head. "One thing I love about her is her quirky sense of humor."

"Hmm." Lauren looked away and rose abruptly. *I didn't need to hear that.* "I'd better check the stew. We'll be ready to eat soon."

"Lauren, I need you to give me a massage," Delphine wailed from inside their tent. After turning the heat down on the stove, Lauren crawled in. She kneeled next to a prone Delphine, kneading her lower back as she had so many times before.

"You have magic hands," Delphine breathed.

Lauren continued to knead as her thoughts drifted. Were Jo and Brenda reconciling? For the last several days, she'd felt tortured with want for Jo. She and Delphine should cut the Yosemite camping short and move on to Sequoia National Park. Then perhaps she could stop obsessing about Jo and what she'd missed and still wanted.

Delphine moaned with pleasure.

Lauren almost pulled her hands away. She had lost all desire for Delphine years ago. Sometimes she succumbed to the call of duty, which only emphasized her lack of emotional connection. On the days when Delphine's mood was stable, she still made Lauren laugh. But there'd been little of that on this trip. Except when they all played Pigs with Jo. Lauren smiled, remembering.

Brenda's laughter at something Jo said told Lauren she was back from the store. "I've got to check the stew," Lauren said, and she gave Delphine a final pat.

After dinner, Brenda read her book by flashlight from the comfort of her camp chair, while Delphine returned to the tent to lie down. A full moon rose just above the horizon as Lauren and Jo cleared the dishes and washed them at the water pump.

"Have you ever seen a moonbow?" Jo asked Lauren.

"Never," said Lauren. "What is it?"

"When the moon is low on the horizon, it catches the mist of a waterfall and creates a rainbow. The conditions are perfect for it tonight, with the full moon rising. Shall we hike up to Lower Yosemite Falls and find one? We'll have to hurry before the moon gets too high."

A frisson went through Lauren. This was just what she'd hoped for. "Sure, I'd love to," Lauren said, tossing the dish towel on the table and grabbing a flashlight and her jacket.

"Bren, are you coming?" Jo asked. Brenda looked up, her headlamp blinding Lauren.

Lauren held her breath. *No, please don't come.*

"No, I'm in an exciting part of my book."

She let out her breath. There wasn't time to tell Delphine.

Lauren hugged herself with excitement as Jo drove them up to the falls' parking lot. Guided by their flashlights, they advanced up the short trail. Lauren stumbled once, and Jo caught her arm.

When they stood before the falls, the cool mist on their faces, Lauren couldn't believe she wasn't in a dream witnessing the magnificence with Jo in the moonlight. The roar of the falls seemed to meld with the pounding of her heart. Even with others nearby, the world contained only the moonlight, Jo, and the water roaring over the edge above them. She reached for Jo's hand and squeezed. Jo returned the pressure and didn't let go. Lauren was afraid to move, lest Jo remove her hand, so warm and strong. Could Jo feel her bounding pulse?

Moments later, Jo dropped her hand and turned. "Shall we head back?"

They'd missed the moonbow. But it didn't matter to Lauren. *I got what I wanted.*

When they were away from the roar of the water, Jo linked her arm with Lauren's, pulling her off the trail at one of the rest stops. Lauren's knees wobbled. She still hadn't recovered from the rush she'd experienced holding Jo's hand at the falls.

"There's something I want to say while we're alone," Jo said.

Lauren searched Jo's eyes in the moonlight and thought she saw an answer to her own longing. *But it can't be.*

"I regret what happened with us," Jo said. "Back then, I didn't have the wisdom I do now. At thirty-one, I believed the world contained infinite possibilities for love. Now, at fifty-three, I realize that in a lifetime, you connect on a soul level with only a few special people. You're one of those people, Lauren."

Tears welled in Lauren's eyes, and she felt as if her chest would burst. "You were always that person for me, Jo." She swallowed hard to suppress a sob.

"I know it's too late for us. Life moves on. You have a partner, a home in France, an exciting job. I'm entangled with Bren. But I needed to tell you this because of how we ended." Jo smiled. "Although maybe you noticed the teapot I carried with me all these years, just like I carried the memories."

Lauren struggled to pull herself together. "I did."

Their faces were so close. Jo looked as if she might kiss her. Then she let go of Lauren's arm. "Shall we continue?"

Lauren followed her to the car, lightheaded and stepping carefully. Tears threatened her vision, and she brushed them away. *It's too late, Jo said. But does she still have feelings for me?* The look on Jo's face in the moonlight suggested she did.

When Jo drove them into camp, Brenda's chair sat empty. Delphine was up and waiting to charge Lauren as soon as she got out of Jo's SUV. "What took you so long? I needed a paracetamol, and they're in your pocket."

Without a word, Lauren reached into her pocket and pulled out a packet, handing it to Delphine. Lauren struggled to make the mental shift from happiness to stoic numbness. She exchanged a look with Jo, who smiled knowingly.

Delphine dry swallowed the pill, took a few steps toward their tent, then stopped and turned. "Coming?"

"In a few minutes," Lauren said, looking over at Jo again.

"Good night," Jo said, letting her gaze linger on Lauren. Then she turned and crawled into the tent with Brenda, leaving Lauren to calm her racing heart.

Lauren pricked her finger and let a drop of blood fall onto the test strip protruding from her glucometer. Despite the recent exercise, her blood sugar was high. No doubt from the adrenaline rush at the falls and Jo's revelation. She gave herself an extra jab of insulin.

She heated water on the stove and plopped a half cube of chicken bouillon into it, stirring thoughtfully. For years she'd been captive to life with Delphine, sometimes tolerable, often demoralizing. When she considered it impossible to return to England, she surrendered to her entrapment with a learned helplessness and depression. She thought of Jo often but wrote to her infrequently. At her lowest, she even believed Jo's rejection of her meant she was undesirable and only deserved someone like Delphine. A belief reinforced by her knowledge that her mother had given her up for adoption a few months after birth.

Jo said I was special to her, that we'd connected on a soul level. She could still feel the thrill of Jo's hand in hers and her dark-eyed gaze in the moonlight. She sighed as a warm glow spread through her body.

chapter twenty-three

BRENDA SAT UP IN HER SLEEPING BAG WHEN JO CRAWLED into the tent. "Hi, baby, I'm glad you're back." She reached behind Jo's head and pulled her in for a wet kiss. Before Jo could protest, Brenda grabbed Jo's free hand and shoved it down into the sleeping bag onto her taut, warm belly. Jo pulled her hand away and leaned back. It didn't feel right to confess her regret to Lauren and then have sex with Brenda. "Not tonight, Bren. I'm worn out from the day."

Brenda flopped back on her pillow. "You're getting to be an old fuddy-duddy. You're no fun."

Jo didn't argue. Brenda had a point. She craved peace and civil normality more than sex. At least more than sex with Brenda.

Jo awoke to hear Delphine's raised voice. "You could've made coffee for us all."

"Make your own fucking coffee. I don't see you doing anything around camp."

Uh oh, Brenda. Jo bolted upright.

"You were happy enough to help yourself to Lauren's chicken stew last night. You're not helping much either. Why don't you make yourself useful and get ice? It's melted, and the food will go bad," Delphine shot back.

Oh god, Delphine just lit Brenda's fuse. I've got to stop this. Jo threw back the top of her sleeping bag and yanked on her jeans. Slipping into flip-flops, she unzipped the tent flap, squinting into the sun.

"Hey there, I'll make us all some coffee. Bren, can I speak with you a moment?" She grabbed the empty pot, took Brenda's arm, and walked her toward the water pump. "What's going on?"

"That lazy bitch is ordering me around like I'm Lauren." She said it loud enough for the entire camp to hear.

Jo's shoulders tensed. "Don't get into it with her, I'm warning you," she hissed. "Or we'll have to leave." With two volatile women, this could easily escalate. "Come with me to the store," she said as she filled the pot. "We'll get ice and any other supplies we need. Let me finish dressing and put on my shoes."

When Jo emerged from the tent, she turned the heat off under the water and poured it through two cone filters filled with coffee. "Coffee's ready," she called to Delphine.

Brenda was slumped in her camp chair, reading.

"Ready?" Jo asked, hovering over her with the ice chest in one hand.

"I won't do her bidding. I'm going to finish this book like I was doing before that bitch annoyed me."

Jo shrugged. "Suit yourself. But stay away from her, okay?"

As she opened the car door, Lauren sauntered toward her from the showers with a towel over her shoulder. "Good morning," Jo said. "I'm driving over to the store to get ice and breakfast. Be careful. Things are tense in camp."

"Can I join you? I need a few things too."

"Hop in."

They drove the short distance in awkward silence. *Did I say too much last night?* Her therapist would not approve.

Jo parked near the front door of the store and turned off the engine. Lauren turned and laid her hand on Jo's arm, the longing Jo thought she'd imagined clear in her eyes.

"I . . . I . . ." Lauren's eyes glistened with tears. She held Jo's gaze, blinking them back.

She wants me. A rush of tenderness weakened Jo's resolve to leave well enough alone. She reached over and stroked Lauren's cheek, her eyes drawn to her mouth. Desire won over her better judgment as she leaned forward and kissed her. Lauren's lips parted as she kissed Jo back, her hand in Jo's hair, pulling her in. Jo melted, oblivious to customers coming in and out of the store.

Someone rapped on the window as they walked by, and Jo pulled away, breathless. "Sorry, I let myself get carried away. Let's shop and get the hell out of here."

"Don't say sorry," Lauren said. "I loved it."

They made quick work of shopping, but Jo's mind whirred and her body still vibrated. She'd let her guard down and followed her heart. *Holy shit, what have I done?* Where could they possibly go with this?

Back in the car, Lauren reached for her. Jo couldn't stop herself from kissing her again, as she'd wanted to do since Lauren had first arrived. Her rapid arousal startled her. *But not here.*

"We need to talk," Jo said, as she reluctantly pulled away and started the car.

"We do," Lauren agreed, keeping her hand on Jo's thigh for the short drive back.

As they approached the camp, Lauren exclaimed, "We forgot the ice!"

Jo didn't answer as she leaned forward, frowning, focused on the scene unfolding before them. Delphine, holding a frying pan in one hand, faced Brenda and was shouting something in French. With her other hand, she grabbed a raw egg from the table and smashed it into Brenda's face. It cracked and splattered, slithering down Brenda's neck into her shirt.

Jo slammed on the brakes, flung open the car door, and charged toward them. Lauren panted right behind.

"I'll show you, you crazy fucking bitch!" Brenda bent to grab a fistful of dirt and threw it at Delphine's face, but Delphine raised the pan of scrambled eggs to shield herself, yelling, "*Casse-toi!*" (Fuck off!)

Brenda, red in the face, grabbed hold of Delphine's wrist with her left hand and raised her right fist.

"Oh my god!" Jo shrieked. "Stop, Brenda!" Jo lunged for her, seizing both her arms.

Lauren gripped a writhing, sputtering Delphine.

Brenda hopped up and down. "She started it!" She wrenched an arm loose to take a swipe at Delphine, but Jo caught her arm before she made contact.

"Stop! You're both out of control." Jo pulled Brenda away and walked her toward the car.

Raw egg dripped from Brenda's cheek, and for a split second, Jo was tempted to laugh. She glanced over her shoulder to lock eyes with Lauren, whose stricken expression instantly sobered her.

chapter twenty-four

LAUREN'S INITIAL SHOCK TURNED TO COLD FURY. "YOU'VE really done it now. Ruined everything. We're leaving."

"I've sprained my wrist. Look, my finger is bleeding," Delphine whined.

Lauren said nothing. She crawled into the tent and started rolling up their sleeping bags.

Delphine called after her, "You don't even care." She plopped down on the picnic table bench, sniveling.

"You're right. I stopped caring long ago." Lauren emerged from the tent carrying both sleeping bags and hurled them into the back of the car. She tossed packets of hand-sanitizer wipes at Delphine for her finger and reentered the tent, kneeling on the air mattress to let the air out.

"She started it."

"Oh, I doubt that," Lauren said, as she dragged the mattress out of the tent. "Help me fold this."

Delphine didn't move. "You're always going off with Jo and leaving me behind with that crazy . . . *putain*. It's your fault."

Lauren gave her what she hoped was a withering look.

"You're still in love with Jo."

Delphine had hit home. Lauren threw the deflated mattress in the trunk, slammed the lid hard, and drove off.

She pulled up to the laundromat in the village. With all the drama, she'd forgotten the wash she put in early that morning. Fortunately, it was still there, and the place was empty. She tossed the laundry into the drier, pulled out her tester and finger prick, and let a drop of blood fall on the test strip. Her blood sugar was sky high. Not surprising, given the adrenaline her body had pumped out this morning. Starting with Jo's kiss.

Lauren stared at the laundry, thump-thumping around in the drier. What did the kiss mean to Jo? To Lauren, it meant everything she'd ever wanted. Was it momentary relief from Jo's tense relationship with Brenda? Yet Jo said last night she felt a special connection with her. And that look in her eyes told her more than words ever could.

But then, Delphine had to ruin it all, before she and Jo could talk. What must Jo think of her that she'd stayed with that self-centered, volatile woman for over twenty years? She'd questioned herself many times over the years, but becoming homeless and jobless again frightened her. Sometimes the devil you know is less scary. But what if she ran toward the woman she wanted, rather than away from a woman she didn't? The US still did not recognize same-sex unions, and neither did the UK or France. And what about Brenda? She shook her head. *I'm getting ahead of myself.*

Lauren rose and searched in the car for the California map and returned to the laundromat. She located Sequoia National Park but then let the map fall onto her lap. She couldn't bear further travel with Delphine.

Too embarrassed to approach Jo after this recent debacle,

she wondered when they'd ever have that talk. What could she offer Jo, who had everything: a lucrative and exciting career, a big house, even her own chef? *Only my heart.* Lauren slumped forward, her head in her hands, and let her tears fall.

She didn't hear Jo enter the laundromat. Not until she sat in the plastic chair next to Lauren and gently touched her on the shoulder did she startle and look up. She wiped her tears on her sleeve and reached in her pocket for a Kleenex.

"I've been looking for you everywhere," Jo said. "Your abrupt departure worried me."

Lauren turned toward her, putting her hand over Jo's. "Sorry about Delphine. I'm so embarrassed. We'll leave as soon as we can."

"I don't want you to leave," Jo said.

"Me neither, but those two can't stay together. I'm afraid of what you must think of me, living with someone like that." Lauren withdrew her hand and looked away to hide the tears welling up once again.

Jo gently touched her cheek, brushing her tears away.

"And I worry what you think of me for the same reason," Jo said. "Maybe we both need therapy."

Lauren smiled and blew her nose.

Jo took Lauren's hand in both of hers, her eyes boring into Lauren's. "I want to be with you, not just now, but forever."

Jo said it so softly, Lauren wasn't sure she'd heard it correctly. Her pulse throbbed in her neck, and she could hardly breathe. She searched Jo's dark eyes, imploring her for confirmation. *Does she mean it? How can we?* Then her gaze flicked to the drier.

The timer showed seventeen minutes left. Lauren inhaled deeply and locked eyes with Jo. "We have seventeen minutes for you to tell me how that could possibly work."

chapter twenty-five

JO RUBBED HER HANDS UP AND DOWN HER THIGHS AND inhaled deeply before beginning what she knew would be the most important closing argument of her life. "I know I screwed up all those years ago. I didn't fight hard enough for us to be together. And I still don't know how we can do it, but I'll give it my all if you're willing."

Jo paused and sensed Lauren intently listening, though she said nothing.

"It's much more complicated now, of course. You have a partner, a home, a job in France. I also have a partner, but not for long. Our relationship has been toxic, almost from the beginning, and now I'm finished. You must decide where you are with yours. We have to deal with our lives as they are right now. Then, when the dust settles, if you're willing, we'll move mountains if that's what it takes to be together."

Jo paused and looked intently into Lauren's eyes. What she saw did not require words, and her heart leaped.

A moment later, Lauren spoke: "I want that more than anything."

Jo reached for Lauren and kissed her, sending waves of desire to her core. Alone in the laundromat, they carried on, kissing and caressing each other until the drier buzzed. Jo reluctantly pulled away. "Come. We can't leave those two explosive women alone any longer."

Back at camp, the combatants had apparently worn themselves out. Delphine sat on the picnic table bench, cleaning out the frying pan with a paper towel. Brenda had washed the egg from her face and neck and was filling her water bottle at the pump. Neighboring campers gave them curious looks as they walked by.

Jo confronted Brenda. "What were you thinking, engaging with her? Nearly getting into a fistfight?" When she got no response, Jo said, "I guess you met your match."

Brenda snorted.

Jo glanced over at Lauren, packing the rest of their gear into the trunk of the car. "We should leave too," she said.

It was such a fine day: sunny, a cool sixty degrees with a slight breeze, the rocky outcrops crisp against the clear blue sky. The falls thundered with water, and crimson Indian paintbrushes dotted the meadows. A couple of mule deer were munching grass a few feet away. It was a day that would normally lure Brenda and her to tackle the strenuous hike to Upper Yosemite Falls. But not today. Not anymore.

"I don't see why we need to leave. I want more time with you."

Jo hesitated. Should she tell Brenda it was over and risk another scene? Before Lauren and Delphine left? *No, I can't deal with that now.*

"I've lost my enthusiasm for camping. I have projects to do at home before I go back to work next week."

"You mean you've lost your enthusiasm because Lauren is leaving?"

Jo hesitated, then opted for a partial truth. "Your anger is still on a hair trigger. I prefer to keep my distance from you."

Brenda's eyes widened. "She smashed an egg on my face," she whined.

Jo stifled a grin. "I heard your exchange with her before we left for the store. You were itching for a fight." Jo gathered the remaining items on the picnic table and put them into a plastic box.

Brenda's face settled into a pout. "Maybe I wanted them to leave. You were getting too chummy with Lauren."

Jo refused to take the bait. "The effect of your blowup is to drive me away. Can you lend a hand in taking down the tent?"

Brenda rose abruptly and made an exaggerated show of pulling up the tent stakes as the mule deer bounded away. She joined Jo in folding the tent.

As Jo was putting the tent and sleeping bags into the back of the SUV, Lauren approached.

"I'm so sorry about all this. It's best we leave. We'll come by later and get our stuff from your house and return the tent and gear. Of course, I don't expect you to put us up. I'll text you when we're back in San Francisco."

"I'm sorry too," Jo said, suppressing her desire to hug her. *Call me as soon as you can,* is what she wanted to say. "Take care," she said instead.

She and Brenda finished decamping and packing the car in silence. Jo took the wheel in case Brenda's silence meant her anger was gathering steam.

An hour into the four-hour trip to San Francisco, Brenda asked, "What's going on with you?"

Jo couldn't remain silent any longer. She pulled the SUV over to the side and turned the motor off. "Bren, I can't take your anger anymore. I've tried to give you a stable home, to be a loving partner, to seek outside help for us. I just . . ."

"You have," Brenda interrupted. "And I'm trying. I'm back on medication, and you said we would see Dianne again." An eighteen-wheel truck whizzed by, shaking the car.

Jo held her gaze. "I can't do it anymore, Bren. I don't *want* to do it anymore."

"But you said . . . Is it because of Lauren?"

Jo thought for a moment. "Lauren reminded me of feelings I'd buried. But no, our relationship became toxic well before Lauren arrived. And I've given up hope it's going to change." She noticed a wasp crawling up the windshield inside the car. She plucked a Kleenex from the box and gently grasped it, opened the door, and let it fly away.

Tears streamed down Brenda's cheeks and she stared at Jo, the hurt in her big blue eyes tugging at Jo's heart.

"What am I supposed to do?" she choked.

"Move out. Get your own place. I'll help you find an apartment, and I'll pay for the movers and your first and last month's rent."

"Just like that? Lauren arrives and you don't care anymore?"

"I do care, Bren. That's why I've hung in there with you so long. But I can't help you. And it's driving me up the wall trying. I've got to stop for my sanity."

Brenda turned away and blew her nose. Her tears still streamed.

Jo reached out and touched her arm. "I'm sorry, Bren."

Brenda yanked her arm away. "Just drive," she said.

chapter twenty-six

LAUREN DROVE IN SILENCE OUT OF YOSEMITE.

"I want to go to Sequoia National Park," Delphine insisted. "It is less than three hours away."

Lauren said nothing as Delphine rattled on, as if nothing had happened, and with no apology. But Lauren wasn't going to Sequoia or anywhere else with Delphine ever again. She would return to Paris and begin separating, even if she had to find a short-term rental.

Lauren parked the car outside a Mexican restaurant in Oakhurst, about twenty miles out of the park. "I need to eat. I gave myself extra insulin earlier and my blood sugar is low." What she was about to say to Delphine gnawed at the pit of her stomach. She had to fortify herself first.

Once inside, they ordered. Lauren checked her blood sugar, found it high, not low, and gave herself a jab of short-acting insulin. She ate her carnitas in silence.

Delphine finished hers well before Lauren. "Aren't you going to talk to me?" Delphine asked.

"When I'm finished." Lauren deliberately chose a public place to talk with Delphine, hoping to temper her reaction.

Eventually, Lauren laid the knife and fork at six o'clock

across her plate in the English fashion to show she was finished. The server took their plates away.

Lauren put her elbows on the table, leaned forward, and looked Delphine in the eye. "I can't live with you anymore."

"What? What do you mean?" Delphine's eyes grew round, and a flush began at her neck.

Lauren braced herself for Delphine's reaction. She only hoped Delphine had some restraint in front of strangers.

"Just what I said. I'm leaving you."

Delphine's mouth hung open as she stared at Lauren. Then she scowled, raised her purse, and whacked Lauren on the side of the head with it. She got up so abruptly, her chair fell backward. Delphine grabbed the car keys off the table. "No, I'm leaving *you!*" She stomped out of the restaurant, nearly bowling over the server. Lauren heard the tires screech as she drove away.

She rubbed her head, shaking.

The server rushed over, picked up the chair, and asked if she was okay.

"Not really, but I'll take the check now, please," she said.

After she'd paid, she went outside and looked around. The sun, high in the sky, seemed too bright. Three women gave her curious looks as they spilled out of the restaurant, and she turned and walked toward the parked cars as if she had not just been assaulted and abandoned.

Suddenly, she remembered she had only a limited supply of short-acting insulin in her purse. The essential long-acting insulin was in the car. Could she get insulin here without a prescription? Did this town even have a pharmacy? Delving into her purse for her phone to call Delphine, she remembered it was still plugged into the car charger. Fear surged in her chest, and her throat tightened. Pacing up and down the parking lot, she tried to think.

Lauren spotted a phone booth near the gas station on the corner a couple hundred yards away and hurried over. She inserted coins and waited for the tone, then dialed Delphine. It rang only once and went to voicemail. *Damn. She's turned off her phone.*

Jo might not be too far away. What was her mobile number? With the adrenaline pumping through her, she couldn't remember. Did it end in 4566 or 4655? She slid more coins into the slot and dialed. A man answered. Wrong number. She fumbled for the last of her coins and tried the other combination. After five rings, Jo answered.

"Lauren, what's wrong?" Jo's concerned voice took Lauren's anxiety down a notch.

"I told Delphine I'm leaving her. She's gone off in the car with my bag, my long-acting insulin, and my mobile phone. I'm stranded in Oakhurst."

"Oh, my god, Lauren. Would she just abandon you?"

Lauren could hear Brenda talking to Jo in the background.

"I have no idea. She still surprises me with what she's capable of."

Brenda's voice became louder: "What does *she* want?"

"What if she doesn't come back?" Lauren asked. Nervous sweat beaded on her forehead. A truck roared by, and she had to ask Jo to repeat herself.

"Listen, there has to be a pharmacy there," Jo said, her voice sounding stressed. "Look in the phone book or ask someone where it is. They might give you insulin in an emergency, even without a prescription."

Jo must have covered the receiver with her hand as there was muffled talking.

"Lauren, I'm dealing with a situation here, and I'm driving. I can't talk right now. Can you call me back later?"

"Okay," Lauren said, her voice quavering. She hung up and, finding no phone book in the booth, she traipsed back to the restaurant to ask about a pharmacy. The sympathetic server had difficulty explaining in English, so he drew her a map.

Once outside, she took stock of her circumstances. She didn't need the long-acting insulin until the evening. Delphine might return, so she should stay at the restaurant. She reached to put the map in her purse.

It isn't here! She gasped. Her whole life was in it: credit cards, passport, short-acting insulin. Fear paralyzed her, her heart pounding in her throat. She remembered the last time she had it was in the phone booth at the gas station. She took off at a run for it, her breath coming in quick gasps.

No purse. Panic gripped her. *Can it get any worse?* Bile rose in her throat, and for a moment she felt she might throw up. She glanced wildly around, a deer in the headlights about to be flattened by a truck roaring toward her. Stranded in a foreign country with no ID, no passport, and no money. And most alarmingly, no insulin. Crossing her arms, she doubled over, trying to calm her panicked breathing.

She raised her head and spied the mini-mart at the gas station. She rushed over, crashing through the door and breathing hard. The astonished attendant and customer turned to stare.

"Did anyone find a purse . . . in the phone booth outside?" she gasped. "I left it there a few minutes ago."

The customer, a prim, gray-haired woman, replied, "Why yes, I found it when I made a call and turned it in."

The attendant said, "And your name is?"

"Lauren. Lauren Robinson."

The attendant reached behind the counter and handed her the purse. Her knees turned to rubber as the tension left her body.

She turned to the woman. "Thank you so much!"

"You're very welcome, dear. I'm glad you came back."

Lauren was still catching her breath when she offered the woman two $20 bills, which the woman refused.

"May I at least give you a hug?" Lauren said.

That, she accepted.

Purse in hand and contents intact, Lauren got more change and left the mini-mart, stopping to slump against the side of the building to consider her options. The adrenaline left her weak, but she recovered enough to trudge to the phone booth, clutching her purse tightly under her arm. She dialed Delphine again. No answer. She wondered if Delphine realized she was without long-acting insulin. Surely, she could see her mobile phone plugged into the car charger. The pharmacy was not likely to close for hours. She'd just wait in hopes that Delphine would return.

Lauren had plenty of time to think as she paced back and forth outside the Mexican restaurant. She couldn't have waited until they were back in France to tell Delphine she was leaving her. Being with Jo, even for a short time, reminded her what it was like to relate to a stable, caring person and yanked her out of the mire of chronic depression. Long-dormant feelings and hope rose to the surface along with the return of her agency to act in her own self-interest. Now, finally, she could imagine a different life.

Who knew if they could ever live as a couple in the US or anywhere else? But Jo, her first love, said she wanted to be with her. They'd kissed. The hope of a better life revived Lauren's spirit. She embraced the change and couldn't wait even one more day to shake off Delphine's emotional and physical abuse and the depression it engendered. Even with the uncertainty of whether she and Jo could make a life together.

Delphine, pulling into the parking lot, interrupted her musing.

Lauren strode to the car, opened the trunk, and grabbed her bag with the long-acting insulin. Quickly rounding the car to the passenger side, she flung open the door and yanked the charger and phone out of the cigarette lighter.

"Get in," Delphine commanded. "You're lucky I came back."

"Nice to know there are limits to your cruelty. But I'm not going anywhere with you."

Delphine smirked. "You'd better. I have the car and both our return plane tickets."

Lauren doubted she needed a paper ticket, and she'd rather walk all the way to San Francisco than join Delphine on the road. "I'm sick of your selfishness, infidelity, and abuse. Goodbye, Delphine."

Lauren slammed the car door and walked away, not looking back. Delphine drove slowly out of the parking lot, as if giving Lauren time to change her mind.

When she was sure Delphine was gone, Lauren entered the restaurant to inquire about a bus station in town. She must get to San Francisco, to Jo. *Then what?*

chapter twenty-seven

HOLY SHIT, LAUREN'S TOLD DELPHINE SHE'S LEAVING HER. Jo gripped the wheel, rolling her head around to ease the ache in her tight neck and shoulders. Things were happening too fast. Torn between wanting to turn around and rescue Lauren and needing to deal with the emotional fallout of her announcement to Brenda, she chewed her lip.

It wouldn't do to have Lauren and Brenda in the same car for four hours. Especially given Brenda's current state, alternating between tears and angry outbursts. More tears than Jo had ever seen her shed in the four years she'd known her. Lauren's call only exacerbated Brenda's anger. Captive in the car, Jo drove as fast as she safely could.

Would Delphine be so cruel as to leave Lauren stranded without insulin? She couldn't fathom it. If Delphine did not return and Lauren called back, Jo could call a physician friend to fax a prescription for long-acting insulin to the pharmacy in Oakhurst. Or Lauren could take a bus to San Francisco. That might be faster than Jo driving another four hours back to Oakhurst. Her friend could fax a prescription to a pharmacy in San Francisco instead.

Brenda interrupted Jo's whirring thoughts. "When are you kicking me out?"

Jo jerked herself into the present. "I'm not kicking you out, Bren. We'll look for a place together. You don't have to leave until we find one."

"I'm super busy at work. I don't have time to search for a place and move." Brenda sniffed and blew her nose.

Jo should have expected her to resist. She had a cushy setup in Jo's Marina District home. "You'll need to make time. I no longer want to live with you. I'll try to make it as easy on you as possible, but I need you to leave."

"You *are* kicking me out. To make room for Lauren?"

Jo understood it might look that way to Brenda. Lauren had opened Jo's eyes to the possibility of a different, healthier relationship. But there were still many unknowns. It was not a given she and Lauren could ever live together. No, her parting with Brenda was separate from Lauren.

"I can't live with you anymore because you run away from me when I want to be close and ask anything from you emotionally. You explode with anger when you feel trapped or threatened by intimacy, and it's dangerous. It has often turned me into an angry person as well, and I don't want to be like that. I can't change you. I can only work on changing myself. That's why I want you to leave."

"Don't you love me?" Brenda said in an anguished voice.

Jo took her eyes off the road to glance over at her. Brenda's big blue eyes filled with tears, beseeching her to change her mind—again.

Jo struggled to keep her eyes on the road, but her vision blurred. *Was Bren so damaged as to be unlovable? Heartbreaking.*

She wiped away a tear with the back of her hand. "I've experienced the sweetness in you underneath all that fear and anger. It's why I fell for you in the first place and stayed so long." Jo plumbed the depths of her heart. "I still care, Bren, but I'm not in love with you. And I can't live with you anymore." How many times would she have to repeat this before it sunk in?

For the next hour, they drove in silence, except for an occasional sniffle and nose blow from Brenda and the hum of the road.

The ringing of Jo's cell phone pierced the silence. She pulled over and answered it. "Hold on." She turned to Brenda. "I need to take her call. Lauren could be in real danger without insulin." She hopped out of the car and closed the door.

"Lauren, are you okay?"

"I am now, although I almost lost my purse with my ID, credit cards, and short-acting insulin. That was terrifying." Lauren's voice sounded choked, and she paused before continuing.

"Oh, no, what happened?" Jo's concern allowed Lauren to get her voice back and tell her.

Jo blew out a breath. "Whew! I'm so glad you got your purse back! What a disaster that would have been. Did Delphine come back with your insulin?"

"Yes, eventually. I snatched my bag with the long-acting insulin and my mobile phone. I refused to go with her, and she took off again. But at least she didn't want to kill me."

"Thank goodness." Jo paused, thinking. *I must keep Lauren safe.* "Can you see if there's a bus to San Francisco today?"

"I've already checked. There is. It arrives at the Folsom Street Station at 1:10 in the morning."

"Take it. I'll be there to pick you up."

Home in San Francisco, Jo and Brenda sat at the kitchen island on high stools eating their prepared dinners.

"Delphine has stranded Lauren outside Yosemite. I told her to take a bus to San Francisco this evening. She'll arrive very late," Jo said, knowing this would raise alarm bells for Brenda.

Brenda threw up her hands and slammed them down on the countertop. "I don't want her here."

Jo didn't respond. *This is awkward.*

"I'm going into the office tomorrow and for the rest of the week," Brenda announced. "Apartment hunting will have to wait." She flounced upstairs to the bedroom and slammed the door.

What a relief. Trying to both apartment hunt with Brenda and look after Lauren would be difficult, and she desperately wanted to see Lauren and spend time with her. They had much to work out.

Jo retired to her office with its soothing dark-green walls and solid bookcases filled with books. She swiveled back and forth in her office chair and gazed out the window at the lights of the city, the water, and the Golden Gate Bridge. Though tinged with sadness, the decision regarding Brenda lifted a weight from her shoulders.

Ellen would likely approve of her leaving Brenda. But what would she think of Jo's renewed involvement with Lauren? A woman who'd been in a committed relationship for decades until Jo came along. Who lived in France with little chance of moving to the US. Would Ellen conclude Jo had plunged into involvement with yet another unavailable woman?

Jo shook her head. No, Lauren was emotionally available and solid. Although she took quite a risk today. Just as she did all those years ago when she put her job on the line to visit Jo in Washington, DC.

Did I cause her breakup with Delphine? Ellen would certainly not approve of that. It was hard to imagine there had been any love between them. But there must have been. Just as there'd been with her and Brenda.

Jo sagged in her chair. *What a day!* And she had to keep herself awake until the wee hours of the morning to pick up Lauren. Then what were they going to do? Jo sighed, leaned back, and closed her eyes.

chapter twenty-eight
Oakhurst

FOLLOWING HER PHONE CONVERSATION WITH JO, Lauren strolled around town, locating the Greyhound bus station for later and a café for dinner. Early that evening, she treated herself to a glass of cabernet and a rib eye steak, enduring Toby Keith singing "Beer for My Horses" in the background. Her spirits lifted with a sense of liberation and freedom she hadn't felt for years. It reminded her of the old days when she would arrive in a foreign country without an itinerary, letting each day unfold spontaneously.

At the bus station, Lauren steered clear of three sketchy-looking characters, one of whom flashed her a toothless smile. On the bus, the seats were upholstered with old scratchy carpeting, the floor was sticky, and the air-conditioning didn't work. A man in his twenties plopped into the seat next to her, earphones connected to his radio and a blank, bored expression on his face.

The next five hours would go faster if she were unconscious. She tried reclining the seat, but it went back only an inch. She took a sweater from her bag and leaned against the window. Eventually, the vibration and motion of the bus lulled her to sleep.

She awakened to a hand slithering up her leg to her thigh. She bolted upright. The pimply young man smiled, his earphones in his lap.

"What the fuck are you doing?" she demanded, flinging his hand away.

"I like older women, and you're pretty," he said, his breath sour.

"Oh, for god's sake. Keep your hands off me. I'm definitely not interested and am old enough to be your mother."

"Aw, come on," he said, leering at her.

Lauren turned to face him. "Look, you wanker, I'm an expert in martial arts. If you touch me again, I'll break your wrist like a twig."

"Bitch." He grabbed his stuff and moved to another seat.

Lauren turned toward the window again, pleased with the return of her moxie. Before she met Delphine, she didn't take shit from anyone. Though the closest she'd gotten to martial arts was watching her brother do judo.

At the terminal in San Francisco, Lauren descended the bus steps to find Jo waiting at the door, wearing a broad smile. She ran into her waiting arms, dropped her duffel, and hugged her tight. The other passengers streamed around them.

Jo linked her arm with Lauren's, grabbed her bag, and guided her to the SUV. Once inside, she moved across the seat and kissed Lauren until her knees turned to rubber.

"Do you remember the night at the mall in Washington?" Lauren said breathlessly.

"Of course I do. But we were a lot younger and more limber. Let's go someplace more comfortable."

Lauren's arousal so roiled her body that she didn't care where they landed—the kitchen floor, for all she cared, as long as Jo wanted her.

She wasn't too far off. Twenty minutes later, Jo entered the driveway of an unfamiliar house. "I called a friend to ask if we could stay here tonight. She left the keys for us under a rock. The bad news is there's no furniture. She's moved out and is waiting for the sale to close." Jo got out and pulled the air mattress and sleeping bags from the car. "There're pillows too, if you want to grab them."

Lauren smiled. "We're camping again. In Yosemite, I laid there in my sleeping bag, wishing I was with you."

"All the while, I wished I was with you," Jo said.

Lauren helped her prepare their bed on the floor. "I haven't showered since yesterday morning, and I . . ."

Jo pulled out a bag. "I brought towels, soap, and shampoo. Go shower. I'll be waiting."

Lauren emerged from the shower with a towel wrapped around her naked body. Jo lay on top of the sleeping bag wearing only a T-shirt. When she slipped it over her head, Lauren's throat grew thick at the sight of Jo's lean, toned body and her small breasts. *Still so lovely.* Jo pulled Lauren down to lie beside her, her face buried below Jo's collarbone, inhaling the creamy vanilla musk of her skin and trembling as she had so many years ago.

The house creaked, and they both looked up momentarily, but it was nothing. Then their lips met in ever-more-passionate kisses until Jo moaned and pulled away slightly, breathing hard. She nipped and kissed Lauren's neck, fondling, then swirling over Lauren's nipples, sending electricity to her core. She continued to slide down Lauren's body, her mouth devouring sensitive skin everywhere as she murmured words of appreciation, working Lauren into a frenzy. Lauren moaned and cried out in pleasure and torment, desperate for Jo inside her.

"I want to look at you," Jo said, before her hair brushed softly against Lauren's inner thigh. Lauren shuddered at the shock of Jo's tongue as her breath caught and she writhed with pleasure almost too much to bear. Just when she might plummet over the edge, Jo looked up, sliding up Lauren's body and locking eyes with her. She slipped her fingers into Lauren's wet center and curled them upward, massaging Lauren's clit with her thumb. Lauren clutched at the sleeping bag, bucking and crying out as waves of hot lightning coursed through her.

When Lauren lay limp and satiated in Jo's arms, she confessed, "I never imagined I could ever feel that way again. Thank you."

Jo breathed into Lauren's ear, her voice husky. "My pleasure, sweetheart."

Lauren nuzzled Jo's neck, then climbed on top of her. Without having to think or to ask, Lauren's body remembered how Jo liked to be touched, how she moved, how she sounded. And already aroused by making love to Lauren, how easily she came.

chapter twenty-nine

JO AWOKE AT FIRST LIGHT AND UNWRAPPED HERSELF from Lauren, who stirred and opened her eyes. "I have to go home. I'll be back in about an hour. You go back to sleep." She kissed Lauren, and her body melted. She'd love to stay and luxuriate in Lauren's arms, but she could not.

It didn't seem appropriate last night to bring Lauren to her house, especially given their loud and unrestricted lovemaking. But she needed a plan to house Lauren without disrespecting Brenda and creating conflict. She wanted to catch Brenda just before she left for work. Something about being dressed in a business suit, a mature adult ready to face the law office, seemed to constrain Brenda's reactivity.

Brenda was pouring coffee into her to-go mug when Jo arrived. Her eyes looked red-rimmed. Jo stood next to her, filling her own cup with the dark French roast.

"Where's Lauren?" Brenda said.

"She stayed the night elsewhere, but that's only temporary. I know it's awkward, but I'd like her to stay here for a few days until she decides what to do. She'll sleep in the guest room, and I'll sleep on the couch."

At first, it appeared Brenda was ramping up for a fight.

Then she shrugged, looking defeated. "Well, it's your house. And you're kicking me out."

Jo inwardly flinched. "Would you be okay with her staying here until she arranges her return to France?"

"Why are you even bothering to ask?"

"Because I care how you feel about it." *And because I want to avoid another scene.*

"Whatever. Let her stay. But I don't want to be around her. Or you. I need to get to work." Brenda turned away, checked herself in the hallway mirror, picked up her briefcase, and left.

Jo closed her eyes and exhaled a long breath. She and Lauren had to talk and come up with a viable plan. An exciting but daunting task for which she felt responsible. She slumped against the refrigerator, lack of sleep catching up to her.

Jo brought Lauren back to her house, and while she settled in, Jo called her office. She wasn't due back until the following week, but she liked to stay on top of things and not get slammed upon her return. As expected, the defendants in the recent trial appealed. The case still lingered, and there would be more delays until the plaintiffs received compensation and medical surveillance.

She phoned Ellen and left a voicemail requesting an earlier appointment. "I'm going to do whatever it takes to be with Lauren," she explained. "She's leaving Delphine. We don't have a plan." She knew this would set off alarm bells for Ellen. It did for her too.

Lauren padded into the office in Jo's bathrobe, her hair damp and tousled, tempting Jo to untie the belt and have her way with her. But they had things to work out. "Let's make breakfast and have a nap. Then let's talk," she said.

Four hours later, fed, sleep-refreshed, and sexually satisfied once again, they lounged on the couch in the living room, with Sarah Brightman on low in the background. Lauren sat with her feet in Jo's lap, moaning over Jo's foot massage. Jo gave her a final rub, then lifted her legs and swung them over the edge. Lauren scooted in close.

"Okay, I'll start," Jo said. "Brenda knows I can't live with her anymore. I feel compassion for her, but our relationship is over. I'll help her find a place and make the move as smooth as possible. Yesterday she resisted, but today she appears more resigned. That could change on a dime."

Lauren rubbed her temples. "I dread going back to France. When Delphine realizes I'm serious about leaving her, she might become vicious."

Jo's eyes widened. "Would she attack you? Physically?"

"She already has. But more likely, she'll squeeze me financially. She worked for a winery until we moved to Paris. Together we had enough to pay off our mortgage. The apartment and our checking account are all held jointly, and she insisted on controlling our finances."

Alarmed by the risk Lauren was taking, Jo said, "I'm not sure how the legal system works in France, but she can't just steal your money and take your half of your property, surely. You should withdraw your money out of the joint account immediately."

When Lauren held her stomach and bent forward, Jo reached to rub her back. "Don't worry, I have enough for us both," she said. *That might not sit well with a woman who has always looked after herself.* She could hardly judge Lauren for getting in so deep with an abusive, manipulative woman. There were many reasons some women found themselves in abusive relationships, and it wasn't because they lacked sanity or intelligence. A controlling and wounding partner can cause confusion, doubts, and self-blame, leading to despair. She'd had experience with that herself.

Where would they live? France was not an option, since Jo didn't speak French and could not practice law there. Lauren hadn't lived in England for over twenty years. Jo couldn't practice law in the UK either. It only made sense for Lauren to come to the US. But how could they make that happen? They had no legal status as a couple, and Lauren did not have unique qualifications for work. Given Lauren's recent traumas, Jo thought it best to postpone the discussion of where they might live.

Jo rolled her tense shoulders, her thoughts racing. *What have I done?* She'd disrupted Lauren's life and didn't know what their future held. Much was out of her control, and she didn't like it one bit.

That evening, she and Lauren left the house before Brenda arrived. They had a leisurely dinner, then made out in the car before cautiously entering the house. Jo tensed when she saw Brenda's briefcase by the door but relaxed when the muffled sounds of the television in the bedroom told her Brenda was already upstairs. Reluctantly, she made up her bed on the couch, leaving the guest room for Lauren.

Tomorrow, she and Lauren would resume their planning. To the extent they could plan. And she'd talk with Ellen.

chapter thirty

EARLY THE FOLLOWING MORNING, JO SUMMARIZED recent major events for Ellen, who listened without comment. But her concern showed in her eyes.

"So, part of you wants to jump into this new relationship, but part of you realizes you still have unfinished business with Brenda?" Ellen said.

"Yes, but you know my relationship with Brenda has been rocky from the beginning. When she threw the beer bottle at me, I was finally ready to call it quits. But she persuaded me to give it another try."

"But you changed your mind when Lauren came along?" Ellen prodded.

Jo fingered her necklace. "She possesses all the characteristics I wanted from Bren and lost hope of ever getting."

"Like what?" Ellen asked, leaning forward.

"Like stability, calmness, normalcy. Like love and caring," Jo replied. "How could I let that go again?"

"On the one hand, you describe Lauren as stable. Yet you said she abruptly left her partner of twenty years with no assurance you two can live together. What do you make of that?"

Jo raised both hands in a gesture of futility. "What's the point of her remaining stable in an abusive relationship? It's self-destructive. Isn't that what you've been telling me about mine for several months now?"

"I have, but you had to get there on your own." Ellen smiled and leaned back. She appeared to be waiting for Jo to say more.

"It's awkward to have both Lauren and Bren in the house. It'll take some time to get Bren settled elsewhere."

"I can imagine. And being the protector you are, you feel you must take care of Brenda?"

"Well . . . yes, I do."

"And Lauren, you say, will leave her home and job and possibly move to a foreign country. Will you take care of her too?"

Isn't that what I always do? Protect and take care of people I love? Jo leaned forward with elbows on her knees, hands clasped tightly together. "Yes, if that's what it takes for us to live together." But would Lauren allow herself to be in such a dependent position? She wasn't sure.

"And who will take care of you?" Ellen asked gently.

Jo shrugged and let out a long exhale. "Me, I guess."

After lunch and a snuggle on the couch, Jo said, "Okay, let's tackle the hard part. Where shall we live?"

Lauren sat up and ran her hand through her hair. "I've given it some consideration. You moving to France is an option on a long-stay visa if you want to retire and learn to speak French. We could eat a fresh baguette every day and sip coffee and wine in outdoor cafés. It could be an adventure and give you a different perspective on the world. I can still work translating French films. You'd be a kept woman, no disrespect intended." Lauren kissed the top of Jo's head. "How'd you like that?"

Jo smiled. "It's interesting you'd suggest it, but I'm only fifty-three. I have petrochemical companies and other corporate polluters to fight. I'm at the peak of my career and not ready to retire."

Lauren flopped back into the cushions. "I know. It was a fantasy." She sighed and stared into the distance.

Jo waited. She wanted Lauren to have as much control as possible in choosing their options. If they had any.

Lauren turned to her again. "I suppose the UK is out for us. With both of us in our fifties, it would be hard to start over."

"We're just barely in our fifties," Jo reminded her. "In the early 1980s, I investigated the requirements for becoming a solicitor in the UK. It looked daunting even then."

"I doubt there'd be much call for French-film translators either." Lauren leaned against Jo's side. "I suppose that leaves the US as our best option."

Jo bit her lower lip. If she were a man, she could marry Lauren and sponsor her. But they could not marry, nor would the US recognize them as a couple for immigration. Regardless, if there was a way, they'd find it together.

Before they could leave the house for dinner, Brenda arrived earlier than usual. "The bitch is back!" she announced, dropping her briefcase in the hall. She stomped upstairs to the bedroom.

Jo and Lauren rushed around, gathering their bags and jackets, and headed for the door. Opening it, they nearly knocked over Delphine.

"Oh," Lauren gasped.

"I knew I'd find you here," Delphine hissed. She shot a venomous look at Jo. "In the clutches of *her*, the vampire."

Jo hesitated to invite her in, but Delphine pushed past them. "You need to get your stuff, Lauren. You're leaving."

Jo tensed, her fingers curled into her palms.

"I'm not leaving, Delphine. Not with you. I'll return to Paris on my own," Lauren said, her voice firm.

A look of disbelief passed over Delphine's face before it reddened, her neck veins bulging. From her mouth came a harangue of French.

Lauren said in English, "I'll talk to you only if you calm down. Right here. I'm not going anywhere with you." She moved into the living room, and Delphine followed until Lauren stopped, and they stood, facing each other, a foot apart.

On alert and not taking her eyes off them, Jo slipped behind Delphine. When Lauren shifted her gaze from Delphine's face to Jo, Delphine whirled around. "Get away from us, vampire!"

Jo stepped back and took several deep breaths. *This is their struggle.* She would not intervene unless Delphine threatened Lauren.

Delphine spoke loudly and rapidly in French. Lauren's firm "No" punctured her barrage.

A creak behind her caused Jo to turn. Brenda was coming down the stairs. She stopped midway and stared wide-eyed. Jo put her finger to her lips, willing her to stay quiet.

Delphine was leaning forward now, furiously shouting into Lauren's face.

Jo clenched her fists.

Brenda crept up behind Jo, whispering in her ear, "What the fuck?"

Delphine whirled around again, wild-eyed. "You two," she spat. "Go away. This is none of your business. You've done enough damage."

"This is my house," Jo said, firmly. "And you're threatening Lauren."

Delphine turned around and grabbed Lauren's arm. When she tried to twist away, Delphine raised her other arm and slapped her hard across the face.

Jo was on Delphine in an instant. Amazingly, so was Brenda. They each took hold of an arm, and Lauren pushed a struggling Delphine from behind to the front door. She almost jerked loose when Brenda let go with one hand to open the door. It took all three to push her out and slam the door.

Tears rolled down Lauren's cheeks, one of which displayed a red handprint. Jo wrapped her arms around her.

"I'm so sorry," Lauren sobbed.

"You have nothing to be sorry for," Jo soothed. "'Hell hath no fury like a woman scorned,' so they say."

"Yeah," Brenda said, "you got off easy with me."

"Thanks for your help, Bren," Jo called after her as Brenda headed up the stairs.

Delphine cursed them all in French on the other side of the door. *Should I call the police?* What a scene this was for the neighbors. She held Lauren, her back against the door, breathing hard, relaxing only when she heard the sound of Delphine's car backing out of the driveway. *So far, this is nowhere near the peaceful, normal life I wanted.*

chapter thirty-one

LAUREN'S HANDS STILL SHOOK FROM RESIDUAL adrenaline when she and Jo got in the car to go to dinner. They sat in the garage with the motor off. Despair gripped her at the thought of returning to Paris and facing Delphine again. She clasped her hands together to stop the shaking, and heat rose to her face as she relived the scene Jo had just witnessed.

As if reading her thoughts, Jo said, "I worry about you returning to Paris. To the same house with that angry, violent woman."

Lauren said, "You need your space to sort things out with Brenda. I can't stay here. I could go to England to stay with my brother for the rest of my vacation. But I'll have to return to Paris, to my job, if only to give my notice. Hopefully, my friend Jane will put me up. There's so much to disentangle."

"I wish I could go with you and help. But I might only make things worse with you and Delphine."

Lauren smiled briefly. "Yeah, she thinks you suck blood."

"Might she threaten me with a crucifix?"

"Or worse," Lauren said, shaking her head. "I need to work things out on my own for now." Tears started, and she threw her arms around Jo's neck. "Oh, Jo, I'm so sorry. And I'm scared."

"Don't be sorry. Her behavior is not your fault." Jo kissed her neck, her mouth, her tears. "Come back to San Francisco as soon as you can manage. Then we'll seek advice from an immigration attorney."

The following morning, Jo nudged Lauren awake. "Delphine's at the front door. She appears calm and wants to talk. What do you want me to do?"

Lauren sat up and rubbed her eyes. She had gotten little sleep. "I'll come down."

"I'll stay nearby and keep out of it unless she threatens you again."

Lauren opened the door a crack. Delphine looked like hell, her eyes bloodshot and her face pale. Underneath all the anger, Lauren surmised there was confusion and hurt. She waited for Delphine to speak.

"What am I supposed to do? We have a week of vacation left," Delphine whined.

"I know this is not the holiday you expected. Go back to Paris. I'm going to London. I'll let you know when I return to Paris."

Delphine frowned. "No! You're coming with me," she demanded.

Lauren straightened. She wouldn't allow Delphine to intimidate or control her ever again. "I just told you. I'm going to London. And I'm not going anywhere with you. Especially after your violent outbursts."

Delphine looked as if she was about to explode again, but then her face fell.

Perhaps she has a little remorse after all.

"Will you pay for my ticket to Paris if I leave tomorrow?" Delphine asked, her voice faltering.

Lauren considered this. Her expenses would mount going to London. But Delphine looked broken. "I will."

"And for my hotel in San Francisco?"

Delphine's frugality appeared to be winning out over beating down Lauren to come with her. "Yes, if you leave tomorrow."

"And you're coming back to Paris?"

Lauren took her time answering. "Eventually."

Feeling less threatened, Lauren stepped outside, and they discussed details, including Delphine's return of the rental car. When Delphine left, Lauren shut the door and pressed her back against it. "That went better than I expected."

Jo strode to her side and pulled Lauren into her arms. Lauren laid her head on Jo's shoulder. "I think we need a few days of respite," Jo said. "We'll let Bren have the house to herself over the weekend."

After lunch, Lauren called her brother, Richard, in London. She explained she was leaving Delphine for good. "I need time to catch my breath and figure out what actions I should take without Delphine badgering me."

"You're welcome to stay with us as long as you like," he said.

"Thank you, Richard, you're very kind."

"And something else." Richard cleared his throat. "We didn't want to upset you before, but nobody in the family liked Delphine, especially our mother."

"I felt it. But she was too diplomatic to say anything."

When they hung up, Jo offered to pay for Lauren's plane ticket to London, and she accepted.

Jo found a hotel in Healdsburg in the wine country north of San Francisco, where they spent two heavenly days strolling the charming town plaza lined with restaurants, tasting rooms, and galleries. Lauren found a tapas bar and introduced Jo to the art of consuming small, artfully presented dishes of mussels, creamy chicken croquettes, and roasted Brussels sprouts washed down with sips of Spanish sherry.

Driving through rolling hills of vineyards and farmland outside town, they stopped to taste world-famous local chardonnay and pinot noir. With the DO NOT DISTURB sign on the door, they made love and slept in each morning. With Jo relaxed and laughing more often, Lauren again floated on the giddy happiness she'd experienced when they were first together in Washington, DC.

For those two days, Lauren suppressed her fear of what lay ahead. But as Jo drove them back to San Francisco on that bright, cloudless Monday morning, her chest tightened, and she had difficulty taking a deep breath. Her flight left at five thirty that evening. She lay her hand on Jo's jean-clad thigh and studied her profile, memorizing her chiseled features, her long neck, and the prominent collarbone protruding from her open-necked shirt. She'd brushed her lips along it less than three hours ago.

Jo caught her staring and flashed her a smile.

"Please don't find everything too hard again and change your mind," Lauren blurted. She hadn't meant to say it quite like that. But the memory of her devastation when she received

Jo's letter all those years ago bubbled up and nearly choked her.

Jo squeezed Lauren's hand on her thigh but didn't take her eyes off the highway as they drove over the Golden Gate Bridge. When they'd crossed, Jo said, "We're going to make a detour to Union Square."

After snagging a lucky parking spot, Jo took Lauren's arm and led her along the sidewalk, stopping in front of Tiffany & Co.

Lauren's eyes grew wide. "Oh, what?"

Jo smiled. "Let's find you a ring. You choose. What would you like?"

Lauren's heart pounded as they approached the counter inside. *What does this ring mean to Jo?*

An elegant, gray-haired woman, smelling faintly of lilac, greeted them.

Lauren looked into Jo's smiling eyes and touched her arm. "I would love a simple gold band," she said.

"For which finger?" asked the clerk.

"The ring finger of her left hand," Jo said with authority.

Without batting an eye, the clerk took out several rings and Lauren tried them on, choosing a plain, solid gold one.

"Excellent choice," said the woman, and she placed it in a velvet box. "Would you like a glass of champagne to celebrate?"

They looked at each other, grinning. "Why not?" Jo said.

In the car, Jo took out the ring and placed it on Lauren's finger. "This is my commitment to you to fight hard for us to have a life together—finally."

Her fears vanquished, Lauren touched Jo's smiling face and kissed her.

All the way to the airport, Lauren kept her hand on Jo's thigh. They'd had a fabulous few days together, but the reality of what lay ahead would hit her the moment she departed for London. At least she would have nine hours of transition. She checked her shoulder bag to make sure she had her insulin, passport, and printed ticket at hand. She'd tossed in a romance novel to read on the plane.

Just before she entered the security lineup, Lauren clung to Jo and buried her face in her open collar. Jo held her tight and stroked her hair. "I love you," she whispered.

"I love you too," Lauren said, looking up into Jo's dark eyes and lingering there, anchoring her soul. When she tore herself away, her vision blurred with tears.

Jo called after her, "Ring me as soon as you arrive, even if it's four in the morning, my time."

As Lauren progressed through the security line, she looked back often to see Jo still standing there, each time smiling and waving, before the final checkpoint swallowed her.

PART III
July 2003–2005

chapter thirty-two
London

RICHARD HAD NO CAR, SO LAUREN HAD TO TAKE SEVERAL trains to get to Forest Hill in South London. He and his wife, Kelly, greeted her with hugs and jolly teasing. They organized her in the bedroom of their elder daughter, who'd agreed to bunk with her sister.

Lauren stayed awake with difficulty through a hearty dinner of chicken and dumplings. She asked Richard and Kelly, and each of the girls, about their lives before the conversation turned to practical matters.

"You should open a bank account here and get your money out of France. You can use our address as your home," Richard said, with his mouth full of salad.

Sweet Richard. When he was a child, Lauren used to say, "Close your mouth when you eat, Richard, or flies will get in." It was hopeless now.

"Good idea. I'll do that tomorrow," Lauren replied. She also needed to confirm online that Delphine had withdrawn no money from their joint checking or her personal savings account. Fortunately, she had the passwords in her address book.

"What about your job? When are you expected back at work?" Richard asked, flicking his too-long sandy hair from his eyes.

"I have another week of leave. I cut the US holiday short, and I'd arranged to have additional time off when we got home to do house projects." She had yet to mention that Jo had an ex-partner still living with her and needed time to sort out her departure. Fortunately, her younger brother, now married to his third wife, had little judgment about Lauren's life choices, except for Delphine. "I plan to give my four-week notice to quit work when I go back to France."

"Brave," her brother said, giving her a look of admiration.

"We can also investigate the requirements for getting a visitor's visa. I know you must apply through the US Embassy here in London," Kelly said.

It pleased Lauren that they appeared to support her desire to live with an American woman in the US, rather than return to England.

Lauren remembered Kelly worked from home. "Right. May I borrow your computer tomorrow?"

"Of course. We'll investigate the visa together." Kelly reached over and put her hand on Lauren's. "Richard and I are so happy you're extricating yourself from that self-centered, controlling, and manipulative woman in Paris. We'll do everything we can to help you."

Exhaustion caught up with Lauren. "Thank you both. I think I need to go upstairs to bed. It's been quite a journey."

Delphine had signature authority for Lauren's personal savings account and would draw upon it occasionally for household expenses. When Lauren checked online, her savings remained intact. The following day, Lauren opened a bank account in London.

Delphine had benefitted from Lauren's income for many years. She might have to go back to work full-time and cut down on massages and dinners out. *It's time to take care of myself.* She reclaimed her savings and transferred her funds to London.

Negotiating to extract her share of the Paris apartment they owned jointly would be far more difficult. Delphine would resist selling it. *I'll deal with that later.*

Finished for the day, Lauren remembered her good friend Claire still lived in London and called her.

She and Claire met for dinner the following evening at a very upscale Central London restaurant, Claire's treat. As a high-powered executive in finance, she could afford expensive meals out.

"Do you still ride your motorcycle to work?" Lauren asked as they sipped a French cabernet.

Claire smiled. "Of course. It's the best way to get into the heart of London."

Lauren smiled. "It must impress your colleagues."

"Yeah. Last week, I was late for a meeting I'd called, and I didn't have time to change. I walked into a room full of men in business suits sitting around the mahogany conference table. I took my place at the head in my leathers and boots and plonked my helmet on the table. They all stared and said nothing. So I broke the ice by hoisting one leg onto the table and said, 'Like the boots?' This got a laugh."

Lauren laughed too. She missed her flamboyant friend. Despite her job in high finance, Claire kept some of her South London moxie.

When it was Lauren's turn to update Claire on her decision to leave Delphine, Claire raised her wineglass, sloshing some on the table.

"Oh, thank goddess! Here's to your liberation. I couldn't stand that bitch. She could be outrageously funny. Aside from that, I couldn't understand what you saw in her."

Lauren clinked glasses with Claire. "Whatever it was, it was long ago and far away. For years, I just felt stuck."

Their food arrived. Filet mignon with a blue cheese sauce for Claire and sea bass on a bed of lentils for Lauren. She uttered appreciative sounds, suddenly starving.

When the server left, Claire said, "So, what got you unstuck?"

"I saw Jo again. We stayed with her in San Francisco. She reminded me who I was before Delphine beat me down."

"Ah, yes, I remember. Jo, the love of your life. The woman you could never forget. And who also broke your heart?" Claire cut a slice of steak and popped it in her mouth.

Lauren flinched at the reminder. "Yes, her. The spark is still there. For us both. In fact, it burst into a four-alarm fire in Yosemite."

"Ooo, tell me," Claire said.

Lauren took her first bite of sea bass. "Yum, divine." Despite Claire's prompting, Lauren was shy about sharing intimate details, so she told her just enough to elicit a salacious smirk. Claire was on her fifth girlfriend since she and Lauren had become friends. Claire relished the seduction part of these couplings but lost interest after a while. Luckily, Lauren was never a target. She might have lost Claire as one of her very best friends.

"What about her being an American? Aside from her obvious cultural deficiencies. How do you expect to live together?"

"I'm going to resign from my job, apply for a six-month non-immigrant visitor's visa, and return to the US."

"Wow." Claire put down her fork and fixed her gaze on Lauren. "And then what?"

Lauren rubbed her hand over the back of her neck. "I have no idea."

"Risky," Claire said.

Lauren sighed. She needed no reminder. "Yes, but she's worth it."

chapter thirty-three
San Francisco

WHEN LAUREN DISAPPEARED THROUGH THE FINAL security checkpoint at the airport, Jo's smile vanished. The emptiness in the pit of her stomach drove her to action. She straightened her shoulders and strode to her car. She had Brenda to deal with and whatever had accumulated at the office in her absence.

Brenda was sitting on a stool at the kitchen island eating a bowl of takeout noodles when Jo arrived.

"I took Lauren to the airport this evening. She's gone. I'll move back into the guest room."

"Okay. Did you cancel our appointment with Dianne this week?"

Jo had forgotten. "I didn't. I think we should still go."

Brenda looked up from inhaling her noodles. She cocked an eyebrow and made eye contact. "You said we're finished."

"We are. I've offered to help you move out. One last session with Dianne might help us negotiate the timing of your move."

Hope disappeared from Brenda's face, and she frowned. "So Lauren can move in?"

Jo didn't respond right away. She didn't know if or when Lauren might move in. Not that she wanted to share this with Brenda. "When you move out, I'll be living here on my own. In peace."

Brenda returned to her noodles, sucking in the last one. "You don't need to come with me to look for an apartment. In fact, I don't even want to be around you," she said, her tone flat. But her voice broke when she said, "It makes me sad."

Jo's face softened. Brenda almost never named a feeling. Jo had been on the receiving end of a breakup enough times to understand the hurt on a visceral level. She wished she could take Brenda's pain away. She reached out and touched her arm.

"Don't." Brenda sniffed and wiped her nose on her napkin.

Jo pulled her hand back.

"Cancel the appointment," Brenda said. "I spent the entire weekend looking for a place. I think I've found one, and I'm going to look at it again tomorrow."

Relief flooded Jo's chest, but she knew better than to show it. "Do you want to tell me about it?"

"It's within walking distance of work. The apartments are above shops and restaurants. It's tiny though. Good thing I have so little," Brenda said, with a trace of resentment.

"If you decide to take it, let me know what you need, and I'll help you buy it."

For the rest of the week, Jo focused on house projects, checking in with her office periodically. She spoke to Lauren daily, with frequent exchanges of emails. They both agreed the visitor's visa that would enable Lauren to live in the US for six months was the best temporary option while they explored others. It also made sense for Lauren to wait until she'd concluded her business in France and then apply for the visa just before she intended to come.

Brenda arrived home midweek with news. "I've taken the apartment. But I need lots of stuff, and you said you'd help."

"I will. Let me know also what I owe you for the first and last month's rent."

"Will you come with me to buy kitchen stuff and living room furniture?"

This surprised Jo. "Sure, we'll do it this weekend."

Jo busied herself with finances and work projects in her office. She sometimes met friends for dinner, unless Brenda wanted to talk. Now that Jo needed nothing from her emotionally, Brenda became the one seeking contact.

The day before Brenda's move, she asked Jo to help her pack her books, outdoor gear, and new kitchen items. Jo looked up from packing a box of camping equipment to find Brenda wiping her eyes.

Jo stopped herself from putting her arms around her.

"It is sad," Jo said. "We had some wonderful times together, especially hiking and camping. We can still be friends."

"Don't count on it," Brenda said and turned away.

The movers came and went while Jo returned to work in her law office downtown. She was dealing with a case of phenol-formaldehyde resin carried in railroad cars that overheated, spewing toxic gas over nearby residents. Information gathering occupied her until early evening.

Late that evening, she passed the closed bedroom door and raised her hand to knock. Muffled crying made her pause. She sighed, lowered her hand, and carried on to the guest room. Her heart ached for Brenda.

In the morning, Jo surveyed the living room, now empty of boxes. She glanced at the two blank spaces on the wall where Brenda's outdoor photos had been and sighed.

When she entered the kitchen, no coffee awaited her. She spied a note on the kitchen island. It read, "I'm out of your life for good. If I've left anything, throw it away. Don't bother getting in touch. I never want to see you again."

Jo pursed her lips and tossed the note in the trash.

The following week, Jo sat on the couch opposite Ellen in her office.

"So, Brenda's moved out. What feelings are coming up for you?" Ellen asked, crossing her legs.

"Relief. And sadness."

"That's understandable. We often have mixed feelings about loss," Ellen said.

"It's doubtful we'll ever be friends."

"Is that what you want?"

Jo stared at a picture just to the left of Ellen's head of ducks swimming in a lily pond, a willow tree bowing over it. It reminded her of a painting her mother brought back from Europe after the war. It hung in the den and gave her a sense of peace when life at home was anything but. She looked back at Ellen.

"I've stayed friends with most of my ex-lovers. That's the lesbian way. But living with Bren was hard." She sighed. "So perhaps not."

"What would you say you learned from your relationship with her?"

Jo took a moment. "Well, I know I can't change my partner to better fit my emotional needs, nor can I fix someone who's emotionally broken. They have to do it themselves. And we'd better mesh well from the start because what you see is what you get."

Ellen nodded. "You've captured a lot of learning in those few short sentences." She leaned forward. "How well do you know Lauren? Can you apply what you've learned to this new relationship?"

Jo sat up straight and rubbed her hands up and down her thighs. "Our circumstances have prevented us from spending much time together, although we've kept in touch for decades."

Ellen raised an eyebrow.

"But I feel I know her. That I've always known her." She paused and held Ellen's gaze.

"Sometimes it's hard to tell if that familiarity might come from old patterns and dynamics in our past," Ellen cautioned.

This startled Jo. "Oh, I don't think it does. We've been long-distance friends for over twenty years. Back in the day, we wrote letters and later emails." She paused, then added, "She's nothing like my mother."

"Let's hope not," Ellen said. "I guess that's part of what you'll discover as you spend more time together. Exciting—and a little daunting too?"

chapter thirty-four
London

WHILE STILL IN LONDON, LAUREN CALLED HER FRIEND and colleague Jane in Paris, who joined the chorus of congratulations on her leaving Delphine.

"I know this is a huge ask, but might I stay with you and Jules for a few weeks, while I give my notice at work and settle things with Delphine? God only knows what she'll do when it really sinks in that I'm leaving for good."

"I'm sorry you'll be abandoning me at work. Who's going to make me laugh? But, of course, you can stay with us. The house has felt empty since our son left for university."

Lauren let out a breath. "Thank you. I'll arrive in Paris early next week, around midday. You'll be working, so just leave me a key somewhere. I'll settle in and have dinner on the table when you and Jules get home."

Lauren's last few days in London fortified her spirit. She'd visited another old friend, played raucous games with her nieces, and relished talks with Richard and Kelly. Everyone expressed delight at her leaving Delphine, suggesting she should have done it sooner. But then she might not have taken that trip to San

Francisco and reunited with Jo. Sometimes important events happen for a reason, and at just the right time.

Lauren traipsed into work on Tuesday, having arrived in Paris the day before. The film-production company's main office buzzed with activity. Film scripts and translations to be checked littered her desk, and the sticky notes plastered to her computer held urgent messages. Coworkers dropped by to welcome her back and inquire about her holiday.

Lauren read a film script over several times, unable to focus. When her vision blurred, she fled to an empty washroom. She shut the door and leaned her back against it, her breath rapid and shallow. *How can I leave?* She'd earned the respect of the directors and producer. Even when life sucked at home, she could laugh and banter with her colleagues at work. It was a rock-solid island in a roiling sea. To leave it for an uncertain future was like parachuting from a plane. Could she find satisfying work in the US?

Lauren tried taking deep breaths through her nose and exhaling through her mouth. At age fifty-one, she'd be starting over in a foreign country. She'd been up to the challenge two decades ago in France, but could she do it again? Her savings might last only six months. Later, she'd have to rely on Jo. But she hadn't depended on anyone to support her since high school. *What if Jo changed her mind?*

Lauren moved to the sink and splashed cold water on her face. She twirled the gold band on her left ring finger. *Jo said she'd fight hard for us to be together.* Lauren had to trust her.

It took hours to track down the film producer. When they met in his office, she handed him her resignation. He leaned back in his chair, laying both hands heavily on his desk. "This is bad timing. You've just been on holiday. Can you at least give us until the fall? Finish the subtitles on the film series?"

Lauren blew out a breath. It was a long time to be away from Jo. But the producer had been very supportive of her over the years. "Yes, of course. I'll do my best," she replied.

The producer stroked his beard. "You're an excellent employee, Lauren. I sure hate to lose you."

"I've loved working with you and the team," Lauren said. *It saved my life.*

Lauren returned to her cluttered desk with renewed vigor, now that she'd taken the plunge.

Jane popped in later that afternoon. "How did it go?" she asked, holding on to the doorframe on either side. Lauren's British friend always looked so well turned out in her clingy dresses and high heels.

"Scary. But it's done. Now all I need to do is extricate myself from Delphine."

"Good luck with that. See you at home tonight? My turn to fix dinner." She turned to depart, leaving behind the scent of jasmine.

Lauren let a week go by before she contacted Delphine, prioritizing catching up on her work and recovering from jet lag. Then one evening, bracing for the inevitable backlash, she picked up the receiver to call. Jane handed her a glass of red wine and sat across from her with a magazine.

"Where are you?" Delphine demanded upon hearing Lauren's voice.

"I'm in Paris, staying at a friend's apartment."

"What friend?"

"It doesn't matter. I've given my notice at work, and I want to pick up my things from our apartment."

"What?" A long string of outraged French exploded in Lauren's ear.

Lauren placed the receiver on the coffee table. Jane looked up and rolled her eyes. When the barrage ceased, Lauren picked it up again.

"You're coming home. Your life is with me," Delphine said in a more normal tone.

"And what a hell it's been."

There was a pause as Delphine changed course.

"Are you going to America to live with her?"

"I don't know." All she wanted Delphine to know was that she was leaving her.

"I've met women like her. She's a vampire and will suck you dry."

Lauren didn't respond. It was remarkable how Jo had morphed from warrior to vampire when Delphine realized it was Lauren, not her, who interested Jo.

"She'll dump you just like she did the first time."

Delphine always lunged for the jugular. The less information Lauren gave her, the better.

"I'd like to come pick up my things in the apartment this weekend. It's best if you're not there. I have my keys."

There was another long pause.

"You'll have only four hours this weekend to pack up all your shit. After that, I'm changing the locks."

When she hung up, Lauren leaned back in her chair and

sipped her wine to soothe her blazing anger. *I deserve better.* All those years of contributing to the household, greater than her share. Until Jo, she'd remained faithful. Not that Delphine valued loyalty herself. She'd even propositioned their family doctor.

She took another sip. Soon enough she *would* have better—much better, if the Fates permitted.

Jane looked up from her magazine. "Bad as you expected?"

Lauren filled her in.

"I'll come with you," Jane said. "She won't mess with me."

Lauren smiled. Though feisty, Jane weighed less than a hundred pounds. "Thank you. Better wear a flak jacket."

That weekend, when Lauren and Jane arrived at the apartment, Lauren could not unlock the door with her key. She rang the bell, and Delphine took her time answering. She glared at them and crossed her arms. To Lauren, she said, "Only you can come in."

Lauren turned to Jane, who said, "I'll be right here. You can pass me stuff and I'll load it into the car."

The two women returned to the car and unloaded empty boxes and garbage bags. Once inside the apartment, Lauren strode to the bookcases and perused her collection of British classics, lesbian literature, and French language books. She grabbed as many as she could, packing them into boxes, too heavy for Jane. For over two hours, she hauled them out of the apartment, filling the boot of Jane's SUV.

Upstairs in the spare room, Lauren passed her hand over the top of her late-eighteenth-century desk of light oak with leather inlays. She sighed with regret at leaving it. Then she removed her antique inkwell stand, pictures of her family in England, and other personal items, packing them in a box surrounded by sweaters. Lauren hurriedly sorted through her files and packed essential documents into the portable file boxes Jane lent her, taking care to locate and make a copy of the closing document for the purchase of the apartment and the deed.

Just as she finished, Delphine loomed in the doorway. "Your four hours are up."

Lauren bristled. "Oh, for god's sake, Delphine, this is my home too. We've been together for over twenty very long years, and this is how you treat me?"

For once, Delphine looked chastened. "You're the one leaving me for that American vampire bitch, and I'm watching you dismantle our life together. It hurts."

Delphine had showed some heart, and Lauren softened, ignoring the dig at Jo. "I'm sorry you're hurting, Delphine. I just have my clothes to pack, and I'll leave." *Forever.*

To speed up the process, Lauren handed Jane wads of clothes to stuff in garbage bags. When they finished, Delphine was nowhere to be found. Just in case she was lurking nearby, Lauren called out, "We're leaving. We'll talk later about settling my share of the apartment."

Once on the pavement outside, Lauren rubbed her shoulder where she'd strained it, lifting heavy book boxes. She gazed up at the apartment with its bright-blue wooden shutters and geraniums in the window boxes. *Was I ever happy here?* She couldn't remember.

"Goodbye, Delphine," she said under her breath when she saw the curtain flutter in the upstairs window.

chapter thirty-five
San Francisco

WITH BRENDA GONE, JO FELT AS IF SHE WAS IN LIMBO until she could reunite with Lauren. Emails with loving and suggestive endearments sustained her most evenings but paled compared to Lauren in the flesh. During meetings at the law firm, she drummed her fingers, jiggled her foot up and down, and couldn't wait for them to end. A colleague caught her staring out the window and had to repeat his question. Fortunately, she was still in the discovery phase of her next case and didn't have to prepare for depositions or trial.

In her home office, Jo investigated requirements for citizens of the European Union who wished to immigrate to the US. It looked as dismal as it had in 1981. The recently formed United States Citizenship and Immigration Service still did not recognize same-sex relationships for immigration. This meant they would have to prove that Lauren had unique professional qualifications not possessed by a US citizen. A hard knot formed in her stomach at each brick wall she discovered.

Jo got up and paced her office. Lacking inspiration, she sat again and flipped through her contacts list. She pictured a plump, animated Latina woman she'd met at a party of lesbian professionals two years ago. She'd given Jo her contact information and urged her to call to have dinner together with their partners. Jo never called, but she remembered the woman mentioned she was an immigration attorney and that her last name started with an "A." She flipped through her Rolodex one more time and found her: Maria Alvarez.

Jo researched her credentials. She'd gone to the USC Gould School of Law and practiced immigration law in a firm with only one other attorney. Her reputation appeared solid. Jo called to set up a meeting. Lauren now had a college degree and more work experience behind her. If they could finagle her work experience as unique and find an employer to sponsor her, perhaps she could at least get a temporary work visa.

Late one day the following week, Maria greeted Jo and offered coffee. Her eyes, intelligent and warm, put Jo at ease. Unlike Jo's law firm, with its well-appointed conference rooms with long tables and plush chairs, they sat in a small windowless meeting room, surrounded by abstract paintings screaming color.

Jo faced Maria across the small table and explained their situation.

Maria pursed her lips. "You face the same dilemma as many same-sex couples of different nationalities. The US Citizenship and Immigration Service will never recognize you as a couple for immigration. Whether Lauren can get a temporary work visa—that's very difficult. The US authorizes only a few thousand H-1B visas at the beginning of the year, usually in February, and the tech companies snap them up right away.

Does she have any specialized computer skills or technical background?"

"No. She works as a project manager for a French film company doing translations."

"Hmm." Maria frowned. "It would be hard to turn that into a unique qualification."

Jo's shoulders slumped as hope drained away.

Maria leaned toward Jo. "I'm sorry I can't offer you better news. I hope one day our country will deem our unions as legitimate as heterosexuals for immigration."

"Probably not in my lifetime," Jo muttered.

"At least she can apply for a B-2 visitor's visa to come to the US for up to six months. It may also be renewed. She can't work, though. Perhaps you two can travel back and forth to the UK? Is your law practice flexible?"

"Not really," Jo said. After a half hour of social chitchat, Jo took her leave, dragging herself to her car. She wanted to go home, flop into bed, and pull the covers over her head.

Oddly, fall in San Francisco was often warmer than summer. Jo reclined on her deck, drinking a glass of chardonnay and talking to Lauren on the phone, who'd called her in the middle of the night Paris time because she couldn't sleep.

"I'm staying one more week to finish up this film series . . . then I'm free to go back to London. I'll fill out the B-2 visa application, have my interview at the embassy, and fly into your arms."

"That sounds wonderful," Jo said, pushing aside her fears. Surely, they would come up with something. "What about your apartment?"

"I've been working on it with a very resistant Delphine. If I force her to sell, which I'm not sure I have the power to do, she won't be able to afford another one in Paris. Even renting could be out of her range. I've hired an appraiser and am still waiting for her report. Then I'll negotiate with Delphine to take out a mortgage for half of the appraised value and buy me out."

"Excellent solution. I hope she agrees."

When they hung up, Jo covered her face with her hands. *Have I motivated Lauren to resign from her job and give up her apartment, only to find out she can't stay in the US?* Her stomach roiled. She might be sick.

The next evening, in dire need of a listening ear, Jo met a friend for dinner. Barb had heard the saga of her rekindled passion for her old lover from decades past. Partnered with Anne for over twenty years, Barb offered wise counsel on relationship longevity, though she approved Jo's split with Brenda.

"I've been reckless and selfish," Jo lamented. "Telling Lauren I want to live together. I love her, but the world conspires against us. She's quit her job and is giving up her Paris apartment. The chances of us living together in the US are extremely low." Jo swallowed hard and took a deep breath.

"Do you really want this woman?" Barb asked, holding her gaze.

"More than anything." Jo sighed.

"Then what are you waiting for? Go to Paris. Travel with her to London and bring her back with you to the US. Show her you're in this together. Wherever it takes you."

Jo sat up straight. "You're right."

Jo booked her flight to Paris. She and Lauren planned to stay in a hotel for the last two days in Paris before driving to London. Jo's law firm complained about her absence, so before she left, she put in frenetic twelve-hour days organizing and delegating work for the week she'd be away.

Once she reclined her seat on the plane and closed her eyes, the tension drained from her body. She'd be in Lauren's arms soon. They'd face whatever unfolded for them together, one day at a time.

chapter thirty-six

Paris

THEY'D HARDLY PUT THEIR BAGS DOWN IN THE HOTEL in Paris before Lauren jumped Jo. They tore off their clothes and indulged their lust before Jo called a time-out for a shower and a brief nap. Making love worked up their appetites, and by early evening, Lauren suggested a stroll to a nearby restaurant for dinner.

"I remember a great place for chicken soup with matzo balls if it still exists," Jo said.

"I think we need something more substantial to keep our strength up. Why don't I take you to my favorite seafood restaurant? How do razor clams swimming in a buttery sauce or scallops atop a *risotto de fregola* sound?"

"It's hard to top chicken soup with matzo balls, but I'm sold. Let's go."

For the next forty-eight hours, Lauren enjoyed taking Jo to the Latin Quarter, the cobbled streets bustling with students from the Sorbonne and sidewalk cafés overflowing with young people arguing, laughing, and smoking while sipping espresso. They stepped into a boulangerie for sweet indulgences, and

Lauren kissed residual *pain au chocolat* off Jo's lips as they wandered the tiny picturesque streets, evocative of medieval Paris. Jo kept looking up and marveling at the architecture, and Lauren had to guide her by the arm so she didn't trip or collide with anyone. She dragged Jo into one of her favorite clothes shops, where she tried on a fitted leather jacket that made Lauren want to take her to bed immediately. In the evening, they lingered to enjoy an impromptu classical music concert on the Place Saint-Michel.

On the last day, Jo insisted they visit the Panthéon, the resting place of Victor Hugo, Voltaire, Rousseau, and Pierre and Marie Curie. Later, they visited the Cathédrale Notre-Dame, but, put off by the crowds, they sat quietly in the Sainte-Chapelle. Lauren leaned back, put her arm around Jo's shoulders, and took a deep breath. The light coming through the magnificent stained-glass windows bolstered her spirit. Their second chance wasn't just serendipity but was meant to be. *Everything's going to be okay.*

On the last morning, they set off early from Paris, planning to take the Dieppe–Newhaven car ferry across the English Channel, since Jo felt jittery about going through the Channel Tunnel. Packing boxes and bags filled Lauren's hatchback.

As they left Paris behind, Jo rubbed Lauren's shoulders while she drove. "How do you feel, leaving Paris?"

"Like I'm starting a whole new adventure. I haven't been this excited for years."

The ferry rocked side to side in rough seas. Lauren noticed Jo was quiet and pale. "Are you okay?"

"I'm trying not to vomit," Jo said.

Perhaps she's anxious.

The traffic snarled as they approached London, but by early afternoon they arrived at the boutique hotel Jo had booked, a restored Victorian pub with rooms above, a terrace, and a lush garden. Lauren approved the king-sized bed, and they showered and made use of it before walking the mile to Lauren's brother's home.

Richard and Kelly greeted Jo warmly with handshakes and hugs. After preliminary chitchat, Richard said, "It's quiz night at the pub around the corner. Shall we grab a bite there and form a team? With Lauren and an American, we should smoke 'em."

It pleased Lauren to see Jo respond enthusiastically. She'd get to show off for her.

Later that evening at the pub, Jo nudged her. "Why do you know so much about everything?"

Lauren winked at her. "I'm a sponge for information."

"You should have been a lawyer," Jo said.

The following morning, Lauren, Jo, and Kelly sat around the computer as Kelly downloaded and printed the application for a six-month visitor's visa to the US. Kelly took several headshots of Lauren against the white kitchen wall and chose the best one. She printed it on photo paper and cut it down to size.

Kelly struggled to match the photo to the designated square on the application, which specified where the eyes should be. She frowned. "Your eyes are too low," she said.

They all looked. Either Lauren's forehead was too high or her eyes were too low.

"Will the embassy deny my visa because my eyes are too low?" Lauren said.

They laughed, all three confident there would be no problem.

Two days later, Lauren and Jo approached the US Embassy in Grosvenor Square in London.

"Wow," Jo said, "Look at that . . . 9/11 has really changed things."

Concrete barricades surrounded the embassy. Atop some of them stood soldiers bearing automatic rifles. A long line snaked out from the main entrance. A tall man in uniform walked up and down the line, shouting, "Make sure you have all your documents and a properly completed application. If anything is missing, you'll be asked to leave."

Lauren and Jo joined the end of the line. The official strode over to them. "Documents," he demanded.

Lauren produced her application and British passport. Then he turned to Jo.

"I'm with her," she said. "I'm a US citizen."

"Only visa applicants can approach the embassy. Stand back."

Jo's mouth dropped open, and Lauren touched her arm. "I'll be okay."

As she watched Jo walk away, a hard knot of anxiety formed in Lauren's stomach. Europeans, South Asians, and Africans stood in the chill fall air, shuffling forward every few minutes. Most wore sober, tense expressions and spoke in hushed tones.

The soldier looming above with his automatic weapon slung over one shoulder made Lauren's skin crawl.

Inside, a glass barrier separated the line from the larger room. Again, a staff member demanded she show her documents and gave her a number. Lauren's anxiety mounted, knowing her future happiness was in the hands of complete strangers, most of whom would be hostile to her desire to live with Jo.

An excruciating half hour later, Lauren's number displayed overhead. She approached the designated window, her heart pounding. A tired-looking middle-aged woman stood behind bulletproof glass. "Documents," she barked.

Lauren struggled to keep her hands from shaking as she placed her application and passport on the counter. *Please, please let this go well.*

The woman pulled them through the opening in the glass barrier. "You've been living in France for decades?"

"Yes," Lauren said.

"Where do you work?" the agent asked without looking up.

"I worked for a film company in Paris."

The woman jerked her head up and peered at Lauren. "Worked? You mean you're no longer working?"

"No." Lauren wiped her sweaty palms on her pant legs.

"Why do you want to go to the US for six months?" The woman fixed Lauren with an unfriendly stare. The room suddenly dimmed and closed in, and Lauren felt she was standing at the end of a long tunnel.

"I'd like a break from working. I have a friend in San Francisco I want to visit. Then do some traveling." Lauren couldn't keep the tremor from her voice. *I should have done this before I quit my job.*

"Will you be returning to France?"

"No. I'll stay with my brother in London and look for another job when I return." *Can she tell I'm lying?*

The woman examined Lauren's face for a long moment. "You're too young to be on holiday for six months, and you just recently returned from the US." She picked up her stamp and banged "VISA DENIED" in big red letters across Lauren's application. She pushed her passport back, looked over Lauren's head, and said, "Next."

Lauren shook her head in disbelief, gripping the counter to steady herself. *What? I'm too young to take a six-month vacation?* Her limbs turned to jelly, and tears blurred her vision as she pivoted and shuffled through the waiting throngs, hearing and seeing nothing but the question looming in her mind: *What now?*

chapter thirty-seven

JO RAN TO LAUREN AS SHE EMERGED FROM THE EMBASSY, looking crestfallen. Fear gripped her chest when she saw tears. "What happened?"

"They... denied... my visa," Lauren said between sobs.

Blood drained from Jo's face. "What? Why?" She held Lauren until her sobs subsided.

"That miserable woman said I was too young to go on holiday for six months after I'd told her I quit my job."

"What kind of reason is that?" *We should have planned this better.* She linked arms with Lauren. "Let's walk." The icy fear in her chest morphed into smoldering anger. "I can't believe it." How could the agent make such an arbitrary judgment? And ruin their plan to be together?

As they walked, Jo's anger turned to rage. She let go of Lauren's arm and slammed her fist into her palm, breathing hard.

Lauren startled. "Are you upset with me?"

"Of course not, sweetheart. I'm angry at my country. Look at those barricades, those soldiers, those weapons. They just want to keep everyone out." She linked arms with Lauren again and they paced around Grosvenor Square, oblivious to passersby and the beautiful fall day.

On their second turn around the square, the maple leaf flag flying over the Canadian Embassy caught Jo's eye. No barricades, no soldiers, no guns. By the third time around, an idea formed. She halted and faced Lauren.

"Let's see what's required to immigrate to Canada."

Eyes wide, Lauren searched Jo's face. "You would move to Canada with me?"

"Ontario and British Columbia just legalized same-sex marriage. Perhaps Canada will recognize us as a couple for immigration." Energized with hope, she added, "Let's find out."

They linked arms again and strode to the entrance of the Canadian Embassy. The door opened. No one stopped them as they walked up to a woman at the reception window.

The woman smiled. "May I help you?"

"Can you tell us how we can immigrate to Canada?" Jo gripped the edge of the counter. *Am I really doing this?*

"Yes, of course. Will you be applying as a couple?"

It amazed Jo how natural the question sounded coming from this pleasant Canadian. She relaxed her grip on the counter. Jo's eyes searched Lauren's. She nodded.

"Yes," Jo said.

Both Richard and Kelly greeted them at the door when they arrived in South London.

"We opened a celebratory bottle of wine for you," Richard said. "How did everything turn out?"

"They denied my application," Lauren said, taking off her jacket.

"What? Because your eyes were too low?" Kelly said. Then she sobered. "I'm sorry."

"The agent said Lauren was too young to take a six-month vacation, so it was about that ridiculous and arbitrary," Jo said. "But we have a Plan B."

"Let's hear it," Richard said, pouring the wine and handing them each a glass.

"We're going to apply to become Canadians," Lauren said. She pulled Jo toward her for a kiss on the cheek. Jo bit her lip, then swallowed hard. How had her life suddenly gotten so complicated?

"Here's to plan B, eh?" Richard said, raising his glass.

The following morning, Jo, Lauren, and Kelly read the pamphlets and information sheets from the Canadian Embassy and looked online.

First, they had to become Permanent Residents. The only avenue open to them was as skilled workers. This required a minimum number of points based on age, language proficiency, education, and work history in Canada.

"They take away points for each year over fifty," Jo said. "And I don't speak French."

"Look, they have a calculator tool," Kelly said. "Let's see if you have enough."

The two women leaned over Kelly's shoulder as they entered Jo's information and added up the points. She fell short of the minimum required.

Jo rubbed her hands up and down her thighs, anxiety blooming in her chest. Lauren massaged her shoulders.

Kelly entered Lauren's age, education, and language proficiency in both French and English. Her younger age and French language skills put her over the minimum by four points.

Jo took a deep breath and let it out slowly. Lauren had the option to immigrate even if she didn't. But what good would that do?

Lauren peered at the screen. "It says that couples can combine their points," she said. She did a quick calculation in her head. "Together we have enough!"

The two jumped up and did a happy dance.

"Wait," Kelly said. "It says for a common-law couple to combine points, you must prove you've lived together for at least a year."

Jo locked eyes with Lauren and sagged into a chair. "How the hell can we do that?"

Back at the hotel, they climbed into bed and Lauren laid her head on Jo's chest, weary and despondent. Jo stroked her hair.

"We must be smarter about this. Theoretically, as a British citizen, you can come to the US for three months without a visitor's visa under the Visa Waiver Program."

Lauren raised her head. "Do you think they'll let me in when they just denied my visitor's visa?"

"They probably won't if you fly back with me now as we'd planned."

Lauren's face fell.

"But if we stack the deck with evidence you're planning to return to England, we'd have a better chance."

Lauren perked up. "Right. Claire might offer me a job."

Jo smiled. "And you'll show them your return ticket to London."

"And my bank statement showing my brother's address as my own," Lauren said, her face brightening.

Lauren's hand slid up Jo's sleeping shirt, and their lips met. Jo dissolved into Lauren's embrace, allowing herself to just be present in the moment.

chapter thirty-eight
San Francisco

JO BOARDED THE PLANE TO SAN FRANCISCO WITHOUT Lauren, contemplating the unsettling turn the visit took when she agreed to immigrate to Canada. Jo loved her work. When she hit corporate polluters in their wallets and forced their accountability, she experienced deep satisfaction. She and her team celebrated many wins. One of the country's most egregious polluters had to declare bankruptcy.

In the past, her work often took precedence over her relationships. Long hours at the office took their toll. Two women walked out on her because she didn't give them enough attention. Since then, she'd prioritized her relationships more, but she'd collided with an emotional brick wall with Brenda. Now she faced a dilemma: her work or the potential of a healthy, emotionally stable relationship.

Landing in San Francisco, Jo took a cab to her empty house. She opened the refrigerator to find no frozen dinners and moldy leftover pizza. A tub of yogurt appeared mold-free, and she ate some directly from the container. She flopped onto the couch and pressed the remote to turn on the latest episode of *The West*

Wing. Jo thought, *if only this were real*. A country and a president who accepted that love is love, regardless of whether it's between a man and a woman or a woman and a woman.

Over the next couple of weeks, while Lauren sold her car, obtained an offer-of-employment letter from Claire, and got more documents mailed to her at her brother's address, Jo fretted about Lauren's arrival. What if the border patrol refused her entry after a nine-hour flight from London? And ordered her to take the next flight back? This would be rough on anyone, but especially someone with type 1 diabetes.

An idea popped into her head. Lauren could fly to Vancouver, British Columbia, instead. If she met Lauren there, Jo could accompany her across the US border by car. In the worst-case scenario, if Lauren was refused entry into the US, housing her in a rented flat in Vancouver might do while they worked out their Canadian applications. She sighed. Sheltering Lauren in Vancouver rather than tucking her safely under her own roof in San Francisco seemed a gloomy prospect.

Jo recalled a gay attorney, Neville, from Vancouver; she worked with him on a cross-border case three years earlier. She found his number and called him.

After catching up on the aftermath of the case, Jo described her predicament with Lauren.

"I've become a marriage commissioner in BC and have performed dozens of marriages for couples coming up from the US. Also for couples where one is an American," Neville said.

"Married or not, Lauren and I must live together for a year to be considered a couple. But there's no country where we can legally do that." She clenched her jaw. This injustice made her blood boil.

"You're not alone. It's so unfair. But I can give you the name of an excellent immigration attorney."

When she hung up, Jo stared out at the Golden Gate Bridge, partially enshrouded in fog on the highway leading north to Canada. Is that really where her life was headed?

Jo scheduled another session with Ellen. When she described the difficulties that lay ahead, Ellen said, "It strikes me you are potentially making an enormous sacrifice to be with this woman. Have you thought about what it will be like to give up your law practice to move to Canada?"

"Lauren has given up her home, career, and probably her country," Jo said.

Ellen paused for a few beats. "Yes, she has. She's taken an enormous risk. But do you feel obligated to do the same? Your law career has been the one constant in your life through all the turmoil of your relationships."

"Of course, I would prefer to continue practicing environmental law and to protect my ability to earn income. But I want to live with her. I don't see how we can do that in the US." Beads of sweat formed on Jo's forehead. She felt like peeling off her shirt. "It's really warm in here."

"Do you think it's the room? Or are you having a hot flash?"

Jo's shoulders sagged. "Oh, no. Menopause is all I need right now."

Ellen's face showed concern. "You've been through a lot lately. Before you make major changes, what would it be like to take a breather? Perhaps let your new relationship develop without so much external turmoil?"

Jo considered this. "Yes, I'd like for us to have time together without so much pressure. It's worth a shot to see if Lauren can spend at least three months in the US."

Ellen held her gaze. "This must be your decision, but I encourage you to think long and hard about moving to Canada. Especially if it means giving up your career that's so important to you."

Jo looked past Ellen at the duck painting on the wall, searching for calm. She tried taking a deep breath, but her chest constricted. Perhaps she shouldn't fill out the Canadian application just yet. She didn't have enough points anyway applying as a single person. She rationalized waiting until it was clear they could combine their applications.

In mid-November, Lauren called Jo. "I have all the documents to show I intend to return to the UK and not remain in the US beyond the three months allowed. I sold my car. Shall I buy my round-trip ticket to Vancouver?"

Jo drew in a long breath before answering, her heart pounding. "Absolutely. I'll make a reservation at a bed-and-breakfast in the Davie District. We can enjoy a night together before facing the US border."

chapter thirty-nine

Vancouver

JO FLEW UP TO VANCOUVER THE MORNING LAUREN was to arrive. She rented a car and waited at International Arrivals, pacing to relieve her impatience. When a smiling Lauren came through, Jo freely threw her arms around her and claimed her.

Lauren melted into Jo's arms and her fears receded. She'd leaped off a cliff and into the arms of this woman whose allure she couldn't resist. That night at the B and B, she let Jo sweep her away in the current of desire with no thought of what lay ahead.

In the cold light of morning, they prepared for the face-off with the US Citizenship and Immigration Service. Lauren pulled out her job offer from Claire and packed it safely in her bag, along with confirmation of her return airline ticket. Claire had surprised her when she said, "I have the perfect job for you. In the event you must return to London while your Canadian application is pending, you will at least have an income."

"So, how do we know each other?" Lauren asked over buttery croissants with raspberry jam in the breakfast room.

"We're old friends who met in London. This summer, we camped in Yosemite together, and now you'd like to explore more of the US before you start your new job early next year," Jo said.

"Why are you in Canada?"

"I'm on holiday and came up to meet you. You'll be staying with me, and I offered to give you a ride back to my home in San Francisco so we can explore the Pacific Northwest on the way." Jo paused. "How will you explain the denial of your visa?"

"The bitch was just jealous of me taking a six-month holiday," Lauren said.

"Probably true. But the facts were: You quit your job, left France, and hadn't lived in the UK for over two decades. Footloose and fancy-free, you might look to settle illegally in the US."

"But I'm not wanting to do anything illegal. I just want to live with you. Somewhere. Legally." Lauren threw up her hands. "Oh, my god. This is so convoluted. How are we going to keep it all straight?"

"Beats me," Jo said. "I've never been straight. That's why this is so hard. If only we had the same rights as other citizens of our countries."

"I'll do all the talking," Lauren said. Frowning, she added, "I don't enjoy being treated like a criminal."

"Let's hope whoever interrogates you is having a good day and is not manifesting a god complex."

Lauren loaded her two duffels into the back of the rental SUV, having left her books and other meager possessions with Richard.

As they approached the US border, Jo squeezed Lauren's thigh. "Whatever happens, I'll be with you."

As the line of cars snaked through the checkpoint at the Peace Arch, Lauren's palms began to sweat. She rolled her shoulders to relieve the tension and tried belly breathing. When they reached the booth, the border guard examined their passports and told them to roll down the back window.

"Where's home?" he asked.

"San Francisco for me and London for Lauren," Jo said, forgetting not to answer for Lauren.

"How do you know each other?" he said, peering into the back seat.

"We're friends. We've traveled together and known each other for decades," Jo said, her tone suggesting to Lauren she was on edge.

The guard scribbled on an orange slip and slapped it under the windshield wiper. "Put on your hazard lights and go to secondary inspection. Everything stays in the car but your documents. Leave the car unlocked."

Once parked, they entered a cavernous room. People lined up to be interviewed in a cordoned-off area parallel to a long counter, behind which uniformed border patrol officers sat. Only a few officers were interviewing travelers. The rest chatted with other officers or stared at their computers.

Lauren hugged her folder of documents to her chest and tried to visualize a calm forest setting. Her scalp prickled. She dared not touch Jo, but she turned to glance at her and they locked eyes. When she advanced to the front of the line, her heart thudding hard against her chest, the patrol officer stared at his computer, ignoring her. *Is he deliberately trying to make me sweat?*

After an interminable five minutes, he motioned for them to approach the counter. The gun on his hip was unnerving, but Lauren tried to ignore it and looked him in the eye.

"Documents," he said, glancing from one to the other.

They both put their passports on the counter. He scanned them into the computer, staring at the screen for another excruciating five minutes.

Finally, he looked up at Lauren. "I see we denied your visa request in October."

"Yes. The agent said I was too young to take a six-month holiday." Lauren struggled to keep the shaking out of her voice.

"And yet, here you are, back again." He smirked at Lauren, looking her over. The back of Jo's hand pressed against her thigh.

"Yes, I'm requesting entry under the three-month Visa Waiver Program before I start my new job in London."

He looked skeptical. "And what new job is that?"

Lauren produced her job offer from Claire. The officer glanced at it briefly and sniffed.

"Do you have a return ticket to London?"

She handed him the flight confirmation.

He examined it, then looked from Lauren to Jo. "What's your relationship?"

"We're friends," Lauren said simply.

The officer snorted. "Friends, huh?" He waved the job offer at Lauren. "I've seen better than this. How do I know you aren't planning to stay on in the US with your *friend* here?"

Lauren stiffened, still looking him in the eye. "Because I've done nothing illegal and don't intend to start now." Then it hit her. "Plus, I'm a type 1 diabetic. I get free health care in the UK and France. Why would I want to stay illegally in the US without medical insurance?"

"Hmm." He stared at Lauren for a long moment, then

stamped her I-94 form and handed her both passports and a slip of paper. "Take this slip to the cashier at the end of the counter," he said. "Enjoy your stay."

Lauren approached the cashier, with Jo close behind. Lauren's hands still shook as she put the documents back in her bag and paid. Neither spoke as they left the building and hastened to the car. Lauren's jacket was not where she'd left it but lay on the back seat. Officers had searched the vehicle. Both women remained silent until they'd passed another checkpoint and were safely on the US interstate south.

Jo pulled off at the nearest exit to hug Lauren, whose body went limp. "Oh, my god," she said as tears of relief slid down her cheeks.

chapter forty
Pacific Coast

JO HELD LAUREN AND RUBBED HER BACK, AWARE THAT many more challenges lay ahead. She could shelter Lauren for only three months. *Then what?* While Lauren eventually calmed, Jo's apprehension remained.

The rhythmic swish of the windshield wipers as they drove south on I-5 in the November rain, and Lauren's steady hand on her thigh, eased her fretting somewhat. *We might as well enjoy the trip.* She remembered a restaurant in Seattle that served up a scrumptious paella.

Over dinner, Jo said, "I'd like you to meet some of my friends. We'll have dinners and parties over the holidays. We can decorate the tree together."

Lauren jumped in with ideas. "I'd love to meet your friends, but perhaps one or two at a time. The holidays inspire my best French recipes. Oysters especially."

Jo's face registered disgust.

"You don't like oysters?"

"Not raw ones. It's like swallowing postnasal drip."

Lauren shot her an amused grin. "I guess there's still a lot to learn about each other."

Jo reached for her hand. "Trivia, my love. We already know the important things."

From Olympia, Washington, they headed west to Aberdeen, then took the coastal route, stopping to enjoy dinner at the Tillamook Cheese Factory, a walk on Cannon Beach in a rain squall, and a fabulous breakfast of blueberry pancakes and apple sausage in Ashland. South of Crescent City in California, they stopped in the Redwood National Forest.

Sunlight filtered through the misty forest of towering giants, a sight never failing to inspire Jo. Lauren seemed equally impressed. They set off together on a trail, Jo's enthusiasm overriding her usual caution. They meandered along the path, taking several forks before Lauren reached for Jo's arm. "I should go back. I don't have any sugar with me, and I think I'm a little low. You go on. I can find my way back."

Jo's instinct was to return with Lauren.

"I'll be fine," Lauren insisted. "You've wanted to stretch your legs for hours. I don't want to hold you back."

"Okay," Jo said. "If you're sure you remember the way. I'll just walk another fifteen minutes, then turn around."

Jo set off at a brisk pace, eager to burn off energy after long hours of driving. She passed no other hikers. The sun that had so gloriously lit her path earlier faded, and the mist grew into fog. In fifteen minutes, she turned to retrace her steps. The fork in the trail didn't look familiar. The fog obscured the rock face she remembered. She chose one path, hoping it was the right one. Though she expected another fork in about one hundred yards, she found none. She broke into a jog, retracing her steps and taking the other fork. She came to another divide that also did not look familiar. The fog swirled in the trees, disorienting her. She chose the left one and increased her pace, running now. Suddenly, a ravine yawned below her. She grabbed a handful of brush to stop herself, breathing hard. *I'm lost.* Why didn't she pay closer attention to the trail instead of gaping at the tree canopy? And what about Lauren? Did she reach the car and sugar?

A cold sweat broke out on her forehead as she tried to calm her breathing and think. She trotted to the previous fork, stumbling over a tree root, and caught herself. The fog cleared slightly, and she noted her surroundings. The path widened on one side of the fork and she took it, keeping up her pace. Ten minutes later, rounding a corner, the outline of a person appeared through the fog.

"Jo?"

Jo ran toward the familiar voice. "Lauren, I'm here."

Lauren emerged, looking frazzled and scared. "I waited for you in the car. But when you didn't come, I was worried."

"Oh, thank god you got back to the car." Embarrassment initially prevented Jo from revealing she'd lost her bearings, and now Lauren was the one coming to rescue *her*.

"Were you lost?" Lauren asked.

"Yes," Jo admitted. "But you found me."

After a night in Eureka, they took the fastest, less scenic route to San Francisco, saving Highway 1 for another day. Jo's law office called several times on the trip, and the requests for Jo's attention mounted daily. A fire hose of tasks would assault her the moment she stepped into the office.

After Lauren organized the contents of her two duffels in the walk-in closet next to Jo's business attire, they heated two frozen meals and ate by candlelight at the dining room table.

"I'm afraid this is the end of vacation for me," Jo said. "You'll get to see what it's like living with a workaholic environmental lawyer."

"Do I have to have dinner waiting and serve it to you barefoot, wearing only an apron?" Lauren asked.

Jo smiled. "Nice image." She reached across the table and touched Lauren's arm. "I'm worried you'll get bored."

"But you worked at home a couple of days a week when I visited this summer," Lauren said.

"Yes, I'll do that at least one day a week. But you better wear something under that apron or I'll get nothing done."

chapter forty-one

WHILE JO WORKED, LAUREN TACKLED THE APPLICATION to become a Canadian Permanent Resident. She had to list the address of every place she'd ever lived and every job she'd ever held. It required a police report from the UK and from France to verify she'd not committed any crimes. Creating the list of everywhere she'd ever traveled took many hours. The request for certified copies of her educational diplomas and licenses required getting Richard to send them from her file boxes in London.

From her downtown office, Jo patched Lauren into a three-way phone consultation with the Canadian immigration attorney Neville had recommended.

After routine background questions, the attorney said, "Lauren, you have enough points to qualify as a skilled worker, but Jo doesn't because of her age and lack of French language skills. Are you applying as a couple?"

"Our understanding is that we must prove we've lived together for a year somewhere to do that," Jo said.

"Yes, that's correct," the attorney said.

"But there is no country in which we can legally live together continuously for a year, not Canada, not the UK, and not the US," Jo said, her voice rising in exasperation.

The anxiety in Jo's voice made Lauren tense. "What if we live together intermittently in different countries but it adds up to a year?"

The attorney paused while he considered this. "I don't think living together for a few months at a time in different countries qualifies. But it might depend on the agent reviewing your application."

Jo sighed again, and Lauren could imagine her rolling her eyes. This news further unsettled her. Jo having to spend time outside the US would disrupt her law practice. Would she be willing to do that?

"My advice is for you to complete your applications separately for now, even if Jo doesn't have the minimum points. Then you can work on proving you're a common-law couple. I should warn you, though. Getting married in British Columbia or Ontario is not enough if you can't prove you live together."

"Catch-22," Lauren said, leaning back in her chair and closing her eyes.

When they hung up, Lauren paced, trying to calm her roiling thoughts. She reminded herself to focus on just one step at a time. What else could she do? So much was out of their hands.

While Jo worked long hours, Lauren filled her days with grocery shopping, food preparation, and gardening. Gone were the chef-prepared frozen dinners. Fresh flowers from the garden festooned the kitchen island and dining room table. Some evenings she and Jo watched a film cuddling on the couch before bed.

Over the next several weeks, Lauren met many of Jo's

friends. Different groups included Lauren in invitations for dinner and parties. The dizzying rounds of introductions and small talk with people Jo had known for years fatigued her. Naturally reserved, she preferred dinners as a foursome, with better opportunities for in-depth discussion. It amazed her how little Americans knew or cared about the world outside the US. She held her own when discussing US politics, film, or literature, but she was happiest sitting before the gas fire with Jo and a good book.

Unaccustomed to unemployment, Lauren enjoyed the first few weeks of relative leisure as a "kept woman." But in early December, over a dinner of coquilles Saint Jacques, Lauren said, "Why don't you let me help you organize your medical records and other documents? If you point me in the right direction, I'm quite good at managing workflow."

Jo tipped her head to one side. "Are you bored?"

"I'm never bored when we're together, but I'm not used to being a house frau."

Jo smiled. "I quite like having a house frau. You outdid yourself with this meal. But I hear you. Come upstairs after dinner and let's have a look at the records I'm wading through for this latest case. Residents are complaining of various medical problems they believe result from living near oil wells in the neighborhood."

After dinner, Lauren sat near Jo in her home office. Jo looked so serious and professional in her reading glasses, poring through the box of files. Lauren leaned against her, dropping kisses on the back of her neck.

Jo shivered and took off her glasses. "Whatever I was thinking has completely flown out the window."

Lauren pulled away and sat up straight. "Sorry, boss, no more distractions."

Jo flashed her a smile before slipping her reading glasses on again. "So, for starters, you can go through these medical records and highlight any history of respiratory symptoms like a sore throat, runny nose, or headaches. Also, lower respiratory symptoms like shortness of breath, wheezing, or cough, and the timing of onset of symptoms. And whether they have any history of cancer and the date of diagnosis."

"Whoa. I don't have any medical background," Lauren said.

"That's okay. We'll have our medical experts opine on the causal relationship of illness to pollutants from the wells, but it helps us organize the constellation of complaints from each person in advance. Then we figure out who to hire as experts." Jo plopped a stack of medical records onto Lauren's lap.

Lauren stared at the intimidating pile. "I might not realize what symptoms or illnesses are significant."

"Include everything if you're uncertain. Think of each person's case as a story. Like the British crime novels you like so much. You're looking for clues to solve the murder, or, in this case, the illness. Let's go through some together."

For hours, they sifted through the records, highlighting and making a spreadsheet of symptoms, illnesses, and time of onset until Lauren got the gist of it.

At 10:30 p.m., Jo took off her glasses and rose. "Come, my love, time for bed." She pulled Lauren from her chair, pressed her up against the wall, hands above her head, and kissed her.

"Is this the way you treat your employees?"

"Only the ones who turn me on."

As they prepared for bed, Lauren mused on her new assignment. Her work with Jo might distract her from obsessing over their immigration problems. And she liked that Jo let her into more of her world.

chapter forty-two

CHRISTMAS LOOMED JUST THREE WEEKS AWAY. USUALLY, Jo flew to San Diego to visit her eighty-nine-year-old mother, Molly, in a retirement home. Sometimes she brought along "a friend," but her mother required that she maintain a respectable veneer of heteronormality for her friends and neighbors. This rankled Jo, but the guilt produced by not visiting her mother at Christmas prevailed over this annoyance. Often, she traveled alone to avoid clashing with Molly. At least, not over that issue. Plenty of other issues elicited controversy, including the cut of Jo's hair, her refusal to wear a dress to dinner, and her insistence on having a glass of wine each evening.

This year, Jo called to inform her mother she was bringing someone special.

"A woman, I assume," Molly said.

"Yes, and she's someone I hope to spend the rest of my life with," Jo said.

Molly's silence suggested she wasn't buying it.

"I'm not interested in meeting any more of your women," Molly finally said.

Molly's words still punched Jo's gut, no matter her age. Jo

tried again, hoping for a better outcome. "She's not just any woman. She's *the* woman I want to live with forever."

"What happened to the last one you foisted on me?"

"We broke up." Jo hated how this sounded. Score another point for Molly.

"That's why I don't want you to bring this one. I get to know them, and then they're gone. I'm too old to want to make friends with any more of your women."

The weariness in her mother's voice softened Jo's defensiveness. "I understand, Mom, but Lauren is different."

"I hope I live long enough to see you in a happy, stable relationship with anyone, male or female. But for now, please don't bring her here."

Jo struggled with her dilemma. What if this was her mother's last Christmas? The fraught, love-hate relationship she'd endured with her mother most of her life had morphed into tolerability over the years, as her mother had mellowed with age. She cherished moments when they could connect and even laugh at themselves. Her mother gave Jo her intelligence, wit, and drive. But also, her loneliness.

"In that case, I won't come, Mom. Lauren's my person. I'd rather not wait years to prove it to you. If that's even possible."

"Suit yourself. You always choose your girlfriend over your mother."

Jo's shoulders sagged. *Why does she make this so hard?* "It's not a competition, Mom. I'd choose both if you'd let me."

Christmas posed problems for Jo most years. Joyful family gatherings of parents, siblings, children, and friends were never part of her holidays. She had only her problematic mother and sister, a few cousins, and no nieces or nephews. Having children hadn't occurred to her. She never had a steady partner long enough to even consider it.

The one constant over the holidays was a gathering of lesbians for a raucous white elephant party at the home of Jean and Susan, who'd been together for decades after leaving their husbands for each other. The guests rotated in and out, but a constant core remained, including Jo, who invited whomever she was with that year. She envied those with long-term, stable partnerships.

Jo and Lauren arrived at the party bearing their wrapped white elephant gifts: pink flamingo yard ornaments from Jo and an inflatable statue of the Virgin Mary from Lauren, a recovering Catholic. Sweet potatoes, salads, homemade bread, garlic mashed potatoes, green bean casserole, smoked salmon, and other delectables lay on the extended dining table along with the hosts' combined wedding china. Lauren added their corn casserole and assorted cheeses to the mix.

With their plates piled high, they squeezed onto a couch with others in the living room. Jo invited Barb to sit in the chair next to her, where she balanced her plate on her knees, a glass of wine in one hand. "I'll try not to dump this in your lap like I did last year," Barb said.

"How's business?" Jo asked. Barb had her own recruiting and talent-sourcing company.

"It's hopping. I placed three managers at big tech companies just this month."

"That's impressive. But I'm being rude. Barb, this is Lauren, the woman I told you about."

Barb reached across Jo's lap to shake Lauren's hand. "I'm so happy to meet the woman Jo crossed an ocean to bring home."

"It's temporary, I'm afraid," Jo said. "Lauren can only legally reside in the US until February."

"Bummer. Can't you find a reason for her to stay?" Barb asked, taking a sip of her wine.

"If we can find an employer to sponsor her for an H-1B visa, she can stay for up to three years."

Barb leaned over to address Lauren. "What did you do before Jo swept you away?"

Lauren told her.

"Interesting. But there's probably little demand for that here." Barb sat back in her chair.

"An immigration attorney told me most of the tech companies snap up the yearly allotment of H-1B visas right away. They're hard to get," Jo said.

"Yeah, the tech companies hire a lot of foreign computer nerds," Barb said and took a bite of turkey and mashed potato.

Lauren hadn't touched her food. Jo squeezed her thigh. *Maybe Barb can help us.*

"If we can find a willing employer to sponsor her and attest that her skills are necessary and unique, we'd go all out applying. We're desperate." Jo explained the necessity for them to live together for at least one year.

"Wow, that's tough. Send me your education and job history, Lauren. I can't guarantee I can find an interested employer, but I'll keep it on file, just in case."

They moved on to other topics and dessert with a choice of pumpkin, pecan, or apple pie, as well as assorted cheeses. Then the women all gathered in the living room for the gift exchange.

One woman opened a package of lederhosen and modeled it. Another received a yodeling fish, to the delight of the crowd. At one point, Jo looked over at Lauren, who laughed so hard tears ran down her cheeks.

Nestled in the warm embrace of her community, Jo's natural optimism rose again. Somehow she and Lauren would become one of those long-term couples she envied.

chapter forty-three

CHRISTMAS AND NEW YEAR'S PASSED IN A BLUR OF holiday festivities. Jo's younger sister Evie flew out from Boston for the holidays. Lauren wondered why Jo and Evie didn't fly down to be with their elderly mother, but neither sister seemed inclined to discuss it.

Evie and Lauren teamed up to convince Jo to hang only red lights on the tree. All three took part in cooking the holiday meals. If Lauren didn't know better, she'd think she'd been part of Jo's circle of family and friends for years. But the inevitability of leaving Jo's cocoon in six weeks lingered in the back of her mind.

In mid-January, still with no long-term solution, she and Jo discussed the possibility of Lauren working for her with the title of project manager. Though they considered it upside down and sideways, no plausible argument that Lauren possessed unique qualifications over an American emerged.

Jo rubbed her temples. "Let's contact Barb and see if she has any ideas after reviewing your qualifications."

She and Barb played phone tag, but in Barb's last voicemail, she said, "I have an idea. I'll call back when I get more information."

Two days later, Lauren accompanied Jo on her daily brisk walk up and down the San Francisco hills. When they both had worked up a sweat, Jo's cell phone rang, and Barb's name came up. She put it on the speakerphone so Lauren could hear, despite the traffic noise.

"I contacted a woman I met at a party who works for a film company in Hollywood to ask if they might have any projects requiring subtitles and dubbing," Barb said. "They didn't, but she referred me to another woman at a larger film company who might."

Jo gave Lauren a thumbs-up. "What did she say?" Jo asked. They leaned their heads together to listen.

"This woman mentioned a French television series they believe will appeal to an American audience. She said she'd check whether they might need someone with Lauren's qualifications."

"Fantastic!" Jo said.

"There is no guarantee of anything. Even if they have an opening, the company may not want to take on the hassle of sponsoring Lauren for an H-1B visa. But I explained your situation to her, as I suspect she's a sister."

"Thank you so much," Jo said.

When they hung up, Jo pulled Lauren into her arms for a jubilant, sweaty hug.

Over the next two days, they discussed again what they might do if Lauren could not get the H-1B visa. Jo called Neville in Vancouver, BC, on speakerphone. She explained their current situation and asked if he had recommendations for a place Lauren might stay for up to six months when she had to leave the US in early February.

"Your timing is excellent," he said. "James's daughter has just moved out of our downstairs suite to attend college in Montreal. Lauren is welcome to stay here."

"That's so very kind of you," Jo said, giving Lauren's thigh a squeeze. "I'll give you an update soon, I hope."

When they hung up, Jo returned to work. Lauren found it difficult to concentrate on the records she was organizing. The thought of languishing in Vancouver for six months, with no job, no friends, and an uncertain future, unsettled her. She would quickly deplete her available funds, and she'd not yet secured her share of the Paris apartment.

Lauren stared at Jo, who was deep in concentration, tapping on her computer keyboard. She'd risked everything to be with her. Jo's love had lifted her out of her depression enough to leave Delphine, but giving up her job and the security of a country with free health care for diabetics made her especially vulnerable. If she was stuck in Vancouver, would Jo go through with their plan to immigrate to Canada? Jo had invested so much in her law practice. Would she give it up for Lauren? She should ask Jo how she felt about that.

Such thoughts swirled in Lauren's brain in an endless loop. She rose abruptly, and her documents fell to the floor. "I need to move and get some air," she said. "I'm taking a walk."

On the third day of waiting, Jo and Lauren were eating dinner when Barb called. Jo answered and put her mobile on speaker.

"Well, gals, I've got good news. The film company has a temporary job for which Lauren is qualified, and if all goes well in your phone interview, they're willing to sponsor you for an H-1B visa. But only if you do the work of applying and pay all the expenses. This took huge arm-twisting from my lesbian contact."

Lauren's heart leaped. She locked eyes with Jo, who was beaming. "Oh, thank god! Or rather, the lesbian network! We'll get right on it."

Lauren threw her arms around Jo's neck. "I might have a job!" But as she let go, Jo's smile had vanished, startling her. A stab of apprehension pierced her joy. "What's wrong? This is good news, right?"

"It is, baby, but we have our work cut out for us to get the visa. I'll try to get an emergency meeting with Maria."

Three days later, after Lauren's successful phone interview with the film company, Lauren and Jo sat in Maria's office as she listed the documentation required from both the employer and the applicant for the H-1B visa. She glanced from one to the other over the top of her reading glasses. "You know, of course, there are far more applicants than visas awarded. The likelihood of your getting one is slim to none."

Jo reached for Lauren's hand. "We know. And time is short. But we have to try. What other choice do we have?"

chapter forty-four

JO TOOK MONDAY AND TUESDAY OFF WORK TO CONCENTRATE on the H-1B application. Lauren phoned the head of HR at the film company to work out the specifics of the job, and Jo used her superb writing skills to fashion a description fitting Lauren's qualifications.

The two women worked together at a fever pitch to get original signatures via FedEx from the film company. When they had everything together, they took it to Maria on Wednesday morning. Their application had to be in the mail by early Friday.

Maria thumbed through the application. "Looking good, looking good," she said. Pausing, she peered at them over her reading glasses. "The university degree. It only took three years?"

"Yes, to get a bachelor's degree in a specific subject, it takes three years in France," Lauren said. "It's equivalent to a four-year degree in the US."

Maria frowned. "I'm afraid the USCIS will find this confusing and reject your application outright."

Jo's shoulders tightened, and she leaned forward. "Don't they know they're equivalent?"

"Don't overestimate the intelligence of the reviewers. They have too many applicants, and they're looking for any reason to reject an application. Even with your work history, they'll not accept it without a relevant college degree." Maria paused. "Hold on." She took out a binder from the shelf behind her desk.

Jo put her arm around Lauren, who looked on the verge of tears.

"Perhaps you can get a US university to certify that your three-year degree is equivalent to a four-year bachelor's degree in the US."

Lauren choked. "How do we do that? We don't have time."

Jo recognized Lauren's desperation. She was on the verge of losing it too. Indeed, time was running out. She squeezed Lauren's shoulders. They'd invested too much to give up now. They were so close.

Maria handed them a sheet from her binder. "Here's a list of US-based organizations that provide credential certification for people who got their degrees outside the US."

Jo took the list and studied it. Then she turned to Lauren, who sniffed and wiped her eyes with her sleeve. "I'll take half and you take the other half. We'll call until we find one who is familiar with your degree and will give us a quick turnaround."

Maria regarded them with sympathy in her eyes. "Good luck. We still have a couple of days."

Jo drove home way too fast. They each called company after company. Most declined to guarantee the degree's equivalency with a quick turnaround.

Two hours later, Jo reached a woman at a company in Chicago. After she explained their situation, she said, "Please, can you review Lauren's university degree and coursework immediately? It's critical we get a response today."

"I'll do my best. It depends on whether the degree meets basic requirements," the woman said.

"Oh my god, thank you. I'll fax the information right away."

When Jo hung up, she gave Lauren a high five. When all the pages went through the fax machine, she looked up at Lauren, slumped in her office chair, wringing her hands. She looked exhausted. Neither had eaten since early that morning.

"Now we wait," Jo said. Once again, their future was in the hands of a stranger. The alternative was for Lauren to hang out in a basement suite in Vancouver for six months. And how often would she get away from work to visit her? Rarely, if she cared to keep up her law practice.

Lauren rose and said, "Come, I'll make us some lunch."

They ate their sandwiches in silence, both casting frequent glances at the clock. The afternoon dragged until it was after five, Chicago time. Jo's shoulders ached, and she jiggled her leg up and down. Lauren paced the living room.

"She might still call," Jo said.

As the clock ticked on past the dinner hour in Chicago, Jo grew despondent. She gave up the show of optimism for Lauren, who'd stopped pacing and now lay listlessly on the couch, staring at the ceiling. Jo shuffled to the fridge and poured them each a glass of chardonnay. Lauren sat up to take the glass, and Jo slumped onto the couch.

Lauren leaned against her. "Will you come with me to Vancouver? Just until I get settled?"

"Of course, sweetheart." Jo's stomach knotted. *Is this the beginning of the end?* She couldn't imagine where they could go from here in the long term. It was a mistake to have lured Lauren to the US with promises of a future together. Especially when Jo had so little control over that future.

A little after nine, Chicago time, the landline rang.

Jo rushed to pick up, her heart racing.

"Hello, Jo, this is Miriam. I've certified Lauren's degree, and I dropped off my letter at FedEx this evening. I used the address you gave me for your attorney. Sorry I didn't call sooner, but I had to rush to meet friends for dinner."

Jo's knees nearly buckled. "Thank you. You can't imagine how much this means to us."

"Oh, but I can. I have a daughter who is in love with a woman. I hope if she were in this situation, someone would do the same for her."

When she hung up, Jo collapsed into Lauren's arms.

First thing the following morning, Jo called Maria to give her a heads-up to expect the certification letter, then went into her law office downtown to catch up. She wrote the same paragraph of a brief several times, unable to keep her mind on her work.

By four in the afternoon, neither she nor Lauren had heard anything. Useless at work, she headed home to sit with Lauren.

She'd just walked in when the landline rang. She dropped her bag in the hall and ran to catch it, but Lauren picked up first and put it on speaker. It was Maria.

"The letter's here. I've prepared everything and checked it over. It'll go out first thing tomorrow morning."

They both exhaled. "Thank you, Maria," said Jo.

"Now what do we do?" Lauren asked, as if there was anything they *could* do.

"We wait," Jo said once again. "And hope we get an answer before mid-February when you're required to leave."

chapter forty-five

A WEEK LATER, RICHARD EMAILED LAUREN TO SAY HE received a letter from Delphine reviling Lauren for leaving her and asking him to persuade her to come home. He wrote back, saying that his sister would decide what was right for her. It was none of his business. *Thank you, Richard.*

Lauren chewed her lip while she considered her options. France did not recognize Delphine and her as a couple, even after twenty years of joint habitation, so the laws regulating divorce didn't apply. The thought of a lengthy civil court battle to secure her half of their jointly held property made Lauren's stomach churn. She'd have to negotiate with Delphine. She picked up the phone to call her in the late afternoon, Paris time.

"Allo?"

Delphine's voice made Lauren cringe. "We need to talk about the apartment," she said.

"Why? You'll be coming home."

"No, Delphine, I'm never coming back to Paris."

Lauren held the phone away from her ear and laid it down while Delphine bellowed in French. She waited several minutes until the volume decreased.

She picked up the receiver again. "You need to pay me for

my share of the Paris apartment. Here is what I suggest: You buy my share of the apartment by taking out a mortgage. That way, you don't have to sell it."

"Why should I? She'll tire of you, and you'll come running back. Then we'll have the useless expense of the mortgage. Plus, I can't afford it."

Lauren rubbed her neck and raised her eyes to the ceiling. "You're not listening, Delphine. Even if she did tire of me, as you say, I will *not* be coming back. Not ever."

Delphine was silent for several beats. Then there was a click and a dial tone.

How did I ever tolerate that woman? Perhaps giving up her equity in the Paris apartment was the price she had to pay for her freedom. But the injustice of it burned in the pit of her stomach.

With only two weeks left before she was required to leave, Lauren did not wish to squander it dealing with Delphine. Over Lauren's home-cooked meals, she and Jo laughed and talked as usual, pretending this happy domesticity could go on forever.

At night, though, more than once, their lovemaking ended in tears. *What if we can never live like this again?* Lauren could hardly bear the thought of lonely weeks in someone else's house in Canada without Jo.

Three days before Lauren was to leave for Vancouver, Jo arrived home looking despondent.

"The train-spill case is gearing up. I'm having difficulty getting someone to cover my depositions next week when I'd planned to go with you to Vancouver."

Lauren's shoulders slumped. Would she have to face her exile alone? Did this foretell their future?

Jo dropped her briefcase, strode to Lauren, and embraced her. "I'll keep trying."

That's the story of our lives. We keep trying. Lauren put on a cheerful front for Jo, but her spirit was flagging as the day of banishment approached. The sense of helplessness she believed she had left behind in France seeped into her, and the high stakes of her gamble for a future with Jo weighed heavily upon her.

The following day, Lauren packed her meager belongings. She was running low on insulin, but she heard insulin was available from pharmacies in Canada without a prescription.

Grocery shopping and preparing a spaghetti Bolognese and salad for dinner occupied only a portion of her mind. She'd just popped the cork on an Oregon pinot noir when the sound of Jo's car arriving and the garage door going up lifted her spirits.

A jubilant Jo burst through the front door. "You got the H-1B visa!" she said. "I wanted to tell you in person. Maria called me at the office just as I was leaving." She held out her arms to Lauren.

Lauren's mouth dropped open, and her eyes widened. Her limbs refused to move. Then Jo closed the distance, enfolding her in a bear hug. "We did it! Maria said it was a miracle."

The weight of the world lifted from Lauren's shoulders as tears of relief stung her eyes. She clung to Jo. "I can't believe it."

Jo lifted her chin and held her gaze. "It's true. I'm so happy. You still have to leave in two days. Your interview will be at the

US Embassy in Vancouver. They'll make the final decision. If approved, they'll issue the visa right away."

Lauren's smile faded. "What if I get another horrible interviewer?"

"We're much better prepared this time. Maria says it's very unlikely they will deny the visa at this point."

"Will you come with me?" Jo seemed so optimistic, but she hadn't been on the other end of the counter when "VISA DENIED" was stamped on Lauren's application.

"Yes. The other good news is an associate attorney will cover my depositions next week. Interesting rumors are floating around the office as to why I'm taking so much time off when I hardly ever did before."

Lauren smiled. "That you're having a child?"

Jo patted her perfectly flat abdomen, a result of her daily workout. She looked way younger than fifty-three. "By now, they must know that's highly unlikely."

"I'll call the film company right away. Let's hope they allow me to do the bulk of the work at home."

Jo's smile never left her face. "It might require special equipment. Whatever it takes, we'll do it."

Lauren squeezed Jo's arms. "You know this means we can live together for a year. Then we can combine our Canada applications to become Permanent Residents as common-law partners." Lauren paused. "Have you completed your application?"

Jo's smile disappeared. Now she had no excuse for not applying. "Not yet, but I will."

A stab of concern penetrated Lauren's euphoria. *Is Jo having second thoughts about Canada?*

chapter forty-six
Vancouver

NEVILLE AND HIS PARTNER, JAMES, WELCOMED JO AND Lauren to their home in Vancouver, a craftsman-style house on a tree-lined street with a purple front door. James served a green curry with tofu over rice, and both he and Neville prodded the women to tell their story.

When they'd finished, Neville said, "You're incredibly lucky. Many of the gay and lesbian couples I've married can't live together legally. For some, the stress is too much and they split. I hope we live to see the day when LGBTQ couples have the same rights as heterosexuals."

Jo wiped her mouth with her napkin. "I can't imagine that happening in our lifetime. I also appreciate that we enjoy a certain amount of white privilege. We speak the dominant language, we're educated, and we understand the culture. We have friends who can help us, and we have the financial resources to navigate the US and Canadian immigration systems. I feel for those couples who do not."

"We also have the will to fight our way through it," Lauren said. "But even so, it's incredibly hard." She took a few bites of curry. "Changing the subject. When we become Canadian Permanent Residents, we'll have to decide where to live. I know Vancouver is gay friendly, but it's so big with so many high rises."

"What about Victoria on Vancouver Island or one of the Gulf Islands? I have a realtor friend in Victoria who could show you around," said Neville.

Jo drew in a sharp breath. She had not yet applied to Canada, and already Lauren was thinking ahead to where they should live.

As if reading her mind, Lauren reached over and touched her arm. "I know it's premature. I haven't even gotten my H-1B for sure. But while we're here, why not look around? Get visual images of the possibilities? A taste of what we might look forward to?"

Jo relaxed her shoulders. As long as it was abstract, it might be fun to explore. "Sure, let's see if your friend has time to show us around Victoria."

Neville texted his realtor friend, Jan, and she called back promptly. She had a client just cancel. The inventory was low, but she'd be happy to show Jo and Lauren around.

Their upbeat mood carried them through an evening of lively conversation. When they'd finished dinner and drunk all the wine, James said, "Let me show you the suite downstairs where you'll stay tonight. I'm sorry you won't be staying longer, Lauren."

Jo waited in a coffee shop a few blocks from the US Embassy. When she'd walked Lauren to the Embassy entrance, no barricades or soldiers with automatic weapons threatened them.

She hugged Lauren and wished her good luck, optimistic the interview would go smoothly this time.

Forty-five minutes later, Lauren appeared in the shop wearing a broad grin. She waved her papers at Jo. "I got it! The interviewer was a friendly young woman. I told her I'd applied to immigrate to Canada. She even apologized for the previous denial of my US visitor's visa."

Despite interested looks from the next table, Jo jumped up and kissed Lauren on the lips. "I'm so happy! Let's celebrate. I found a popular dim sum restaurant for us." She linked arms with Lauren. "It's just down the street."

As they sipped jasmine tea and enjoyed bites of shrimp and pork dumplings, steamed pork ribs, and radish cakes, Lauren shared her dream of living on an island.

Jo listened as her thoughts swirled. She liked access to excellent restaurants, a lesbian community, good medical care, and the cultural opportunities of big-city life. What would she do on an island? Perhaps Lauren's penchant for island life resulted from growing up British. *We're not deciding today,* she reminded herself. *Just throwing out possibilities and riding high on the wave of success. Who knows what might happen in three years? And perhaps her H-1B visa could be renewed...*

Lauren interrupted her musing. "Jo, are you listening?"

Jo pulled herself back to the present. "Yes, love."

"Shall we ask the realtor to show us something on one of the Gulf Islands?"

Jo preferred looking at houses in Victoria. At least it had a couple of universities, theaters, and a symphony orchestra. She'd enjoyed an excellent seafood dinner there and tea at the Empress Hotel when she'd visited years ago.

"Let's look at Victoria first," said Jo. But since this was just a fantasy, she added, "And then visit the islands if we have time."

Lauren almost bounced off her chair. "Let's leave this afternoon. I can't wait."

Buoyed with success and Lauren's enthusiasm for adventure, they said goodbye to Neville and James and found a hotel room in Victoria. On the hour-and-thirty-five-minute ferry ride to Vancouver Island, they enjoyed an early dinner onboard at the Pacific Buffet. The waterside view of several sparsely inhabited islands, snow-capped Mount Baker to the south, and an eagle soaring overhead lulled Jo into a peaceful tranquility.

By the time they checked into their hotel, Jo had succumbed to the allure of their fantasy tour. Jan met them that evening to show what she'd found. The following day, they'd do a quick survey of homes in Victoria. "There's also a home on Saturna Island. A bit off the grid, but well worth a visit," Jan said.

The houses for sale in Victoria did not inspire them. Jo especially disliked the stucco exteriors. When Jan showed them a rundown million-dollar home she said was a teardown, Jo called a halt to further viewing.

"Let's go see the house on Saturna," Lauren said.

Jo groaned. "Why don't we just spend a day in Victoria? Go to the Royal BC Museum. Get some fish and chips at that famous place in the harbor?"

Lauren gave her a pleading puppy-dog look.

Jo smiled. "Okay. It'll be an adventure." Jo hoped the house wasn't too spectacular or the house of Lauren's dreams. She wasn't quite ready yet to plant her flag on Canadian soil.

chapter forty-seven

LAUREN BROUGHT JO COFFEE IN BED. SHE SLIPPED IN next to her with her own steaming mug. "I looked up Saturna Island on the internet. It's only twelve square miles, with a population of around 350 people."

Jo choked on her coffee, and Lauren patted her back, waiting until she stopped coughing. "There are four ferries daily to Vancouver Island," she said in case Jo worried about the isolation.

"Is there a ferry to the mainland?" Jo asked when she could speak.

"Yes, but it stops at other islands, so it takes two or three hours," Lauren said. Sensing Jo's concern, she added, "But we're just looking, remember?"

"Right," Jo said.

They stood outside on the ferry's deck, the sun weak in a partially cloudy sky. Lauren zipped her puffy jacket and swung the scarf around her neck against the chill air and breeze. The ferry passed close to the Gulf Islands, and the windows of waterfront homes glinted in the winter light. Seagulls followed the ferry, hoping for snacks, and the white head of an eagle stood out against the evergreen branches of a nearby tree. The distant snowy peak of Mount Baker showed itself as they rounded a bend.

Lauren held on to Jo's arm. "It's like a cruise. Can you imagine living here?"

"It's beautiful for sure. But it feels more like a vacation destination," Jo said. "I wonder what people do to keep themselves sane, especially if they live on one of these islands year-round."

"They probably go boating, garden, and read a lot. Maybe some work for the government in Victoria or companies that allow them to work from home."

"If there's reliable internet," Jo said.

Jan joined them from inside the ferry. "Almost half the island is protected by the Gulf Islands National Park Reserve," Jan said. "Before we look at the house, let me show you some of the natural beauty."

When they arrived at Lyall Harbour, they watched the walk-on passengers with dogs, bicycles, and motorcycles disembark. As Jan drove them through town, they passed two general stores, a post office, a liquor store, artists' galleries and studios, and a pub.

Jan carried on to a marine park on the tip of the island, where they walked along the grassy bluff, leading down to a small beach and sandstone rock formations. On the eastern side they faced the Strait of Georgia, with views toward the San Juan Islands and majestic Mount Baker in the US. "On this part of the island, you can see whales from the shore, especially during the summer months when the southern resident orca pods J, K, and L pass by. Transient orcas visit the area year-round, as do Dall's porpoises and harbor seals. During certain times of the year, humpback whales bring their calves to feed."

"Wow," both women said in unison. The natural beauty and the promise of marine-life viewing stirred Lauren. She cast glances at Jo to gauge her reaction. Her face revealed calm contemplation and occasional delight. This encouraged Lauren, and she urged Jan to show them the house.

Five minutes later, they drove into the driveway of a blue house with a sloping roof surrounded by an old-growth forest of Garry oak, arbutus, and Douglas fir. It looked much smaller than the description, perhaps because it perched on the edge of a cliff overlooking the water, with the lower floor hidden from the street.

When they entered the front door, an open floor plan with a river-stone fireplace and soaring ceiling greeted them. The enormous glass windows yielded a spectacular view of the sound. When the realtor ducked around the corner to pick up the detailed flyer, Lauren nudged Jo in the ribs. She appeared as stunned as Lauren. "Wow," Jo mouthed, squeezing Lauren's hand.

The spacious bedroom on the main floor also revealed sweeping views of the water and the San Juan Islands in the distance.

"The owners tell me they often see orcas and other marine animals swimming by. Also, boat traffic. Hence the high-powered telescope in the living room."

A pine-paneled downstairs held a woodstove, another bedroom, and a bathroom and gave a more intimate, rustic feel. Lauren could not stop grinning, though she tried not to tip their hand to the realtor. She prayed to whatever goddess might be listening that Jo loved it as much as she did. The house exceeded her dreams. She could see them spending hours looking out the window at the water and marine life, hiking the nearby trails, and reading by the fire...

Jan interrupted her musing to hand them the information sheets. After reading for a moment, Jo quirked an eyebrow in surprise. "Um, why is the price so low? With a drop-dead water view, I would expect this house to command a ransom."

"Many people don't want to live so remotely. Or rely on the ferry system," Jan said.

"I can understand that," Jo said.

Lauren's heart sank. "What about internet access?"

"For some areas of the island, broadband access is limited. However, the owner tells me it is pretty good here," Jan said.

"But I still don't understand why the price is so low. Are there any problems with the house?" Jo asked.

"Water on this part of the island is scarce. Rather than a well, the house uses a rainwater catchment system for most of its water supply."

"Oh," Jo said, frowning.

Lauren's hopes sank further. "How does that work?" She hoped the discussion wouldn't end here.

"The rain collects in gutters that channel the water into downspouts that lead to two enormous cisterns to supply the entire house. Regular maintenance is required, and it's best to have water delivered for drinking, cooking, and brushing your teeth."

"Is that why the owners are leaving?" Jo asked.

Jan looked from one to the other. "No," she said. "They've lived here for over a decade and love it. But they're older now and need to live close to medical care, so they've moved to Vancouver."

Lauren studied Jo, but her face gave nothing away. A skill she'd probably honed as an attorney. Her own face probably broadcasted everything. She wanted a home. This could be *their* home. They could start afresh, together in a new land.

Jo continued to study the information sheet without speaking and seemed to mull over the details. She raised her head.

Lauren held her breath.

"Thank you, Jan, for showing this to us. The house is beautiful. It will make a great vacation home, but it's not for us."

Lauren slumped against the nearby wall and stared across the water at the USA, a country that didn't want her. *When will we find a home?*

chapter forty-eight

LAUREN'S SILENCE ON THE WAY TO THE FERRY betrayed her disappointment. As they waited in the lineup, Jo twisted in her seat and took Lauren's hand. "I know you want the house. I could see us living there as a vacation getaway, despite the problems with the water. But it's only the first house we've looked at and liked, and we're not buying, just looking. Remember?"

"Yes, but it's so perfect," Lauren said, tilting her head and gazing at Jo with those puppy-dog eyes.

"Yes, perfect, if I were retired. But I'm still working and you're starting a new job. Plus, it's unclear if Canada will grant us Permanent Residency." *Clearly they would not if she didn't get a move on and complete her application.*

"Could we buy it as a vacation house until the Canadians accept our applications? I will contribute all the funds I still hope to get from my share of the apartment in Paris." Lauren frowned. "Although I may have to hire an attorney to get it."

"Right. We just climbed over one major hurdle getting your visa. We still have issues to work out. Let's celebrate our win without additional complications for now."

Lauren shrugged and produced a half-hearted smile. "Okay."

But Jo saw the disappointment in her eyes and relented.

"We'll talk more about the house. I doubt someone will snatch it up right away, given the challenges. It's been on the market for months."

At the San Francisco airport, they separated to go through border security. Jo waited for Lauren in baggage claim, hoping it would go more smoothly for her this time. Soon, a smiling Lauren joined her with a fresh I-94 form in her passport.

The following morning, Jo struggled to keep afloat amid a deluge of emails and phone calls to return. Her law office buzzed with excitement as a judge had granted several of her motions in her absence. The train-spill case would advance to trial sooner than expected and in a favorable jurisdiction. It was midafternoon before she checked in with Lauren to see when she'd get started on her job with the film company.

"They want me to start immediately," Lauren said. "I'll fly to LA and spend a week getting to know the script, the equipment requirements, and the voice actor for the dubbing. They said I could work at home, probably flying to LA once a month. The show has four seasons, so I'll have plenty to do."

"I'll miss my assistant, but I'm pleased you can do so much at home," Jo said. To Jo's relief, Lauren said nothing further about the Saturna house.

That weekend, Jo gave the Canadian application her undivided attention. The tedious and intrusive process took most of the weekend to complete. She opened her file cabinet and dropped the application into a folder, then closed the drawer and leaned her back against it with a sigh. She could not bring herself to mail it. Downstairs, Lauren was clattering around in the kitchen. Perhaps she should talk with her about her fears and reluctance to leave her law practice. But she put it off for now, picked up the phone, and left a message with Ellen requesting an appointment.

A week later, Jo sat in Ellen's office twirling an unraveled paper clip in her fingers. "I haven't mailed my application to become a Canadian Permanent Resident," she admitted.

Ellen cocked an eyebrow. "What do you think is getting in the way?"

"We've been fortunate with Lauren securing the H-1B, which means she can remain in the United States for the duration of the contract but no longer than three years. I'll be living with Lauren and practicing law. At least for now, I have everything I want."

Ellen tipped her head to the side, waiting.

"I could happily continue this way. I dread having to uproot my life to move to Canada."

"Tell me about the dread."

"I'd probably have to give up practicing law. In my mid-fifties, I'd have to start all over, pass eight different examinations, and do a year of tutelage at some law firm. I've fought and struggled to get where I am, a senior partner doing work I love. It terrifies me to think of giving that up." She put the paper clip aside and rubbed her hands on her thighs.

"I can see it is frightening for you. Have you considered other work you might do in Canada?"

"Even to consult with my law firm in San Francisco, I'd

probably have to be admitted to the bar in BC. I've heard the Canadians are really picky about any advisory activities that cross a boundary into practicing law. I have yet to find out if I can advise or serve on the boards of environmental justice groups or consult on cross-border environmental litigation."

"How does the possibility of consulting feel to you?"

Jo gazed at the duck painting, trying to imagine a role outside the practice of law. "I'm a lawyer for those who have little power against the big guys, who only care about profit and rape the environment with near impunity. It's who I am. It's so much a part of me I don't know who I'd be without it. I can't imagine languishing on the sidelines, advising others to do what I know I can do."

"Well, it's clear the prospect frightens you. What happens when you think of not moving to Canada?"

Jo's throat tightened, and she couldn't take a full breath. She struggled to say the words out loud. "I might lose Lauren. Again." Tears welled up. She brushed them away.

Ellen leaned forward and handed her a box of tissues. "Have you talked to Lauren about your fears?"

Jo took a tissue. "I just can't bring myself to tell her I'm having doubts about moving to Canada."

"Are you afraid of how she might react?"

Jo wrung her hands and looked up at Ellen. "She's given up everything to be with me. She'd freak out. I can't do that to her."

"How do you think she'd react if a year or two from now, you tell her you're not moving with her to Canada as you both had planned?"

This broke the dam and Jo sobbed. "I'm stuck. I want . . . her. I want . . . my career. How can I . . . have both?"

"You have a difficult dilemma with no straightforward choices," Ellen said, her voice soft. "But can you conceive of finding a way forward you've not yet imagined?"

Jo composed herself, took another tissue, and blew her nose. "That's why I'm stalling, waiting for a miracle."

chapter forty-nine

WHEN SHE RETURNED FROM LA, LAUREN SET UP HER workspace in the guest bedroom. The light was good, with a view of greenery and trees. Already tulips, daffodils, and hyacinth were popping up in the small back garden. She enjoyed working at familiar tasks, and the script frequently made her laugh.

Sometimes she missed the French markets and bakeries. She loved buying fresh bread and croissants daily back when she could eat those carbs. But San Francisco offered many food options, and Jo expressed appreciation for every culinary creation she presented her, even if Lauren just opened the refrigerator and made it up on the spot.

A continued irritant was that Delphine had not come through with her share of the apartment in Paris. So now Lauren had the added expense of a French attorney. When her irritation peaked, she called Delphine.

"What is the holdup now, Delphine? My lawyer said you had worked out a payment schedule." It amused Lauren that the word for "lawyer" in French was the same word for "avocado."

"It's not fair. I'm the injured party. You should compensate me for all the years I wasted as your faithful partner looking after you. Then you just dump me for that American bitch. You owe me spousal maintenance payments."

Lauren bit her lip to keep from laughing out loud. *Her faithful partner? Taking care of me?* She was thankful she'd downloaded the bank statements documenting her greater contribution to the running of the household. Also, that she'd resisted forming France's *pacte civil de solidarité* (PACS), or civil union, when it became available in 1999. Lauren never considered Delphine spouse material, especially after all her affairs.

Before she could respond, Delphine said, "Has she dumped you yet? She will, you know, and then you'll be glad you still have a home to come back to."

The woman is delusional.

"If some court must arbitrate this, and you lose, you'll pay my lawyer's fees," Lauren said. "Wouldn't it be easier to settle this between us, give me what's mine, and move on with your life?" Appealing to Delphine's penchant for the cheapest option was always an excellent strategy. At least it used to be.

"No. You'll come back. I know you will."

Lauren ended the call. She hesitated to discuss this problem with Jo, as she still hoped to contribute financially to their Canadian home. She'd seen that the Saturna house remained on the market. Maybe the isolation and water issue were a deal-breaker for most people, but for her, the house was perfect.

The next two months passed pleasantly. Jo made them coffee and smoothies each morning. On the days both worked at home, they made lunch together and often sat on the deck watching the fog roll back out to sea as the Golden Gate Bridge slowly emerged in the distance. Lauren usually made dinner, and afterward they snuggled on the couch, their bodies entwined, reading or watching a movie. Their lovemaking became even more thrilling as they knew what gave the other the most pleasure.

Lauren made two trips to LA to work on the film script. The Americans didn't have the same sense of humor as her British colleagues in Paris, but she got along well with the voice actor doing the English dubbing. Her work sufficiently absorbed her attention, so she had little time to obsess over the lack of communication from the Canadians about their applications.

In May, as they cleared the dinner dishes, Lauren said, "The Saturna house is still on the market. Would you consider popping up for the weekend to have another look? We could keep it as a vacation home until they approve our Canadian applications. I would contribute all the funds I hope to get from the Paris apartment."

Jo was rinsing dishes with her back to Lauren, but she could see her shoulders tense.

"Maybe we should wait until you get your money from Delphine before we buy a house in Canada," Jo said, turning to face her. "That house is a bit remote if we are continuing to work in the States."

Lauren understood Jo might not want the expense of maintaining two homes. But having a place to land when they became Canadian Permanent Residents would solidify their intention to immigrate, moving it from the abstract to the concrete. Was Jo's reluctance to take a second look only about the money and the practicality of working from the island? Or was there something else she wasn't telling her?

"We could just go to the house on holidays," Lauren said. "We don't have to work from there. And it would be comforting to know where we'll live when the time comes to immigrate."

Jo appeared to weigh this. "Sure. Let's fly to Victoria some weekend and take the ferry over. We'll find a B and B for the night."

Lauren leaped from her chair. "Let's go next weekend. I'll call Jan right away."

The realtor apparently smelled a potential sale and gave them one better: "The owners suggested you stay the night in the house," Jan said. "They gave me instructions. Buy food for dinner and breakfast, as you might not want to leave until the last minute."

The three women arrived at the Saturn house with groceries and drinking water. They changed the sheets on the upstairs bed and received instruction on the workings of the water system. Then Jan bid them farewell, saying, "I'll be back in time to get you to Victoria for your late flight home. Enjoy and ring me with questions. You should have good cell phone coverage from the US."

No sooner had they settled on the couch facing the water when Jo leaped up and exclaimed, "There's a pod of orca!" They swam less than fifty feet from shore. The women took turns looking at them up close with the powerful telescope, but Lauren preferred to see the entire group traveling at speed without the scope. The two larger upright dorsal fins slicing through the water marked the males. A much smaller dorsal fin closely flanked a female, probably a calf. The sun glinted on their black backs, and an occasional white patch appeared as they surfaced to blow.

"Magnificent," Lauren exclaimed, and Jo agreed.

"It's a sign. We belong here," Lauren said.

Jo squeezed her shoulder. "Maybe." Then she added, "I think these are the southern resident orca. I wish I could save them from excessive noise exposure from boat traffic and the depletion of the king salmon stocks they rely on. They need an excellent lawyer."

They stood in awe until the whales vanished. Lauren sighed and leaned her head on Jo's shoulder.

"It's so quiet," Jo remarked. "I can almost hear my heartbeat."

"I can hear your heartbeat too, especially when you're about to . . ."

Jo elbowed Lauren in the ribs. "Come, let's make dinner. Then you can tend to my heartbeat."

The next morning, a brilliant orange and magenta sunrise reflected off the water before the sun rose above the clouds.

"Wow, I don't think I've ever seen a sunrise like that in San Francisco," Jo said.

"I wish we could wake up to this every day," Lauren said.

"It would be lovely, but let's not rush. I still have a few things to work out," Jo said, turning Lauren over to spoon her.

Like what? She decided not to press her. Maybe Jo would be more amenable to buying the house when Lauren received her money from Delphine.

chapter fifty
San Francisco

BACK HOME, JO WRESTLED WITH HER CONSCIENCE. Shouldn't she share with Lauren that giving up her law practice frightened her? As did living on an island away from friends and city amenities. What sort of partner would she be if she lost her purpose and life's work? Lauren didn't seem to worry about what she might do in Canada. What if neither of them found meaningful work? It just wasn't in Jo's nature to make such a gigantic leap without more advanced planning.

She made inquiries into international environmental law, emailing organizations such as Greenpeace and the World Wildlife Fund to explore the possibility of legal consulting. She also investigated what might be required to do US-Canada cross-border consulting on legal issues related to shared environmental hazards.

Another month passed, and she still had not mailed her completed Canadian application. It lurked in her file drawer, her guilt growing stronger by the day, while she struggled to secure a soft landing.

Desperately needing a friendly ear, she scheduled lunch at an Italian restaurant with her friend, Barb. After asking her about how she and her partner were getting on with their kitchen remodel, Jo uncorked her concerns.

"I don't know what scares me most, giving up my law practice to move to Canada or telling Lauren I'm reluctant to do it."

Barb dipped her bread in olive oil and garlic. "What are you afraid of?"

"In the first case, I'm afraid of losing my identity." Jo took a moment. "But Lauren has risked everything to be with me. She relies on me to be the rock-solid foundation on which to build our new life. I'm afraid she'll lose faith in me if I tell her I have doubts about my ability to pull off what I've promised her."

"What have you promised her?"

"That we'll immigrate to Canada together."

Barb wiped the olive oil off her fingers and held Jo's gaze. "Wow, that's a huge promise. But do you want to start your relationship with secrets and lies by omission?"

"No, I don't.

"Talk to Lauren about your fears. She sounds like a reasonable woman. Maybe you can work out a solution together."

"I'm not used to doing that," Jo admitted. "I've never really had a partner with whom I could share my vulnerabilities."

"Time to start, my friend. That's the joy of married life."

When Jo returned to the office after lunch, an emergency meeting was underway in the conference room. Jo's paralegal motioned through the glass for her to come in. As she settled in a chair, one of the other senior partners addressed her: "There's been a major pipeline rupture and spill in a remote region of Alaska near where a caribou herd is migrating northward."

Jo brought her hand to her throat. Just what she'd feared.

"Since you're our expert on oil company litigation, we were wondering if you could accompany the attorney from Anchorage to a remote indigenous village to assess the situation. Decide whether we should take part in any legal action."

Jo took only a moment to think. Most of her cases were waiting for discovery records, and no trials were imminent. "Of course, I can do that."

"The Anchorage attorney is hoping you can leave this evening so you both can head out by private plane tomorrow."

"Not much time to tie things up here then," Jo said.

Her paralegal piped up: "I'll let the partners know where we are with your cases."

One of the other senior partners added, "I'll assign an associate attorney to cover for you in your absence. It should only take about a week."

Jo rushed home to pack. She hurriedly informed Lauren of her plans.

"Tonight?" Lauren said, sounding alarmed.

"Yup, I guess the Anchorage firm wants us to get there before anyone else does."

"I'll throw something together for you to eat before you go," Lauren said, heading for the kitchen.

"What does one wear to the Arctic Circle in May?" Jo said to herself as she descended to the garage to raid her backpacking supplies for a jacket, gloves, hat, and fleece-lined boots.

Once she had filled a duffel, she strode back to the kitchen to wolf down a chicken Caesar salad. Between bites, she told Lauren, "I won't have cell phone coverage, so you can't call me. I may find a satellite phone to call you, but don't know when."

Lauren said, "I worry about you flying in a small plane to some remote place where I can't call you. Will you be safe?"

Jo reached up and caressed her cheek. "Don't fret, love. This is what I live to do. I always come back safely."

"How long will you be gone?" Lauren's voice sounded strained.

"Probably eight days with travel time. But I don't know for sure."

Lauren didn't look happy, but the cab was outside, and Jo had to go. She hoisted her duffel onto her shoulder and grabbed her rolling file case.

"Bye, sweetheart. I'll call you when I can."

Lauren gave her a full-body hug. "I'll miss you."

Jo got into the cab, buzzing with excitement. This was what she loved. Battling oil companies, making them accountable for destroying the planet. She couldn't wait.

chapter fifty-one

THE MORNING AFTER JO LEFT, LAUREN TIDIED UP THE house, removing the clutter of Jo's work files on the coffee table. Carrying them upstairs to Jo's office, Lauren rifled through the first drawer to find the right spot and filed a brief. As she was closing the drawer, she spied a manilla envelope peeking out from a file labeled "Canadian Permanent Resident Application." She pulled it out and read the mailing address. A jolt of alarm made her heart leap into her throat. *Jo didn't mail her application.*

In disbelief, she racked her brain for explanations. Maybe this was a duplicate? Maybe Jo meant to send it, but then forgot? Or...

Then it hit her like a freight train: *Jo changed her mind. She's not joining me in Canada.*

Her knees buckled, and she slumped into the chair. This discovery challenged everything she'd previously believed about their relationship. *Why didn't she tell me? She said she wanted to be with me, to live together forever. Was it all a lie?* She remembered Jo's lack of enthusiasm for buying the Saturna house. Was it because she never intended to move to Canada?

Lauren gripped the sides of the chair, her breath coming in quick gasps, too lightheaded to think properly. Jo never actually told her she'd mailed the application, but Lauren assumed she had after she worked on it for an entire weekend. Lauren had put everything on the line to be with her. She'd trusted her despite Jo's devastating breakup with her all those years ago. *How could she lie to me?*

Lauren stared out the window. This couldn't be happening. And where was Jo when she desperately needed to talk to her? Unreachable in the wilds of Alaska. She put her head in her hands and cried hot, angry tears. *How could I have been so gullible?*

She wanted her mother, although she was dead. She wanted her family and her friends. All the people she knew in San Francisco were Jo's friends. Maybe they knew all along that Jo never intended to live with her in Canada and were keeping Jo's secret or, worse yet, were laughing at her.

Should she stay and wait for Jo to return and hear her explanation? Why had Jo kept this from her? Lauren had assumed they shared everything.

With the loss of trust in Jo's intentions, the reality of her situation washed over her like a tsunami. She was homeless, a diabetic without health insurance, living and working temporarily in a foreign country that didn't want her, with no friends of her own. She had given up a job she loved for a temporary job with reduced pay. Even her ties to the UK were tenuous because she'd not lived there for over twenty years. She had no guarantee of becoming a resident of Canada. When she had envisioned a secure and long-term future with Jo, she could suppress the reality of the risk she'd taken. Now that future was in doubt.

Staying in Jo's house, stewing in her anxiety, was unacceptable. Anger propelled her to her feet. *I'll go home to London and be with people who love me.* This decision dragged her partly out of the quicksand of despair. She called the film company and left a message that she must make an emergency trip to London for a death in the family. That's what it felt like: the death of her hopes and trust.

She made a plane reservation to leave for London the following day. Then she packed everything she owned into her two duffel bags.

When Lauren arrived at Richard and Kelly's house in London, both expressed sympathy for her alarm. And when she spent long hours alone in the bedroom vacated by their elder daughter, they didn't draw her out, sometimes leaving a lunch tray at her door. However, they insisted she join the family for dinner, and one quiz night at the pub, where she embarrassed herself by not responding even when she knew the answers.

Four days into her stay in London, they were sitting at dinner. Richard finished his mouthful of shepherd's pie and cleared his throat. "Are you going to speak to Jo when she returns from Alaska?"

Just the mention of Jo's name made it hard to swallow her food. "She lied to me by not telling me she didn't send in her application. I'm not sure I can get beyond that, whatever her reasons."

"I can understand your sense of betrayal, but what do you intend to do now?"

Lauren completely lost her appetite. "I don't know. My funds are running out. I hired a lawyer to get Delphine to give me my share of the Paris apartment, but she's still resisting."

"Would you consider going back to Paris? Renting a flat and trying to get your old job back?"

Lauren sighed. "My friends tell me they've promoted someone from within as my replacement. Someone I trained."

"Maybe you could find similar work here for the BBC? Like you did in the US?" Richard suggested.

"I don't know." The thought of starting over again in London in her early fifties gave her a splitting headache. Plus, Claire had already hired someone for the job she said months ago would suit Lauren. "I'm not feeling very well. I think I will retire early." She rose to leave.

Richard said, "Sorry. We brought all this up too soon. Right now, you need to recover."

On day five of her stay, Lauren got her first restful night's sleep. She rallied her energy sufficiently to call Delphine.

After initial frosty greetings, Delphine said, "What are you doing in London? Did the bitch dump you?"

Delphine's gloating rankled her. "No. It's none of your business."

"So, are you coming home?" Delphine's voice softened.

"No, Delphine, I am never returning to Paris. I need my share of the apartment. Now."

Delphine was silent for so long, Lauren wondered if she'd hung up on her again.

"If you've come to your senses and left that vampire bitch, why aren't you coming home?"

False hope. "Because I have no desire to be with you. Not now. Not ever. Even if I spend the rest of my life alone. I've wasted far too many years putting up with your bullshit."

Click.

Lauren sagged in her chair. The call to Delphine took all the energy she could muster that day. She shuffled to the bedroom and lay on the bed facing the wall.

Less than forty-eight hours later, the jangling of the landline interrupted dinner. Richard answered, then put his hand over the receiver. "Do you want to talk to Delphine?"

Lauren shrugged and reached for the phone. "What?"

"Is that any way to speak to me when I've done your bidding?"

Lauren sat up straighter. "Yes?"

"Your lawyer can draw up the papers for you to sell me your half of the apartment," Delphine said.

Lauren let out a long breath and gave Richard and Kelly a thumbs-up.

"But you must come to Paris to sign the papers with me."

Of course, there would be a fly in the soup. "I'll come to Paris, but—"

Delphine interrupted, "That's my condition. We sign them together."

It didn't surprise Lauren that Delphine had to have the last word and ounce of control. Had she finally accepted that Lauren never intended to return to Paris, regardless of what happened with Jo? Did she wheedle money from her parents for Lauren's half? *No matter, I'll be free!*

Then she sobered. *Free to do what exactly?*

chapter fifty-two
An Inupiat Village

THE ANCHORAGE ATTORNEY, JOHN, A LANKY MAN WITH an unruly mop of dark hair, arrived panting just before they were to board the Cessna taking them to a remote village on the North Slope. He and Jo climbed aboard and exchanged greetings with the pilot, who motioned for Jo to take the seat next to him.

The small plane dipped and swayed as it navigated through the crisp, cold air of Alaska, its engines humming steadily against the backdrop of the vast, untouched wilderness below. Jo pressed her face against the window, her breath fogging up the glass as she took in the sprawling expanse near the Arctic National Wildlife Refuge. She had read about this place, seen pictures, but nothing could have prepared her for the raw beauty and the sense of isolation it evoked.

As the plane descended toward a small makeshift runway, Jo's heart raced. This was it. She was about to step into a world far removed from courtrooms and legal libraries. The plane bumped and jostled as it landed, kicking up snow and ice. Jo gathered her briefcase and duffel and stepped out into the biting cold as John unwound his long body from the seat behind.

The village was a collection of modest homes, smoke curling up from chimneys into the clear blue sky. The people of the village, wrapped in thick coats and fur hats, greeted them with cautious curiosity. She and John were outsiders, a fact she was acutely aware of as she introduced herself and explained their mission. "We're here to listen, to learn, and to document the impact of the oil spill on your land and way of life," Jo said to the group.

An old woman, her face tanned and heavily lined, took Jo by the arm and nodded to John. "Come, let's have a hot drink and talk. Elders have gathered to speak with you."

The next day, several villagers took Jo and John on snowmobiles and on foot to areas where the effects of the oil spill were most evident. A chilly wind whipped at Jo's face as they traveled over the frozen landscape, the snowmobiles' engines loud intruders in the silent wilderness.

When they arrived, the sight that greeted Jo was heart-wrenching. The frigid air was heavy with the scent of oil. A thick black sludge crept across patches of once-pristine snow, a stark contrast to the untouched beauty that lay just yards away. A group of oil-soaked birds lay dead, their feathers matted and heavy with crude oil.

Jo dismounted and picked her way through the sludge, her boots soon soaked in oil. In her peripheral vision, she saw movement and hurried to kneel beside an exhausted young fox, its fur slick and dark. Gently, with trembling hands, she wiped at the oil with her handkerchief as the creature whimpered and struggled weakly to get away. Tears stung her eyes as she choked back a sob. "Poor little guy. What can I do for you?"

The village elder who accompanied her placed a gentle hand on her shoulder. "We'll not let him suffer," he said as he led her away.

Later, they found a small group of caribou, their coats matted with oil, struggling to navigate a marshy area that was now a potential death trap. Their movements were sluggish and uncoordinated as they attempted to free themselves from the sticky substance clinging to their hooves and fur.

Jo's sadness morphed into anger. *In a court of law, how much is a dead animal worth? Probably nothing, unless humans are also affected.* This rankled, and her resolve to right this injustice hardened. The spill was a call to action, a stark reminder of the delicate balance between nature and human greed and folly.

Back in the village, a smiling young woman offered Jo and John caribou soup, followed by a dish of whipped fat mixed with berries. The villagers relied on subsistence hunting and fishing, and caribou were a main staple of their diet.

When the attorneys were alone for a few minutes, Jo said, "Oil will probably contaminate the lichen and other vegetation that caribou feed on. Already Indigenous people living above the arctic circle and relying on traditional food sources have higher levels of persistent organic toxins in their bodies—even more than urban dwellers."

John shook his head sadly and commented, "The spill may also interfere with the migration of the larger caribou herd."

Yet we're here only to determine how much impact that would have on humans. The ecosystem they all depended on was suffering a wound that would take years, perhaps decades, to heal.

As she ate her soup and berries, surprisingly good, Jo reflected on her law career defending people affected by corporate and government polluters. *Who defends creatures like these oil-soaked animals who have no voice?* Though she'd dallied with the idea of defending animals and their ecosystems over the years, it now took on a new urgency. Jo vowed to fight, not just for the cleanup, but for the prevention of future disasters. For the villagers, for the wildlife, for the untouched lands that lay beyond the reach of the spill, she would be their voice.

Three days into her village stay, Jo secured a connection via satellite phone. She looked forward to sharing her eye-opening experience with Lauren. But the landline rang and rang with no answer, so she left a long message. She also tried Lauren's mobile phone, but it went immediately to voicemail. This surprised and frustrated her. *Where is she?* Maybe the film company had called her to LA to work and Lauren had no way to let her know. This seemed a likely explanation, and she stopped worrying. Her work totally absorbed her attention until she boarded the Cessna with John and the pilot bound for Anchorage.

As the plane sliced through the cold Alaska air, Jo gazed out the window at the white and brown expanse, happily anticipating her reunion with Lauren. She'd share her idea of eventually changing her career focus, and how they could research possibilities with international environmental organizations in Canada together. At last, she would send in her Canadian application to become a Permanent Resident.

The landscape below shifted from the stark, icy expanses of the Arctic to more welcoming green vistas until they entered clouds. The pilot warned of potential turbulence because of a storm system moving across the region, and Jo tensed. This was the part of flying she dreaded.

Suddenly, the small plane shuddered violently, its frame groaning and cracking against the relentless wind. From Jo's window seat, the world outside became a blur of white and gray. The pilot's voice, usually calm and reassuring over the intercom, took on an edge of urgency as he announced their descent. "Hang on," he said.

Jo glanced over her shoulder at John, white-faced and clutching the back of Jo's seat. "Fuck," he mouthed.

The turbulence intensified, a wild dance that tossed the plane like a toy, and Jo's seatbelt strained against the sudden shifts. She closed her eyes, trying to calm her breathing. Memories of Lauren, family, and friends flickered behind her eyelids, a montage of moments, each suddenly precious in the face of potential oblivion.

A powerful gust tilted the plane alarmingly to one side as the wind howled and the engine strained. Jo opened her eyes to catch a quick glimpse of the ground, a patchwork of white and dark where snow-covered fields met forest. Her heart leaped into her throat, a silent prayer forming on her lips. She closed her eyes tightly again. *Don't let me die. I have important work to do and a new life with Lauren.*

The plane lurched violently, a sudden drop causing Jo's stomach to churn as she let out an involuntary gasp. She tried to remain calm, focusing on the rhythmic whir of the engine, but her heart pounded in her throat.

And then, as suddenly as it had begun, the turbulence eased. The plane steadied, gliding more smoothly as the pilot navigated the last stretch. Jo opened her eyes to see the lights of the runway appear in the gloom. As they touched down and rolled along the tarmac, Jo's adrenaline ebbed, leaving her limp and shaky. She had just enough time before her next flight to call Lauren. She couldn't wait to talk to her and tell her again how much she loved her.

chapter fifty-three

Anchorage Airport

AS SOON AS SHE CHECKED IN FOR HER FLIGHT TO San Francisco, Jo called Lauren to let her know she was on her way. Still no answer. Worry marred her excitement at returning home. She called the number she had for the film company. They told her Lauren was on leave for a death in the family.

Who died? Her anxiety mounted as Jo imagined plausible scenarios all the way back to San Francisco. When the cab pulled into her driveway, she opened her front door to a dark house. Flipping on the lights, she searched for a note of explanation, but found none. Upstairs, she noticed Lauren's clothes were missing, which sent her into a panic. *What's happened?* Lauren would surely have left a note or a voicemail.

Jo's pulse raced as she struggled to remember where she might find Lauren's brother's phone number. Why didn't she make sure they each shared their emergency contacts? She rushed into her office, and that's when she saw it lying on her desk: her unmailed Canadian application.

Her hand went to her throat as alarm shot through her. *Oh my god.* She sank into her office chair, dropped her face into her hands, and rocked back and forth. How she wished she'd had that talk with Lauren as she intended before she left. Now Lauren only saw evidence of betrayal—an outcome far worse than Jo exposing her fears. *I must talk to her.*

She booted up her computer and searched for Richard's number in London. After an exhaustive and circuitous search, she found it and dialed. It was four in the morning in London. The call went to an answering machine. She didn't know if Lauren was there, but maybe Richard knew where she was. Jo left an urgent message that if he knew where Lauren was, would he please ask her to call?

Jo paced the floor. She whacked her forehead with her palm. *Stupid. Stupid. Stupid.* She'd fucked up again and hurt the most important person in the world. Lauren trusted her. Now she'd damaged that trust, and it could be irreparable.

Too upset to unpack or eat dinner, Jo paced, wringing her hands and berating herself until seven in the morning London time. She called Richard, and again the call went to the answering machine. This time, she couldn't keep the tears out of her voice. "Please, if you know where Lauren is, please have her call me. It's urgent."

Hours later, at 1:30 a.m. San Francisco time, the jangling of the landline jarred Jo from a half doze. She dashed for the phone. Hearing Lauren's voice, she blurted. "Oh, thank god, I was so worried I'd—"

Lauren interrupted. "You lied to me."

"I didn't lie to you. I was afraid to—"

"Tell me you never intended to immigrate to Canada with me?"

"No, I just wanted to line things up before I sent in my application." Jo's palms sweated, and she wiped them on her trousers. She didn't really have a good excuse, so she told the truth: "I was afraid to tell you I had doubts about giving up my law practice."

"You didn't think to share your doubts with me? Aren't we supposed to be a team?"

Jo sighed. "I guess I'm not used to being vulnerable in that way."

There was a long silence before Lauren said, "This is not what I expected of you. I'm disappointed and more than a little sad. I need time to figure out what I'm going to do."

"What do you mean?" Jo's knees grew weak. *Is she leaving me?*

"We should spend time apart until you decide if you're committed to a life with me or not."

Lauren's words stabbed her heart. Tears welled up. "But I am."

"Show me," Lauren said, and she hung up.

What have I done? Jo rushed to the bathroom and threw up.

After a few hours of restless sleep full of bad dreams, Jo shuffled downstairs to make coffee. She waited until seven thirty to call Barb.

Jo filled her in on her situation: "Lauren's left me and has gone back to London." She choked on the last sentence.

"Oh, I'm sorry, girlfriend. What are you going to do?"

Grateful Barb did not say "I told you so," Jo said, "I must prove to her I'm committed to being with her permanently in the only country that might have us."

"How will you do that?"

"I have an idea. But it's going to take some quick work." She bounced her plan off Barb.

"Sounds like it might convince her. But do it in person. Go to London."

"Right. I'd better get to it," Jo said, and she hung up, fired up to save the most important relationship of her adult life.

chapter fifty-four
London

LAUREN MET CLAIRE FOR LUNCH AT HER FAVORITE INDIAN restaurant and ordered *matar paneer*, her comfort food. After Lauren explained she'd left Jo, Claire probed, "Was Jo waiting until she could find a job in Canada?"

"I don't know. Maybe."

Claire tore off a piece of garlic naan and chewed thoughtfully. "I'd have a hard time giving up my career to be with a woman."

"Yes, but you've always been upfront about the fact your career comes first."

"Maybe that's why I can't keep a relationship longer than a couple of years." She gave Lauren a rueful smile. "What about your job in LA?"

"I usually stay in a film editor's rental cottage when I'm on site. Maybe she'll let me stay longer. Until Delphine comes through with the cash, I need the money."

"Stay for how long? And try some of this fish curry. It's delicious." She pushed her plate toward Lauren.

"I'll continue to work until I finish the project. I owe them that, since they came through for me on the H-1B visa." Lauren swallowed a forkful of fish curry, then fanned her mouth. "Wow, I forgot how hot this stuff is in London." She followed it with a spoonful of yogurt. "Oh, and Delphine insists I come to France to sign the legal papers together."

"Of course she does. Just don't let her trap you into going back to her because you're hurting."

Lauren coughed and swallowed. "Never in a million years."

Two days later, Lauren was editing translations online, trying not to get too far behind at work, when an email from Delphine popped up: *I'm ready to sign. We have an appointment with the attorney on Wednesday. Be there.*

That was the day after tomorrow. Lauren quickly arranged her travel.

She hadn't heard from Jo again since their phone conversation. Perhaps she, like Claire, put work above all else. Lauren regretted not probing Jo's thoughts about giving up her law practice to move to Canada. But since immigrating had been Jo's idea, she just assumed she was okay with it. Big mistake.

Jane picked Lauren up at the airport in her Citroën. On the smooth, comfortable ride to her house, she informed Lauren of the latest office gossip as she deftly maneuvered through rush-hour Paris traffic.

"We miss you. Your replacement is not nearly as efficient and effective as you were. That Hollywood film company is lucky to have you."

"I hope they feel that way after I return from my sudden disappearance."

Jane discreetly asked little about Lauren's love life. As they neared her flat, Jane said, "Would you consider moving back to Paris? I mean, not with Delphine of course."

Lauren did not respond right away. She sighed. "I used to love Paris, the cafés, the shops, and the nightlife. I loved my job and my friendship with you and some of our pals at work. But I'm done with Paris, just like I'm done with London. I might move to a small community somewhere to experience a slower pace of life. Maybe an island." The mention of the island pained her, and she looked away.

Jane pulled into her parking spot. "Yes, I can relate. Sometimes, Jules and I fantasize about moving out of Paris to somewhere more peaceful too."

Lauren arrived at the lawyer's office before Delphine. She was tempted to just sign the papers and leave, but what if Delphine refused to sign? She had to stay and witness it.

Delphine burst in fifteen minutes late, huffing about the traffic. She eyed Lauren up and down. "You look unhappy," Delphine said.

Lauren bit her tongue. *Please, let's just get this over with.*

"She must've really fucked you over."

Lauren took several deep breaths, determined not to take the bait.

"Shall we proceed?" The lawyer, a no-nonsense middle-aged woman, handed a black pen to Lauren, and she quickly signed. She handed the pen to Delphine.

Delphine smirked. "I've changed my mind. I've hired my own attorney and I'm going after you for spousal support."

Lauren gasped. This whole thing was a farce? Her neck and face grew hot. She should have known when Delphine agreed so soon after their last conversation that it was too easy to be true. But she doubted the penurious Delphine had hired an attorney. "That's ridiculous, Delphine. I was never your spouse."

Lauren's attorney looked nonplussed but quickly recovered. "That's not possible. French law only provides for civil solidarity pacts, which allows civil partnerships between two persons without regard to their gender. However, these do not grant the same rights as marriage, including the right to sue for spousal support."

"Just sign it, Delphine," Lauren said and held her breath.

Delphine clenched her jaw and gave Lauren a hard stare. "You'll regret this." She snatched the pen and signed, then slammed it onto the table.

The lawyer jumped, and Lauren let her breath out.

Delphine stood up, looking deflated. "Just because it's my apartment now doesn't mean there's no place for you. I told you she'd dump you. Come back to Paris." Delphine paused, and her tone changed from demanding to wheedling. "I need you."

It didn't surprise Lauren that Delphine needed her—mostly to fix a plumbing leak, paint a room, or tile a shower. Not to mention grocery shopping and cooking. No doubt, Delphine struggled on her own. *Not my problem anymore.* "I'm never coming back," Lauren said for the umpteenth time. "Thank you for signing the transfer." She grabbed her bag and as she opened the office door to leave, she turned. "Goodbye, Delphine," she said, hoping this was, finally, the last time.

Later that day, she accessed her bank account on the internet to find the money from the apartment had landed. Jane popped the cork on a champagne bottle, and they toasted her success. Bittersweet now, because she could imagine presenting Jo with the proceeds so they could buy her dream house. She pushed the thought aside with a large swallow of champagne.

In the comforting bosom of her friends and family, Lauren could put despair and sadness on hold for part of the day. But in her quieter moments, it haunted her. In just a few days, she'd be on her way to LA and her job in Hollywood, bypassing San Francisco. In a foreign country, away from family and friends, could she navigate an acceptable future? Alone?

chapter fifty-five
San Francisco

THE SHOCK OF LAUREN'S RETURN TO LONDON JOLTED Jo into considering her priorities. Winning back Lauren's trust shot to the top of the list, and she could think of nothing else. What would her life be like if she remained married to her career and stayed in San Francisco without Lauren? She couldn't bear it. Finally, she'd found someone caring and emotionally available. How could she have put that love at risk?

The morning after her phone call with Lauren, she got to work on her plan. Lauren's challenge—"Show me"—rang in her ears. Several calls and faxes later, she made plane reservations for London. She put in two back-to-back eighteen-hour days at her law office so she could leave for five days.

Jo had little time to think, eat, or exercise, but when she paused even briefly, her mouth felt dry and her heartbeat throbbed in her ears. She visualized standing at the edge of a cliff, preparing to plunge headfirst into water of uncertain depth.

Two days later, before leaving for London, Jo took the day off work to complete her plan.

She emailed Lauren: *Are you still in London?*

She received a reply: *No, I'm in Paris.*

Jo tensed. Was she thinking of returning to Paris? To her old job? To Delphine? But Jo had already taken the plunge. There was no turning back.

Jo wrote: *I'm flying to London tomorrow.*

She received no reply.

The following afternoon, Jo boarded the plane for London. She did not know if Lauren would return to London or stay in Paris, but she'd follow her to Paris if she had to.

Too exhausted to read or watch a movie, Jo slept fitfully on the ten-hour flight, arriving in London late in the morning the following day. Shuffling through the lineup for Passport Control was dreadfully slow. In the restroom, she brushed her teeth and dabbed makeup on the dark circles under her eyes.

Dragging her carry-on behind her, she aimed for the cab stand. When she'd entered the cab and closed the door, she gave Richard's address rather than the hotel. She wouldn't sleep until she found Lauren.

On the way, Jo composed her speech to Richard and Kelly. When the cab pulled up to their terraced house, she stumbled out, climbed the steps, and knocked on the door. Her heart thudded against her ribs as she waited.

Kelly opened the door. She didn't smile, but she didn't close the door either. "What are you doing here?"

Jo swallowed. "I need to talk to Lauren. In person."

"She's not here. But she's due back from Paris later this afternoon. I'm not sure she wants to see you." Kelly kept the door half-closed.

"I know. I fucked up big time. But when we talked, she asked me to show her I'm committed. I'm prepared to do that now. In person."

Kelly appeared to weigh this. "You might as well come in. Can I make you a cup of tea?" She swung open the door.

"Thanks, that would be lovely." The tension drained from Jo's body, and exhaustion took its place.

chapter fifty-six

OVER TEA AND CRUMPETS WITH BUTTER AND JAM, JO told Kelly of her plan.

When she finished, Kelly put down her teacup. "Well, that would convince me. You really look exhausted. Richard and the girls won't be home for another couple of hours, and Lauren probably won't either. Why don't you go upstairs and freshen up? Lie down in the first room on the right for a little nap?"

With a belly full of tea and sugar, Jo immediately fell asleep. Two hours later, she awakened to the sounds of excited little-girl voices downstairs, followed by a deeper male voice. She sat up, disoriented, then remembered her purpose. She listened for Lauren's voice, but it wasn't there. Jo sprang off the bed, popping into the bathroom to apply lip gloss and a little makeup before descending the stairs.

"Feel better?" Kelly asked.

"Yes, much," Jo said.

"Lauren called forty-five minutes ago as she was leaving the airport. She should be here any minute." Kelly must have revealed her plan to Richard, as he greeted her with a warm hug. The girls gave her shy smiles. They all sat in the living room, awaiting Lauren's arrival. While the family chatted, Jo clasped her hands around her briefcase, too tense to make small talk. Her plan had to work.

Ten minutes later, a cab pulled up outside, and Lauren got out with her small suitcase. Through the front window, Jo watched her climb the stairs, and her heart leaped. Richard opened the front door for his sister and got a hug in return. When Lauren caught sight of Jo over Richard's shoulder, her eyes grew wide.

"Jo." Lauren let go of her brother, letting her suitcase fall to the floor.

"I have something I need to show you," Jo said, stepping toward her.

The entire family gathered around expectantly. *It looks like I'll have an audience.* She reached into her briefcase and took out a small piece of paper. "I FedExed my completed Canadian application, and here is the acknowledgment of receipt."

She handed the paper to Lauren, who read it silently, her face inscrutable.

Jo's heart sank. *Too little, too late?*

Jo's mouth felt dry, and she licked her lips. Her heart pounded in her ears. "And there's more." She reached into her briefcase again and pulled out legal-size papers. She offered them to Lauren.

Lauren locked eyes with Jo as she took the papers, her expression neutral. She examined the papers for only a few moments before she gasped. "It's the purchase and sales agreement for the Saturna house!" She looked up, smiling. "We're buying the house! I can't believe it. We're *actually buying* the house!" She bounced on her toes, waving the papers.

"All it needs is your signature, if you agree, and both our names will be on the title." Jo's excitement rose to match Lauren's.

Lauren rushed forward and threw her arms around her. "Of course, I agree!"

Smiling, Richard and Kelly applauded. The girls danced around Lauren, tugging at her trousers. "What house? What does it look like?" the younger one asked.

Lauren pulled apart from Jo, still holding on to her arms. "Oh my god, it has the most fabulous view of ocean and whales and mountains and..."

Lauren kept her eyes locked on Jo's as she excitedly described the house to her family. Jo saw love and forgiveness there, and warmth filled her chest.

On the plane back to San Francisco, Jo and Lauren occupied seats side by side in premium economy. They each had a glass of red wine, settling in for the long haul.

Jo pushed her seat back and turned toward Lauren. "Here we are, suspended in a metal tube over the Atlantic Ocean. It's like our lives. We're buying a home, but we don't even know if Canada will accept us both."

Lauren reclined her seat too and rested against Jo's shoulder. "Yes, we've taken off, hoping there will be a place for us to land. The most important thing, though, is we're flying toward that landing together." She turned toward Jo. "I've failed to discuss with you what moving to Canada will mean for your career. I regret that. From now on, will you talk with me about your concerns, so we can problem solve together?"

"It's a novel experience for me, having someone to work with me. Rather than just react," Jo said.

"It is for me too."

"Perhaps I needed those years since we first met to mature. And to learn what's most important," Jo said.

"That's a positive way to look at it," Lauren said. "Though I've always known what *I* wanted."

Lauren took a last sip of wine and snuggled against Jo's shoulder while Jo shared her experience in Alaska and how it had jolted her into considering a new direction for her career.

chapter fifty-seven
San Francisco

WHEN JO AND LAUREN HAD LIVED TOGETHER IN SAN Francisco for a year, they amended their Canadian applications to apply jointly as a common-law couple. But to do so, they had to submit proof of their living together with additional documents and testimonials from friends and family.

Jo called her mother in San Diego. After hearing Jo's lengthy account of all she and Lauren had gone through, Molly said, "If you've gone to that much trouble to be with this woman, I suppose I should meet her."

Jo and Lauren flew to San Diego, and for two days they shopped, cooked, and ran errands for Molly. From the beginning, she had opinions on all aspects of Jo's life, but she behaved graciously toward Lauren.

On the second night of the three-day visit, all three were sitting at dinner when Jo leaned forward in her chair. "I'm thinking of changing the focus of my career," she said. "I'd like to advocate for animals and saving their habitats."

Molly paused, her bread halfway to her mouth. "Why would you want to do that?"

"I've spent most of my career advocating for humans harmed by corporate negligence. Humans are not endangered. We're the dominant species. But we're wiping out other species at an alarming rate with complete disregard of their right to exist alongside us."

"I doubt there's any money in that. Do animals even have rights?" Her mother took a big bite of her bread.

"Humans treat other animals as property to be used and exploited. Just like women used to be—and still are in some parts of the world. There are laws about treating such animals humanely but very few protecting animals' rights to live as they wish, independently of humans." Jo eyed her mother, knowing she was about to commit blasphemy. "And I don't care about the money."

Looking alarmed, her mother stopped chewing. "What?" She swallowed. "What about that big house of yours? Your law practice? You wouldn't give up your successful career, would you?"

Raising Jo as a single mother, she'd prodded her to gain the education and skills to become self-sufficient, so she never had to rely on a man. But sometimes her fears were too much for Jo. Like now. "I'm selling the house, Mom. We've bought a home in Canada on an island."

"And what will you do there? How will you make a living?" Molly glanced accusingly at Lauren before glaring at Jo.

"Our living expenses will be much less, and I have considerable savings, especially after I sell the house in San Francisco. Living on an island will be a new adventure and each time we go there, I love it more. I'll volunteer and consult for international organizations working to save the environment for both humans and other animals. That's where I am most needed now. I've already made inquiries and have some good leads and interviews set up."

Her mother stared at her, slower with age in gathering verbal ammunition. Jo mused that she'd probably become such an excellent attorney because she so often had to resist and come up with arguments to counter her overbearing mother.

But before her mother could further object, Jo said, "I've always toed the line with my career advancement, and I've done well financially. I've taken very few risks, and because of that, I almost lost the love of my life."

She glanced at Lauren, who was watching her intently. Jo reached over and squeezed her hand. Lauren squeezed back.

"I'm fifty-four years old, Mom, and I want a different life. My relationship with Lauren is my highest priority. Even if I never become a Canadian resident and Lauren does, I can still spend six months in Canada. She can then spend six months in the US. We'll make it work. I'm actually looking forward to life on an island and the shift in the focus of my advocacy."

Molly shook her head in defeat. "I think you're making a big mistake. But you always do what you want, regardless of my opinion."

Not true. But this time, her mother was right. Jo was doing what *she* wanted.

Hoping she'd not stirred up too much controversy for one night, Jo said, "Mom, I have a favor to ask. Would you be willing to write a letter to Citizenship and Immigration Canada affirming that Lauren and I are a committed couple?"

"Oh, honey, you know I'm nearly blind and too shaky to write."

Jo's defensiveness vanished in a wave of compassion for her aged mother. "That's okay, Mom, you dictate and I'll type."

Molly was silent for several minutes, seeming to withdraw into herself with her eyes closed.

Lauren put her hand on Jo's thigh under the table, and Jo tried to swallow, but her mouth was too dry. Had her mother nodded off?

Then Molly uttered the words Jo had waited decades to hear: "Of course I will. I recognize your love and commitment. I give you both my blessing and, as always, wish for your happiness."

epilogue

IN AUGUST 2005, WHEN JO AND LAUREN EACH RECEIVED their confirmation of Permanent-Resident status from Citizenship and Immigration Canada, they clutched each other, tears running down their cheeks.

"We did it!" Lauren said, laughing and crying at the same time.

"Fantastic!" Jo said, now perfectly comfortable with her choice to emigrate.

Lauren finished her temporary job in LA, and Jo eventually left her law practice and sold her house in San Francisco. Living on Saturna Island full time, they made new friends by joining a book group, a hiking group, and a conservation group. Jo served on the board of several environmental-justice groups and helped to plan their legislative agenda. Busier than ever, she found many opportunities to advocate for creatures with no voice.

A burgeoning film industry arose in Vancouver and provided Lauren part-time work when she wanted it, which was rare. They fostered dogs for the local animal shelter and Lauren worked with Jo, advocating for animals.

In 2006, they were married in their home in British Columbia. Afterward, as they stood together on their deck watching their friends and family line up for the French buffet, Lauren linked her arm with Jo. "Being together with you is what I've always wanted, ever since you looked into my eyes in that pub in London," she said.

Jo smiled and pulled her close. "I finally realized I deserved your love, and you were worth fighting for. Marrying you and being officially recognized as a couple with the same human rights as everyone else is a bonus I never imagined I'd live to see."

In June 2013, the Supreme Court of the United States struck down the Defense of Marriage Act, and Homeland Security declared that same-sex couples were to be treated the same as heterosexual couples for visas and immigration.

Jo and Lauren remained in Canada, the country that first welcomed them as a couple, eventually becoming citizens.

author's note

Although this book is a work of fiction, real-life events inspired it. I've used my imagination to create the characters, dialogues, and certain scenarios to better serve the story's themes and emotional journey.

The US did not start recognizing same-sex unions for immigration until the Supreme Court's decision to strike down Section 3 of the Defense of Marriage Act (DOMA) in 2013. While official recognition of the unions of same-sex couples for immigration is currently the law in many western countries, same-sex couples still struggle with unique challenges.

For example, though the United States Citizenship and Immigration Service (USCIS) will view same-sex marriages the same as opposite-sex marriages in deciding on family green card applications, couples must show that their marriage is legally valid. Civil unions or domestic partnerships don't qualify.

Although all couples must satisfy these requirements, they can create special challenges for same-sex couples, particularly in providing the documentation necessary to prove they have a bona fide relationship. A couple may be asked to show knowledge of their spouse's parents and family, letters from coworkers who have seen the couple together, and lease or deed documents showing that they live together. With the rising backlash against LGBTQ people in the US, this can be harder for same-sex couples. This is especially true in some communities in which making their relationship public might have adverse consequences, such as job or housing discrimination, or for individuals who are alienated from their families because of their sexual orientation.

The other requirement—that the marriage must be legal in the country in which it was performed—is now easier, since over twenty-five countries recognize same-sex marriage. However, this becomes a problem in India, for example, or in one of the many other countries where such marriage is still not legal.

Although it is now the law that same-sex couples be processed the same as heterosexual couples in US immigration proceedings, some LGBTQ people still worry whether USCIS officers will treat them with dignity and respect, given the persistent prevalence of prejudice.

Finally, many same-sex couples do not have the financial resources or cultural knowledge necessary to go through the arduous process of legal immigration. Some may come from countries in which they were severely traumatized, discriminated against, and feared for their lives.

Here are some resources for LGBTQ immigrants in the US:

- National Center for Lesbian Rights
- The LGBT Asylum Project
- Immigration Equality
- National Immigrant Justice Center

acknowledgments

Readers are at the top of my gratitude list for this novel. When I wrote my debut memoir, *Making the Rounds: Defying Norms in Love and Medicine*, I was an unknown author with no readers, gripped with anxiety about putting something so personal into the world. But then many readers and reviewers graced me with comments that the book was "enthralling and brutally honest," "engaging and immersive," and "I did not want it to end."

This gave me the confidence to further study the craft and try my hand at writing a novel, *Golden Years and Silver Linings*, which I coauthored with my partner. Again, I received heartwarming comments from readers that gave me the impetus to write this recent novel, combining experiences from real life with fiction.

As an indie author without the publicity and marketing backup of a big publisher, I rely on readers like you to leave ratings, reviews, and comments on social media to help other readers find and enjoy my books.

A book project is a long slog filled not only with energizing creativity but also with drudgery, revision after revision, and self-doubt. I am so grateful to the following people who, like supportive bystanders at a marathon, provided feedback and cheered me on.

Thank you to my beta readers, Deborah Moncrief Bell, Christine Oliver, Elke Scrimshaw, Georgina Patko, Gretchen Staebler, Judy Kiehart, Morgan Elliot, Grethe Cammermeyer, Katherine Forrest, Kathryn Guthrie, David Logan, Adele Holmes, and the Lake Forest Park Writing Group: Linda Lockwood, Anu Garg, Helen Wattley-Ames, Mercedes Roberson, Sara Kim, and Connie Ballou. I appreciate the support of other aspiring writers, Barb Glen, Jean Anton, Jan Leonard, and Ginger Rebstock. All gave feedback to help me create a better book.

The hardworking team at She Writes Press, including my indefatigable project managers, Shannon Green and Lauren Wise, and publisher, Brooke Warner, brought me back to She Writes for the second time. The encouragement from other She Writes Press authors has been and continues to be an invaluable part of the journey. Being part of this distinguished and supportive writing community fills me with immense pride and gratitude. The connections and stories we share remind me of why I write— to inspire, to heal, and to stand up for our passions and ambitions. Here's to the power of words and the communities that support us in telling our truths. Whether you're a lover of memoirs or fiction, know that your story matters, and you are not alone.

Editors are crucial to clarify and pick up mistakes that become invisible to an author after repetitive readings. Thank you, Barrett Briske, Margaret Morris, and Anne Durette.

Most of all, I thank my wife and fellow author, Linda M. Ford, who provided the inspiration for this novel and supported me with love, encouragement, editing, and delicious meals every step of the way.

about the author

Patricia Grayhall is a retired medical doctor and author of *Making the Rounds: Defying Norms in Love and Medicine*, published by She Writes Press, which garnered a starred review in Kirkus Reviews, which also listed it as one of their Best Indie Books of 2022. The memoir won the 2024 National Indie Excellence Award for LGBTQIA Nonfiction and Memoir, the 2023 Best Indie Book Award in LGBTQ Memoir, and the 2023 Readers' Favorite Book Awards Gold Medal in LBBTQ Non-Fiction. Other awards included silver Nautilus Award in Medical Memoir, and it was a finalist in the American Book Fest "Best Book" Awards, the Nancy Pearl Best Book Awards, the Canadian Book Club Awards, and the Goldie Awards.

She and her wife, Linda M. Ford, are the authors of the second-chance lesbian romance novel, *Golden Years and Silver Linings*. Patricia has published articles in *Queer Forty*, *The Gay & Lesbian Review*, *The Millions*, *Lesbian Game Changers*, and *Seattle Magazine*, among others. You can find her podcasts and NPR interviews, articles, and blogs on her website, www.patriciagrayhall.com where she enjoys connecting with readers.

Patricia splits her time between Seattle and Vancouver Island, where she enjoys other people's dogs, hiking, birdwatching, and her second career as an author.

Looking for your next great read?

We can help!

Visit www.shewritespress.com/next-read
or scan the QR code below for a list
of our recommended titles.

She Writes Press is an award-winning
independent publishing company founded to
serve women writers everywhere.